The Pregnancy Test

The Pregnancy Test

Erin McCarthy

KENSINGTON PUBLISHING CORP.
http://www.kensingtonbooks.com

BRAVA BOOKS are published by

Kensington Publishing Corp.
850 Third Avenue
New York, NY 10022

All Kensington titles, imprints and distributed lines are available at special quantity discounts for bulk purchases for sales promotion, premiums, fund-raising, educational or institutional use.

Special book excerpts or customized printings can also be created to fit specific needs. For details, write or phone the office of the Kensington Special Sales Manager: Kensington Publishing Corp., 850 Third Avenue, New York, NY 10022. Attn. Special Sales Department. Phone: 1-800-221-2647.

ISBN 0-7582-0847-2

First Kensington Trade Paperback Printing: October 2005
10 9 8 7 6 5 4 3 2 1

Printed in the United States of America

For Meaghan and Connor,
my pride and my joy

The Pregnancy Test

Prologue

"Oh, honey, su-gah, I see sweet things ahead for you."

"Really?" Mandy Keeling found there was something really fascinating about listening to the predictions of a cross-dressing psychic wearing designer shoes.

Especially since Beckwith Tripp had so far predicted a long life, an increase in personal assets, and sweet things for her. Of course, that could mean anything from receiving a cute greeting card to inheriting a candy shop from a previously unknown ancient aunt.

"But what do you mean?" Mandy knew it was blather, hogwash, coddle, but that didn't stop her from leaning across the coffee table as Beckwith stroked her palm between his huge hands. There were worse ways to spend an utterly miserable February day in Greenwich Village with her three roommates.

In fact, it was highly entertaining.

"That's not very specific," Allison Parker said, skepticism dripping in her voice. "I could tell your fortune, Mandy, if all you're looking for is vague assurances. Or better yet, I'll run down to Hunan's and buy you a bunch of fortune cookies."

Beckwith, built like a professional wrestler, and wearing a vintage Chanel suit, shrugged a broad shoulder. "I'm like Ripley, honey. Believe it or not. Doesn't matter to me."

What was unbelievable was that he wore that outfit better than Mandy ever could. She always had something of an absentminded, windblown look and was a far cry from elegant, as her mother had told her often enough. Yet Beckwith looked like Jackie O on hormone therapy. "Can you give me more details, Beckwith?"

"I can be as specific as you want. You're British, born and raised."

Allison snorted. "Gee, what gave it away? Not the accent or anything."

Jamie Peters, who believed in anything involving crystals, karma, or the supernatural, and who had brought Beckwith to their apartment, shushed Allison.

Mandy shifted on the floor, the seam of her jeans digging into her calf, and decided it didn't really matter if Beckwith was a few billiard balls shy of a game. There was something exciting and amusing and hopeful in hearing about her future, however vague. At twenty-six, she had been confronted lately with the rather alarming feeling that she had frittered away her twenties, living off her parents' money and coasting breezily through each day.

It was time for a change, she knew that, but up to this point she had been avoiding giving it any serious thought. Beckwith's appearance was fortuitous, in that maybe his predictions could give her a push in the right direction.

Caroline Davidson's eyebrows had shot up almost to her blond hair, pulled back in its usual tidy knot. "Where do you find these guys, Jamie?"

Jamie fingered her necklace, a silver Chinese character that meant happiness, and jutted her bottom lip out. "Come on, y'all, just give it a chance. He *knows* things, I'm telling you." She patted Beckwith's arm as if he was a cute toddler instead of a thirty-year-old hairy male in women's clothing.

Beckwith didn't look the least bit offended by Allison and Caroline's cynicism. He gave Mandy a smile, his hand still making those same smooth, warm glides across her skin.

"Born and raised on the country estate, quite a bit of

money, Daddy works in the big city, gone all the time, Mom has horses . . . and I see women, lots of women, talking, laughing, standing, passing teacups—and you, legs together, back straight, hands in lap."

Mandy's throat went dry, and goose bumps rose over her flesh where he was touching her. Beckwith stared at her, a faint smile playing about his mouth, shiny lip gloss hovering over five-o'clock shadow.

What he had said . . . it was her childhood, summed up in one sentence. Her father always in London, carrying on the Keeling tradition as head of the financial division of a world banking conglomerate. Mother alternating between raising her horses and hosting various charitable and social events. There were always women in their house, The Acres, soft, muted, proper, and Mandy expected to behave properly, sit quietly, or entertain Mother's guests with her rather dubious piano talents.

"Yes, sweet things ahead for you. Your life will change, but in a good way. Selfless. Enriched. With a man who makes you just melt."

Ben. Mandy wondered if Beckwith meant Ben, the man she'd been seeing for six months. She didn't think of him as her boyfriend, because it seemed ridiculous to label a man in his forties that way, but that's what he was. And she thought maybe he was going to ask her to marry him.

That would make her happy, wouldn't it? Ben was kind, stable, albeit a little distracted sometimes. He was a fellow Englishman in New York. He was punctual. Respectful. Intelligent. She cared about him a great deal, but she wasn't sure if she was ready to marry him, or if he could ever make her melt. Soften a little, maybe, but melting seemed a bit beyond Ben's reach.

"Pastries."

Mandy blinked. "What?" What did Ben have to do with pastries? When she thought of him, cream puffs and tarts did not come to mind. Ben was a biscuit.

Beckwith closed his eyes. "I see pastries. Baked goods. All lined up in front of you." He shook his head and met her gaze. "Have you ever thought of opening a shop?"

"She already has a store," Allison said, tucking her feet under her long legs as she sat on the butter-colored easy chair wedged in the corner of their minute living room.

"It's true," Mandy told Beckwith, feeling almost guilty. Here he'd been doing so well. "I run a children's toy shop." Opened with her parents' money, and only now breaking even after three years.

"No bakery?" Beckwith bit his lip.

"No bakery. Though when I tossed around ideas for starting the business, I wanted a toy shop or a bakery. But I knew I would have to rely on hired help if I started a bakery. The toy shop didn't require as much staff."

But lately she had been bored with the shop, which catered to tourists and upscale customers who wanted higher quality offerings than what was mass marketed at Toys "R" Us. She had been daydreaming about starting something new. A tea shop really, not a bakery, but serving scones and biscuits and sandwiches along with all the dozens of varieties of tea.

If there was one thing she knew, it was high tea, done the proper way.

Maybe Beckwith was onto something. Maybe it was the right time to make a change, to stop being so complacent and to embrace something that she was passionate about.

"That's odd, because I really see something sticky and sweet, sugary." Beckwith adjusted the strap on his dress.

"Maybe it's a fruitcake," Allison suggested in an innocent tone that didn't match the wicked gleam in her brown eyes.

"Allison!" Jamie looked horrified.

But Beckwith just blinked, solemnly and mysteriously, a self-proclaimed prophet in Prada shoes. "Wait until it's your turn, Allison Agnes Parker, and we'll see if you're still laughing."

Allison's feet fell to the hardwood floor.

Jamie's jaw quickly followed. "Your middle name is *Agnes?*"

"No." Allison tossed back her dark hair. "It's Elizabeth."

"Sure, whatever." Beckwith rolled his eyes and scratched his chin.

Mandy laughed and pulled her hand from his. "You've definitely given me something to think about, so thank you, Beckwith. I do believe Jamie is right. You have a gift for pointing people in the right direction."

"I've never been wrong yet." He peered at her intently from beneath mascara-laden eyelashes. "Trust me, Mandy. Pastries. It means something."

Chapter 1

Mandy clutched her roiling stomach and pondered the irony of it all.

Beckwith Tripp had been right.

Only no bake shop for her. Beckwith's pastries had in fact been buns. Or more specifically, *a* bun. In her oven.

God help her, she was pregnant.

"Are you okay?" Caroline asked as she strode through the lobby, heading to the offices of NY Computing. Mandy inched along behind her, wishing there was a wall she could clutch.

"I'm just lovely, really, other than the fact that I'm being sick every three minutes."

Caroline stopped walking and spun around, her black pumps squeaking on the hard glossy floor. There wasn't a wrinkle anywhere on her charcoal gray suit, and not a single hair dared escape the twist into which she had expertly maneuvered it. Her skin and makeup were flawless, a discreet winter tan giving her color.

"You're not going to throw up during this interview, are you?"

"No, of course not." At least she hoped and prayed she wouldn't. "I was being sarcastic and bitter."

Feelings that came quite easily to her now, since four weeks ago when that stick had turned pink and her whole life had been tossed upside down and around like a Tilt-a-Whirl. Before that moment, she had been blithely considering selling her shop and contemplating her feelings toward Ben. She had been wondering if perhaps it was time to stand on her own two feet separate from her parents and their pocketbooks and grow up just a little bit.

That had been four weeks ago.

Now she was going to be a mum.

Ben had gone bye-bye.

And growing up was no longer an option, but a necessity.

She'd sold the shop, receiving an offer much quicker than she had expected, and while her parents had assured her she could keep the capital gains when the closing went through next month, it was still absolutely necessary to get a nine-to-five job. With health insurance.

She wanted this baby badly, despite its unexpected timing. And she wanted to raise her child on her own two feet, without running to Daddy and Mother for help. She wanted her child to have a self-reliant and responsible mother, with a stable income.

"Good. No throwing up allowed. And save the bitter for later. Right now you need to project confidence and intelligence. Remember what I told you—Damien Sharpton is an impatient man, a total workaholic. He doesn't tolerate weak women."

Mandy remembered. She remembered every horrible thing that Caroline had said about the man, from the grimace she always gave when she brought up his name, to the fact that he had run through four assistants in the previous year.

"He made his last assistant cry almost every day for two weeks until she quit."

"Nice guy." Mandy concentrated on taking little tiny breaths and swallowing slowly. Her fingers quivered as the nausea rose up for one frantic moment, then settled back down again. "I can't wait to meet him."

"And don't forget," Caroline said as she reached forward

and brushed something off the shoulder of Mandy's black suit jacket, "you're not pregnant."

It was still so incredibly bizarre to think that she was, in fact, pregnant. She didn't feel maternal, so it shouldn't be that hard to fake. She felt as though she had a horrific case of the flu, but she couldn't really fathom there was a baby growing inside her. She touched her stomach, brushing her hands over the button on her blouse.

She was thrilled. She was terrified.

She was going to be sick.

Mandy clamped her lips tightly shut and breathed through her nose.

"Mr. Sharpton won't hire you if he thinks you're pregnant. But if he hires you and we hide the pregnancy from him for a while, well, when the truth finally becomes obvious, he won't be able to fire you because of discrimination. And he absolutely hates to think there was something his superior intelligence didn't pick up on, so he'll never, ever admit that he didn't realize you were pregnant when he hired you."

It sounded all rather complicated to Mandy at the moment, when she was fighting to stay vertical and not slide to the floor like a narcoleptic. She had never been so tired in her entire life. Vampire victims probably had more energy than she did.

"But won't he be angry when he finds out?" And given how pleasant Mr. Sharpton sounded, Mandy didn't think that would be a fun day in the office.

"We'll just act like we told him you were back in the beginning. I told you, he'll never admit he didn't know."

Caroline started walking toward the elevators, and Mandy followed, shuffling in her boots. She had heels in the bag on her shoulder to change into, unwilling to tromp through the slushy March snow in them. Somehow Caroline had managed to stay completely intact on the two-block walk from the subway, whereas Mandy felt rumpled and pimply and swollen. She felt like she was thirteen and facing her mother over the table.

How could you have wrinkled that blouse in the three minutes it takes to walk from your bedroom to the dining room?

"Thanks, Caroline, for getting me this interview. It couldn't have been easy since I have no marketable skills to speak of."

Caroline looked outraged. "Mandy! Check that defeatist attitude at the door. You have run your own business for three years. Everything Mr. Sharpton asks you can be answered in some way with that. You have computer experience; employee management experience; you've dealt with distributors and done your own marketing. You are overqualified for this job. Besides, I got you the first interview with HR, but you passed that round and got yourself the actual interview with Sharpton."

Mandy managed a smile. Caroline, Allison, and Jamie had rallied around her, the true friends that they were, offering support and a shoulder to lean on. Allison and Jamie had staunchly assured her she could stay in their two-bedroom apartment after the baby was born, since Caroline, whom she shared one of the bedrooms with, was getting married in July and moving out.

And now Caroline was risking her reputation at NY Computing, where she was a marketing manager, by securing Mandy an appointment with HR, which had led to this interview with Demon Sharpton, her hopefully soon-to-be boss. The fact that he had been given that nickname by the executive assistants on his floor, based on the freaky little boy Damien from the classic horror movie *The Omen*, was unimportant. About as frightening as getting caught under a kicking horse, but unimportant. This was her future, and she could do this.

"You're right, you're absolutely right. I will project confidence, and I won't run out screaming or burst into tears unless a jackal pops out from under his desk. Then I'm out of there."

Caroline laughed as they stepped onto the elevator. "Remember, eighteenth floor. I'm getting off on twelve. HR has screwed up the amount they're withdrawing on my taxes again." She shook her head. "I can't wait to see how long it will take for them to change my name after the wedding."

"I'm so happy for you, Caroline. I can't believe it's only a few months until the wedding."

"Sixteen weeks. Give or take a day." Caroline grinned. "Brad and I are booking our honeymoon to Paris tomorrow."

"Paris in the summer will be lovely. I haven't been there since I was sixteen. I fell wildly in love with a Parisian. He was eighteen and played in clubs . . . he made music with office supplies. I thought it was very deep."

She had always been attracted to the rather flighty types, the artists, the musicians, the modern day Einsteins. That's why it had seemed like Ben was such a mature choice, such an improvement, a stable alternative to passion and poetry.

There certainly hadn't been any passion when Ben had looked her straight in the eye, offered her a five thousand dollar cash compensation for their mutual mistake, and informed her not to call him ever again.

The elevator slid open on twelve, and Caroline and another man moved into the hall. "Don't forget to change your shoes, and good luck!" Caroline gave her a smile and a wave before strolling off with a professional and confident walk.

Mandy glanced down at her thick sheepskin-lined boots peeking out from under her suit skirt. "Right-o. Change the shoes. I remembered that."

No, she hadn't. She couldn't remember her head from her hind end these days. She dug her heels out of her bag as the elevator stopped on fourteen, and the remaining three passengers got off. For one exciting second, she thought she was actually going to get privacy to hop around one-footed tugging her boot off, but then a man got on the elevator, stopping the door from closing with his foot.

Damn.

He was good-looking.

With dark hair, expensively cut. Pricey, but conservative gray suit. Shiny shoes. The *Wall Street Journal* tucked under his arm and a cup of coffee in his hand.

The kind of man who worked with her father, who always made her feel a bit inadequate, dismissed. Like her father himself had.

This man wasn't dismissing her—he wasn't even acknowledging her existence. He glanced at the number panel and gave a firm push to the eighteenth floor, which was already lit.

As if *her* pushing it wasn't good enough. Somehow his pushing it would get them there faster.

Pompous you-know-what.

Mandy dropped her bag to the floor and held on to the handrail. Lifting her leg, she tugged a boot off and let it tumble on top of the bag. Then she hooked her toes into her shoe and hopped a little as she tried to push the heel in. The motion made her stomach heave.

Of course, even wiggling her pinky finger made her stomach heave these days. Forget complicated maneuvers like crossing her eyes or touching her toes.

Or putting on heels in a moving elevator.

She lost her balance and hit the wall with her shoulder. "Damn."

The man glanced her way, but didn't turn far enough to actually see her. His leg tapped impatiently. He watched the buttons climb floors, glanced at his watch, patted his pocket, probably making sure his mobile phone was still intact.

She had one pump partially on and one winter boot, and it looked as though it was going to stay that way unless she got some assistance. Setting her foot back down, she tried to ram her heel in. Nothing happened, so she let go of the handrail, bent over, and used two hands to wedge her heel in the shoe. All the blood in her upper body flooded into her face in a hot, dizzy rush.

"Oh, no." This was bad.

Shiny black shoes turned toward her.

She was afraid to move. If she did, it was highly likely her breakfast of tea and toast would come hurtling up onto her shoe, her bag, and the tired mauve carpet.

"Is something wrong?" He had a hard voice, clipped, reserved. There was reluctance in his question.

The elevator dinged, and the doors opened.

"I think I'm going to be sick." Mandy wondered if she could hobble forward off the elevator, still bent over at the waist. She might have managed it if her bag wasn't lying on the floor two feet away, and her footwear scattered left and right. Her wallet was in her bag, just out of reach.

"Well, get off the elevator then."

He said it as if this was obvious, which it would be if she could move.

Even with her hair falling in her eyes, Mandy could see the black shoes and pant legs were in front of the door, holding it open.

"I can't. If I stand still, I think I'm okay. If I move, I think I'll . . . well, be sick." It seemed inappropriate to say "puke my guts out" in front of this frosty businessman. Or in front of his feet anyway.

"You can't just stand there all day," he said, with a touch of disbelief.

Well, no shit, Sherlock.

The door tried to close, and he pushed it back open.

"I suppose I can't." Mandy raised herself a half inch. Her

head swam, but her stomach only lurched. "I have an eight o'clock appointment—a job interview—and I've got this bad case of"—*Morning sickness*—"the flu."

Nothing but silence came from shiny-shoe man.

Oh, my God, this was a nightmare brought to life. She couldn't think, she couldn't move. She was nauseous, she was mortified. She was stuck on a bloody elevator with her head around her ankles and her bum in the air.

She really didn't think that was the confident side Caroline wanted her to be projecting.

Chapter 2

Damien Sharpton usually knew what to do in any given situation.

But he didn't know what the hell to do about the woman bent completely over in the elevator, ass up, head down.

His first urge was to step out in the hallway and let the door close on her.

Despite what people said about him, however, he wasn't quite that heartless.

He was impatient. Calculating. Aggressive. Consumed by his work and utterly devoid of a personal life.

He was okay with all of that. Yet regardless of the past three years, and everything he'd been through, he wasn't inhumane.

So he hovered, holding the doors open, and wondered what exactly he was supposed to do now.

"Do you want me to call someone?" He reached for his cell phone, pleased that he'd thought to foist her off on someone else. Let one of the executive assistants deal with her, until her husband or boyfriend or friend came and retrieved her. Not his assistant, since he didn't have one at present.

That dippy little girl Lanie he'd hired out of total desperation had not worked out at all. Even the most simplistic of tasks like using the copier had been a struggle for her, and when he'd pointed out ways to increase her efficiency, she had burst into tears on him.

But he could call Jim's assistant, Terri. She was very maternal and sweet and would know what to do with a potential vomit situation.

"No, no, I'm fine, really. I have to get to this interview. I really need this job for the health insurance."

Obviously, since she was sick as a dog. Damien tried to remember what she looked like when her light brown hair wasn't covering her face, but he hadn't really noticed her when he'd stepped on the elevator. He had been thinking about his nine-o'clock conference call with the Atlanta team and hoping that his eight-o'clock interview would result in an assistant who could actually use Instant Messaging without inserting giggling smiley faces every other word.

Lanie had been fond of those.

Damien cleared his throat and flipped open his phone, trying to remember Terri's extension.

"Can you hand me your coffee cup?"

"For what?" But he was already leaning down and sticking his coffee cup under her hair in the direction of her hand, figuring it wouldn't be wise to upset her. The door tried to close again, but he held it with his foot and hip, hoping it wasn't creasing his suit.

"I'm going to stand up, but I need something to catch it, just in case I get sick."

Oh, good God. He was sorry he'd asked. And while he'd gotten a grande, he didn't think the cup was that big. And it was still half full.

A little fist of nausea curled in his own stomach, and he lifted his eyes up from her head to distract himself. Her suit jacket had slid down toward her neck, given the pull of gravity, and he could see her bare back above her waistline. Her flesh was smooth, slightly pink, her waist tapering in above her skirt, in a way that was very . . .

Damn.

Damien nearly thunked himself on the forehead. What the hell was he doing?

In three years, he'd never once felt the stirrings of attraction for a woman, and now he suddenly found a woman's bare back sexy. A faceless, flu-striken woman. It was ludicrous.

"Thanks. I really appreciate this. The job I'm interviewing for, I've heard the boss is a complete and total ogre. He's scared off all his other assistants and is completely unreasonable. I don't mind, because well, I need the job, but I don't want to cancel last minute with someone like that. So I've got to go, hell or high water."

She stood up with a shaky surge, and as her eyes locked with his, Damien realized he was looking at his eight A.M. interview appointment.

He was the ogre.

She wanted to be his assistant.

And she was gorgeous.

With a heart-shaped face, chin-length hair that tumbled in soft waves, bangs sticking up a little from her previous position. Her brown eyes were huge, warm, vulnerable. Her cheekbones were high, her lips bowed, her skin a flushed pink and her breath rushing in and out on shaky little bursts. There were slight dark circles under her eyes, and her cheeks were a bit hollow, like she'd lost weight from the illness she was battling.

Germs were probably leaping off her and onto him even as he stood there, but he didn't retreat into the hallway. In fact, he let go of the door and stepped forward. Found himself bending over to pick up her bag and her shoes.

Shoving them in her hands. "Here," he said gruffly, as the elevator closed and started to ascend.

"Thanks." She brushed her bangs back, making them stick up even more. Then she passed the coffee to him and kicked the brown Eskimo-looking boot off her foot. "You can have your coffee back. I don't think I need it after all."

Damien took the cup and tried not to curl his lip in distaste. He'd never look at a grande coffee from the cafe downstairs in quite the same way. Nor could he believe that somehow this woman had heard he was difficult, unreasonable, an *ogre*, before she'd even been hired.

When she bent partially to put on her black dress shoe, she made a small sound of distress. Afraid he'd be stuck on the elevator indefinitely, Damien grabbed her arm and balanced her before she wound up on the floor or worse. He wasn't sure his dry cleaner could remove vomit.

"I'm okay, I'm okay."

He admired her tenacity. While it would have been simpler and probably smarter for her to just reschedule the interview, she had toughed it out. Probably assuming that he would dismiss her as irresponsible for canceling and that he wouldn't be willing to give her a shot.

Not that he would do that. He didn't think. He mentally went through his tight calendar. He wasn't the most patient of guys, and he'd had it with incompetent and lazy assistants. Being totally honest, he probably wouldn't have rescheduled with her, assuming she wasn't serious about the job.

Which annoyed him that his ogre reputation might actually have some minor basis in fact.

The elevator opened on twenty-four, and an older man got on.

Reaching over, Damien punched the eighteenth floor. No sense in riding this thing all the way to the ground floor again.

Then he watched the woman tuck her boots in her bag. He narrowed his eyes. He fought irritation. Attraction. Admiration.

Time to clear his morning. "Mandy Keeling?"

She looked up in surprise. "Yes, how did you . . ." Horror descended on her face, her fingers rising to clutch at her throat. "Oh, no. No, no, no, you can't be . . ."

"I'm Damien Sharpton." The door opened behind him. "The ogre."

"Eighteenth floor," the older man said when neither of them moved so much as a muscle.

Damien put out his hand in a polite gesture for her to lead, but his voice was the one he used in the boardroom. The one that was ten times colder than the tone that had reduced Lanie to tears. "After you, Ms. Keeling. My office is at the end of the hall, last door on the left. I'll try to be brief."

He expected her to wither. Stammer. Cry. Retreat. Shake her head no, let the elevator door close behind her, and ride her little germ-infested self right out of his life.

She didn't.

Through tight lips, she simply said, "Thank you," and started down the hall, listing to the right a little like she was on a ship at sea.

His interest and respect rose another reluctant inch or two.

Mandy bit back a whimper and clutched her bag in one hand, her stomach in the other.

Bugger it. Now, what were the odds of encountering Damien Sharpton on the elevator? And her calling him an ogre, of all things. It was so heinous it was almost funny.

She winced, and not from the pinch of her swollen feet in heels.

So much for a nine-to-five job that would make day care easier to secure. She wasn't going to be given this position, for obvious reasons, but she needed to at least try and redeem herself on the interview so there weren't repercussions for Caroline.

Which meant no referring to Damien as Demon Sharpton.

The door to his office was closed, which didn't surprise her. In the minutes they'd been on the elevator together, she had sensed his tension, his tightness, his impatient energy brimming beneath the surface. Behind her now, she could feel his presence. Looming, firm, judging, his feet making hard strides, his suit rustling as he slowed down to keep pace with her snail speed. His breath coming out in exasperated bursts that he covered with a cough.

She knew his type. Her father was one. A man with no patience, no interest in anything other than his work. A man who didn't understand why the whole world didn't move at the same frantic, obsessive rate as he did.

Leaning around her, he opened the door and strode past her, tossing his phone on his desktop, dropping his coffee into the trash under it. He smoothed his rich blue tie, flipped open the lid on his laptop, and reached for a file, all before he had completed his descent into his chair.

"Have a seat, Ms. Keeling."

Gladly. Mandy sank into a leather armchair and took a deep breath. "Please, call me Mandy, Mr. Sharpton."

"All right. So, tell me why you think you're qualified to be my assistant?"

No offer for her to call him Damien. No comment on the elevator incident. Right to business. She should let it go, the whole embarrassing ogre thing. But she just couldn't. Not because of the job, but because of Caroline's reputation, and because it seemed that if someone insulted her character, she would like to hear an apology.

"Listen, Mr. Sharpton, I need to apologize for the rather unfortunate comments I made in the elevator."

He pinned her with a stare. "There's no need. Really."

While Mandy heard his almost palpable need to keep this interview clipping along so he could move on to the next task of the day, she could also see that there was more to Damien Sharpton than met the eye.

He was fabulously attractive, with dark hair cut very close to his head, strong, sharp cheek and jawbones, and the palest blue eyes she had ever seen. They matched his tie and set her heart racing with feelings that weren't particularly maternal.

But even a mum can appreciate a good pair of electric blue eyes on an attractive man.

Not that she was a mum yet. And not that she had a husband or boyfriend, so the strange fascination she was feeling wasn't wrong exactly.

But it didn't matter in the least, because she wasn't shopping for a man to fill either role. After Ben, she was done. It was time to concentrate on her child and being the best parent her inadequate self could be.

But blimey, he had nice eyes.

And behind the impatience, there was a touch of something that made her rethink Damien Sharpton. There was pain there, hiding behind his efficiency and elegance and hardness.

"No, there is a need for me to apologize, because I was completely out of line gossiping about you. I don't know you, so I have no reason to believe any of those rumors are true, and it was small of me to be talking like that. I'm sorry. My only excuse is that I was nervous, and not feeling well, obviously, since you were witness to that, and when I'm nervous, I tend to babble." Like now. Good God, Mandy felt her cheeks start to burn.

Damien's eyebrows had shot up, and his hand froze on his computer mouse. If disdain had a name, it would be Damien.

"Fine. Thank you. Moving on, then. Why would you like the position here at NY Computing?"

Okay, then. Mr. Happy didn't like to chitchat. Duly noted. Mandy crossed her leg and settled her bag on the floor and launched into the perfectly poised bullshit response that Damien was expecting.

Twenty minutes later, her answers were getting shorter, her bullshit less poised, and her stomach was doing an imitation of Chinese acrobats. He was relentless. He didn't even give her five seconds after a response before he fired the next question at her.

And every single question seemed designed to force a confession out of her.

Why do you want to relinquish your own business and work for me?

Are you available for business travel?

Where do you see yourself in five years?

The baby she could not feel suddenly seemed like a gigantic white elephant under her skirt. She didn't want to lie—she didn't want to deny her child before it was even the size of a grape.

She knew it was practical to keep her pregnancy to herself, yet she still felt like standing on her chair and screaming, "I'm having a baby! I'm going to be responsible for another human being!"

But first she needed to throw up.

"Excuse me, Mr. Sharpton, where is your wastebasket?"

"What?" His head snapped up, but Mandy didn't wait.

She dropped to her knees and stuck her face under his desktop. As she tossed her tea and toast onto his discarded coffee, it occurred to her that she had followed Caroline's instructions. Her friend had told her to make a knockout impression, and this was certainly that.

Weak and horrified, Mandy lifted her head and found herself face-to-face with Damien Sharpton's crotch.

"Oh, dear, God," she whispered.

Chapter 3

He wasn't sure why he had hired her.

Maybe it had been desperation. There had been no other candidates even remotely qualified.

Or maybe it had been admiration. She had hung in there until the bitter end, finally halting the interview by yaking into his trash can, right smack between his legs. He respected that kind of grit.

Plus, prior to that, she had handled the interview well.

And she was very nice to look at when she wasn't throwing up, not that appearance had any bearing on his decision.

Of course, he never saw her, so that was irrelevant.

Besides, regardless of the reasons why he had hired her, she was working out quite well. She was a stellar assistant, even if she was as elusive as a taxi in the rain.

In the two months since she had started, he'd seen her approximately four times.

It didn't seem to affect her job performance. She was a whiz at instant messaging and e-mails, often responding to his messages in less than a minute. She did everything he asked of her on time and cleanly, and had even gotten to the point where she was anticipating his needs.

Like now. He was sitting at his desk, and suddenly a guy

from the deli had knocked on his door and brought him a turkey sandwich on whole grain.

So he IM'd her.

Is this turkey sandwich for me?

Before he could even get it unwrapped, she had replied.

Yes, it is. Enjoy.

He should let it go at that. Really, it didn't matter. He had the sandwich. He could eat it and not worry about being interrupted in the middle of his twelve-o'clock Web conference regarding the updates to the product roadmap at First Financial. Yet this conference call was taking three times as long as was necessary, and he found he couldn't stop himself from instant messaging Mandy again.

How do you know I would want turkey?

You always eat turkey on Tuesdays.

He wasn't sure if he was pleased or annoyed. Probably annoyed. Because he found that for all the hiding she did from him, it didn't stop him from wasting a great deal of time thinking about Mandy Keeling, trying to figure her out.

Which puzzled him first, pissed him off second.

Maybe next Tuesday I'll have pastrami.

You don't like pastrami.

How did she know if he liked pastrami or not? She never even spoke to him, hiding in her cubicle like she was afraid to come face-to-face with her ogre boss. Maybe he loved pastrami.

He didn't, but that wasn't the point.

He bit the turkey sandwich with more force than was necessary and nearly ripped through his tongue.

How do you know I don't like pastrami?

You said it smelled like armpit when I was ordering party trays for the user group meeting.

How the hell she could even remember he said that was beyond him. He went two years with assistants who couldn't even remember what floor they were on, and now suddenly he had one with magic memory.

He should be thrilled. She was a dream secretary come true.

And maybe he would be thrilled if she wasn't avoiding him like week-old fish.

That shouldn't bother him either. Wasn't he happiest when people were leaving him alone? Hadn't he rearranged his whole life so that he had the least amount of interaction with other human beings as possible aside from work? She did her job, and she did it with minimal contact with him. A perfect working arrangement.

Which didn't explain why he was searching his brain for an excuse to force her into his office face-to-face, so he could puzzle out why he was spending so much time thinking about her.

Do you want me to order you pastrami next week?

Oh, now she was just being a smart-ass. He could practically hear the sarcasm in her typed words. And it made him fight not to smile.

No.

Then what do you want, Mr. Sharpton?

He didn't know what he wanted, aside from thoughts of Mandy Keeling to evacuate his head. And he definitely didn't want pastrami.

I want to order my own sandwich.

Damien chewed the food in his mouth and reread his words. Now, that was a stupid thing to say. He sounded like a three-year-old. And he didn't want to order his own food—that was the whole point of having an assistant, to free his time up for more pressing concerns. What the hell was he doing?

That can be arranged.

He actually laughed out loud. Something he never did. Ever. There hadn't been a whole lot to laugh about in the last three years.

"So that's how she gets all her work done," he murmured to the screen as his laughter dwindled down to a chuckle. "She turns it all back around to me."

"What was that, Damien?"

Oh, shit, he'd forgotten he was on a conference call.

"Uh, nothing, sorry." Christ, he sounded like an idiot, and when the hell had he ever forgotten that he was on a call?

Impulsively, he pressed star six to mute the call and picked up his phone. He had to see Mandy. He had to reassure himself that he was not feeling any sort of attraction whatsoever to his invisible assistant. He had to know that she wasn't any different than any other woman he'd encountered since Jessica. He had to look her straight in the eye and feel nothing.

She answered the phone in that clipped British accent of hers. "NY Computing, this is Mandy."

"I need to see you in my office. Now."

There was a pause. Then she said, "I was just going for lunch. I've an appointment."

Damien was annoyed. How convenient that she had an appointment. And how coincidental that she never seemed to be at her desk when he was walking by. "When you get back then."

"Mr. Sharpton . . ." She sounded nervous and as if she were scrambling around for a plausible excuse not to see him. "I have rather a busy afternoon."

He was a suspicious man. Cynical. Inclined to think the worst. He hadn't always been like that, but life had a cruel way of beating the trust out of a man, and he didn't think he was overreacting in thinking something was really strange about his assistant's behavior.

Clearly, she was avoiding him. And he wasn't sure why it mattered, but he just needed to reassure himself that it wasn't because she thought he was an ogre.

He wasn't necessarily a nice guy, but he wasn't a bastard either.

If he had made an assistant or two cry, it had never been *intentional.*

"A busy afternoon working for me."

"Well, yes."

She didn't sound nearly as confident and efficient on the phone as she did in her e-mails. Damien could practically hear her squirming. And it didn't make him feel any better. It just proved she didn't want to get anywhere near him.

Maybe she was embarrassed about throwing up under his desk. It had been an awkward first meeting, to say the least. Or maybe she had something wrong with her, like a phobia. But what the hell would explain her sprinting down the hall to get away from him, like he could swear he'd seen her do two days before? Fear of Technical Executives?

"Since you're busy working for me, I'm telling you that you can take five minutes out of your task-filled schedule to come to my office."

"Mr. Sharpton, I need to leave for my appointment immediately."

That was the tone he had come to expect from Mandy, even if he never heard it in person. That sort of mildly reprimanding, prim and proper voice.

It kind of turned him on.

Damien shoved the sandwich away so he could rest his head on his hand. Man, oh man, he'd lost his mind. He'd thought that he'd held insanity at bay, but clearly it had snuck up on him when he wasn't looking.

"Fine, I'll just tell you what I want over the phone, then. I'm leaving next week for the Caribbean."

"Yes, I booked your flight last week."

"Get back on the phone and get yourself a seat as well. I need you to accompany me on this trip."

Not really. And he wasn't entirely sure where the idea had come from, but it was brilliant. Whatever little secret Mandy Keeling was hiding from him would be revealed if they spent five days working in the Caribbean together. She couldn't avoid him. There would be no high-speed Internet for her to rely on instant messaging. No maze of cubicles to dart around when she saw him approaching.

Nothing but sun and sand and rum. And Mandy in a bikini.

Damien tried to picture it, but he saw Mandy so infrequently, his mind couldn't quite dredge up enough details to make the image complete. All he had was a cute upturned nose, wavy brown hair, and sheepskin boots.

"What?" she said, her voice squeaking as it hit the T. "I thought you won this trip for your productivity. It's supposed to be a holiday."

He would go absolutely freaking crazy if he had to sit in a beach chair for five days and not work. His body didn't know how to be idle, and his brain, well, too much time to think and there might be images of Jessica popping in there.

That was something he couldn't let happen.

"I don't need a vacation. But I can appreciate the sun and a dive into the ocean. So I'm planning on making it a working week, just at a slower pace. Only I need you there, with me."

"No, I couldn't possibly!"

Was the prospect so horrible? He thought most employees would jump at the chance to hit the islands, all expenses paid for. He couldn't quite keep the irritation out of his voice. "I'm not really asking you."

"I see."

There it was again, that disapproving schoolteacher voice.

He settled back in his chair, satisfied to have the upper hand again. "Do you feel our business relationship is working, Mandy?"

"I don't have any complaints, Mr. Sharpton." She paused. "Do you?"

Only one. "I think it's working well overall. I'd like to make a few adjustments, though, with the idea that we'll be working together long-term." She really was a damn good assistant. He just wanted to see her more often.

Which sounded incredibly odd, like he was a mother neglected by her grown children. A mortifying comparison, to say the least.

"But we'll discuss that on the trip." He'd already wasted the better part of a half hour accomplishing nothing more than forcing her to share the same space with him.

"Fantastic," she said, sounding so unenthusiastic that he hung up before she heard him snort in amusement.

Mandy dragged herself up the two flights of stairs to her apartment, wondering if her body realized that according to *The Everything Guide to Pregnancy*, she was supposed to have left first trimester fatigue behind. Someone upstairs hadn't got the message, because she still felt like hell.

It was probably the stress of her new job. She had been working hard to make a good impression on Damien Sharpton, worrying that any minute he'd fire her without notice or just cause. Besides, she was expending a lot of energy dodging him, popping into the rest room or behind a cubicle wall when he came out of his office, so she wouldn't come face-to-face with him.

In the eight weeks since she'd started as his assistant, she'd stuck to that pattern of hide and never seek, but lately she realized her reasons for it were changing. First it had been because she'd thought he was a beast, capable of making her work environment hell, and because she had seen the wisdom of keeping her pregnancy from him until it was no longer possible. But to her surprise, she was finding that while Damien was arrogant and impatient, he wasn't a bad sort at all.

He was demanding, but he also had a sharp wit and an intelligence that astounded her. It was obvious why he was good at his job—he was aggressive and a perfectionist, but she had expected that. What she hadn't anticipated was the sense of humor that was lurking somewhere in that stodgy exterior. It showed up randomly in his e-mails when she was least expecting it and intrigued her.

The truth was she actually enjoyed the rapport they shared via technology.

And to her horror she'd been having incredibly vivid dreams featuring his blue eyes gazing at her as he performed all manner of sexual acts. To her. With her. Under her. Over her. In her.

The *Everything Guide* said intense dreaming was common and expected in pregnant women, with dreams about the baby and sex topping the list. She'd had a couple of dreams about holding the solid weight of her child in her arms, but mostly, pervert that she was, she was dreaming about her boss getting her off.

It was phenomenally embarrassing.

And a good cause for staying away from him. Any time in his presence might either fuel the fire of her lusty dreams or have her stammering, convinced he could read her mind.

Or worst of all, make her want him during waking hours, too.

That's why this little trip to the Caribbean was nothing short of a major catastrophe.

Mandy grabbed the railing and took a deep breath, wishing for a little air circulation in the hallway. She was burning up. "Just two more steps, then we're home. I can do this." She heaved herself up toward her front door and took a minute to rest while searching out her key.

Maybe it was time to read that *Yoga for Mothers* book Jamie had pressed on her about two minutes after the stick had turned pink. She felt like an anemic turtle.

The door opened, and Allison walked out, wearing a hot pink sundress and heels that sent her over six feet tall. Her long brown hair was pulled back in a sleek ponytail, and she looked cool, classy, put together.

Mandy remembered feeling like that a long time ago. Well, she'd never rivaled Allison for that supermodel look, but she had been cute in a blowsy jean jacket kind of way, with a good complexion and high metabolism. Now she had zits and undereye circles.

Allison jumped. "Jesus, what are you doing lying on the wall? If you lost your key, you should have buzzed us."

"I was just taking a minute to rest. I think I'm having triplets or something. There's no reason why I should feel this tired." Fifteen weeks into this gig and she already sucked at it. Other women were bouncing around looking adorable at this point—pink cheeks, shiny hair, showing off their little bubbles with low-waisted jeans.

She, on the other hand, was becoming really familiar with loose, concealing clothes since the morning sickness had hit her hard and fast. Elastic was her friend.

"You do look kind of bad." Allison leaned over and peered at her. "Maybe you should take a nap. But hey, at least you're not puking all the time anymore."

"Yippee, lucky me." Mandy tried to peel herself off the wall, feeling emotional and crabby. It was the idea of going to the Caribbean with Damien Sharpton, spending days and days in his company in the hot sun, blue sky and ocean waves lulling her, music wafting over the sand. And her trying to pretend she wasn't pregnant and alone.

"Remind me never to get pregnant," Allison said, shifting her clutch from one hand to the other.

Suddenly, without warning, Mandy felt tears well up in her eyes. "It's not like I did this on purpose, you know! Ben was using protection and yet I still got pregnant, and now this poor baby is stuck with a mother who doesn't know what she's doing and can't even walk up the damn stairs!"

Allison's eyes widened as Mandy sobbed, swiping at her cheeks. She didn't know why she was crying except that it just seemed as though there had been so little in her life she'd been successful at that the odds were against her being a stellar mother as well.

"Oh, shit, Mandy, I'm sorry, I didn't mean . . ." Allison

stuck her head in the open door of the apartment. "Jamie, come fix this! I made Mandy cry."

"I'm fine," she said, even as her eyes swelled up and her cheeks went damp with tears.

But she didn't protest when Jamie came and put her arm around her and led her into the apartment, clucking and cooing. "What's the matter, honey? Did that nasty boss of yours do something horrible to you?"

She nodded, plopping onto the couch and hugging a velvet sage green pillow when Jamie gave her a gentle push down. "He's making me go to the Caribbean with him for a week."

"The bastard!" Allison said, then pressed her lips together when Jamie shot her a dirty look. "What? I would kill to go to the beach and get a real tan instead of paying fifty bucks to get sprayed with fake color. What's wrong with going to the Caribbean? It's been a lousy spring. It's May, and most days it doesn't even crack fifty degrees."

"It doesn't stop you from wearing a sundress, though," Jamie remarked, bundled up in a chocolate brown hoodie and pants.

"I have to show off this fake tan."

Mandy tucked the pillow under her chin. "I know it sounds stupid, but the thing is, he doesn't know I'm pregnant. I'm not sure I can hide it for a whole week."

"But you're barely showing at all. A man is never going to notice that, and you're not getting sick anymore." Allison shrugged her shoulder. "I say you go and relax, soak up some rays and hit the spa. Pamper yourself a little—you deserve it."

"Do you think so? I mean, he has to find out sooner or later that I'm pregnant, but I'd rather it be later." Preferably after the baby was born and she was in the hospital. "I actually like working for him, you know, but keeping this a secret is stressing me out."

"Stress is not good for the baby." Jamie had moved

around the back of the couch and was massaging Mandy's shoulders.

Jamie's light fingers kneaded the knots in her muscles, and Mandy whimpered. "I feel completely overwhelmed. There is so much I'm supposed to know. Fetal development, what to ask the doctor, what foods to avoid, how to know when you're in labor . . . I can't keep up."

"So take all your reading material with you on this trip and just kind of take stock. It's a lot to learn, but some of it is just common sense. And what's important is that you be relaxed and stress-free, not whether you know which kind of bottle to buy. That stuff is trial and error."

"Listen to Jamie," Allison said, perching on the coffee table, her long legs crossed. "She's the only one of us who knows a damn thing about babies."

"I know you shouldn't swear in front of a baby," Jamie said.

"The kid's not even born yet! And damn isn't a swear word, it's a pejorative."

Mandy's eyes were half closed, and she rubbed the last of the tears off her cheeks. Jamie's slow and steady massage was lulling her, relaxing her. Maybe she could do this.

Motherhood was common sense, that's all. She knew not to swear in front of a child, just like she knew babies could drown in mop buckets. She knew babies needed powder so their bums didn't get sore, and she knew a fever in an infant meant a visit to the pediatrician. She could handle this, one day, one diaper at a time.

She wanted her baby with a fierceness that surprised her. She wanted to love this child unconditionally and guide it to be a responsible, ethical, confident person.

It was scary, but exciting.

Now if she could just stop having sex dreams about Damien Sharpton giving her multiple orgasms, she would really have a handle on things.

Chapter 4

"Mother, I'm trying to pack for this trip for work, can I call you later?" Mandy tossed a pair of khaki pants aside. She'd never get the button closed on those.

"What trip for work? What is this all about?"

"I thought I told you . . . my boss is going to Punta Cana and needs me to accompany him." Linen skirts were a good choice, comfortable and cool. She stuck two in her open suitcase.

"Punta Cana? Isn't that in the Caribbean? That doesn't sound safe in your condition. They don't wash their fruits and vegetables there, you know. And no air-conditioning, rough roads, huts . . ."

Mandy rolled her eyes, glad her mother couldn't see her. "Mother, I'm not staying in a hut. It's a resort, catering to Americans and Canadians."

"Just as bad. Think of all those French-Canadians in thongs, dear."

Now she did laugh, tossing her blow-dryer into her bag. "There's nothing wrong with wearing a thong. It means they're comfortable with their bodies. It's probably very liberating. Maybe we should try it—I'll get Daddy a thong for Christmas, and he can wear it to the lake."

Mandy knew she shouldn't tease her very proper mother like that, but she was feeling so much better, she was almost giddy. It was as though the minute her pregnancy hit the sixteen-week mark, the curtain on her fatigue had lifted. And her stomach had popped up like a waffle in the toaster. She rubbed her waist, the Capri pants she was wearing digging into her flesh.

"Mandy, you've lost your mind."

"Possibly. Do you think I should go topless on the beach? I finally have a chest worthy of baring." Not that she would, ever in a million years, but shocking her mother brought a sick sort of glee.

"On a business trip! Good God, you really have gone off the deep end. It's the result of being left pregnant and alone by that old man you were dating. You never should have gone out with a man so much older than you. They're all having their midlife crises in their forties . . . it doesn't surprise me he didn't want a thing to do with real responsibility."

The conversation was no longer amusing.

But before she could tell her mother to take a long walk off a short pier, she followed up with a slur on Mandy's toy shop.

"At least you finally have a real job. I know you've always enjoyed your hobbies, dear, but now is time to settle down and do what's best."

What made her feel the lousiest was that she really couldn't argue with her mother. The shop had never felt like a hobby, but after diddling around with it for three years, it hadn't turned a profit, and she couldn't say that she had ever really aggressively sought its success. It *had* been a hobby.

"I still wish you'd come home and let your father and I help you out."

About as appealing a prospect as self-mutilation with a rusty knife. Thanks, she'd pass.

"I'm fine, Mother. And while I miss you both"—when she got in the wine and was feeling nostalgic, but otherwise never—"I need to stand on my own two feet."

Her mother sniffed. "Well, I'm proud of you for working so hard. But I can't help but worry."

"You don't need to worry."

"Promise me you won't eat anything while you're there."

She was supposed to go five days without eating?

Mandy clamped her lips shut so she wouldn't giggle. "All right, I won't eat anything."

"Where are you staying? I should know how to reach you."

Against her better judgment, Mandy lifted the folder off her nightstand and recited the hotel contact information. If her mother showed up in the Caribbean when she was on a trip with her boss, Mandy would disown her.

If parents could disown their mortifying children, surely she could do the same.

"And be careful your boss doesn't try anything funny with you. Businessmen view these kind of resorts as sexual buffets."

What her mother knew about businessmen and their sexual habits was a mystery to Mandy.

"Sexual buffets? Have you been watching those news programs again?"

But at any rate, Mandy wasn't the one who had to worry.

It was Damien Sharpton. Because Mandy's dreams had intensified, if that were possible, and the thought of a sexual buffet, with Damien as the main course, had her body tingling and her breath racing.

And if she had her way, that buffet would be all you can eat.

Damien had his suitcase in the corner of his office and was clearing out the last of his e-mails before he caught a cab to LaGuardia when Rob Turner stuck his head in the open door.

"Hey, Damien, what's up?"

"I'm just about to head out. What can I do for you?"

Damien stood up, hitting the button to shut down his laptop. He was much more eager to take this trip than he ever would have thought when he won the thing.

The last two years he'd taken these incentive trips and spent the whole time wishing he were back in New York. But this time, it was different. He wanted to go.

And it didn't take a brain surgeon to figure out why.

"So you're really taking your assistant with you on this trip?" Rob came into the room and sat down in the leather chair in front of Damien's desk, like he planned to stay awhile.

"Yes. Why?" Damien was suspicious of the casual tone Rob had employed. He leaned on his desk and crossed his arms, alert to any antagonism.

Rob shrugged. He was one of those guys who always had a grin, a charming compliment, an easy-going confidence. He looked comfortable in an expensive suit or a T-shirt to go jogging in and could switch from beer to wine and back again depending on the crowd.

"This is a prize trip. Most guys take their wives or their girlfriends, or if neither of those are available, their brother or something. No one ever takes their secretary, unless she falls in the girlfriend category."

"She doesn't." Damien's answer sounded sharp even to him and he felt a hot rush of angry embarrassment. It did look odd that he was taking Mandy, and he knew it. But he hadn't been able to resist the impulse to spend time with her, assure himself that she didn't think he was the boss from hell.

It had never bothered him before, what anyone thought. Yet it did now, with Mandy. But he would toss his laptop into the East River before he would ever admit that. "You know me. I can't stand being out of touch. We're going to get a jump on some of next month's projects."

"You really mean that. You're not sheet diving with your secretary." Rob looked at him in total disbelief.

"I really mean that." He didn't sheet dive with anyone, not anymore. And Rob was probably the only one who knew that, since he was the only person who had known Damien from before, when he'd lived in Chicago with Jessica.

But that wasn't to say that part of Damien hadn't been much more, well, *alert*, since Mandy Keeling had been hired. He wouldn't go so far as to say he wanted to have sex with her, but he was attracted to her.

That alone was something of a miracle given that he had thought himself incapable of any emotional or physical interest in another human being.

"Maybe you should."

"Should what?" Damien had lost the thread of their conversation.

"Have sex with your secretary. A little island fling under a tiki hut."

"That would be professional."

Rob crossed his feet on Damien's desk, making him itch to shove them off. His sense of neatness and order was offended by Rob's shoes nudging his inbox of papers a little to the left.

"She's hot."

"Excuse me?" Damien stared at Rob, not sure he was following him again. His foot tapped impatiently on the carpet; his hand rattled the change in his pocket. He needed to get to the airport.

"Mandy. Your assistant. She's hot."

"Is she? I hadn't noticed." And he really hadn't. He remembered finding her pretty in that initial meeting, but now he couldn't even dredge up a memory of what she looked like, not in any detail anyway. The niggling attraction he felt had more to do with her wit, her intelligence, her sharp sense of humor.

"If you haven't noticed, I'm worried about you." Rob dropped his feet to the floor, relieving Damien's blood pressure. "She's got that simple rich-girl look going on, like she went to a girls' school during the day, then snuck out at night to go skinny-dipping."

"You've given my assistant a lot of thought." Which somehow infuriated him. A feeling he had no right to claim. Rob was probably more Mandy's type anyway.

"Just scoping chicks for you, man, since you won't do it for yourself."

"Maybe there's a reason for that. Maybe I'm not interested."

"Damien." Rob's voice was soft, serious. "This isn't healthy for you . . . You've got to move on, do something besides work twenty-four/seven. She died, not you."

As if he didn't know that. He fucking felt that guilt every day. And it had eaten a piece out of his soul that could never be replaced.

Damien just stared at Rob, coolly, eyebrow raised. He didn't say anything, didn't blink. Until Rob squirmed and straightened his tie.

"I just think you work too much. There has to be more to life than that."

Picking up his suitcase, he nearly cut Rob down with a cruel remark, a dig at Rob about male bonding. But there was genuine concern on his friend's face, one of his only friends. Most had abandoned him during the investigation, and since he'd lived in New York, he hadn't bothered to make any new friends.

"I'm fine. My life is the way I want it."

But if it was, why was anticipation coursing through his veins for the first time in over three years?

Chapter 5

Mandy finished washing her hands in the miniature sink in the airplane loo and smoothed her hair back off her face. She had been doing so wonderfully. Until the plane had taken off. Then her stomach had stayed at ground level while they'd shot straight up to thirty thousand feet.

She hadn't waited for the seat belt sign to go off before rushing to the rest room and reacquainting herself with kissing the porcelain throne. Or in this case, stainless steel.

When she opened the door to stagger back up the aisle, Damien was standing there, his fist up as though he'd been about to knock.

"Are you okay?" he asked, leaning forward and studying her closely.

Mandy almost cringed under his scrutiny. The mirror in the rest room had not shown good things. Her hair was limp and her cheeks pale. So indignant at being sent hurdling back into morning sickness, Mandy gave no thought to politeness. This stupid trip was his idea, so it was his fault she felt as if she'd been tumbled in a hot clothes' dryer.

"No, I'm not okay. I just threw up in an airplane loo, which means my face was hovering over a metal toilet. All of humanity deposits their filthy germs in an airplane rest room. It's horrifying."

"Sorry," he said, dropping his hand. "But you're starting to worry me . . . It seems like you're always getting sick around me. Maybe I make you nauseous."

Though it was meant to be a joke, ha ha, Mandy just wasn't in the mood. "Don't worry, it's not just you. All men make me nauseous."

His mouth dropped, and she suspected it was the first time Damien Sharpton had been at a loss for words.

Great. She sounded like a man-hating lesbian.

"I'm kidding. I'm just not feeling well. I get airsick."

"You should have told me."

"Then what? You'd have let me stay home? Taken a boat?" The plane bounced a little. "I need to sit down."

"Of course." Damien put his hand on her elbow, and they both froze. She ground to a halt first; then he did, clearly uncertain why she was stopping so soon after starting.

But his touch, such a simple meaningless gesture, seared through her flesh and lit a slow-burning fire in her belly. She had almost convinced herself that her fevered dreams had exaggerated his attractiveness. Then he'd met her at the gate before boarding, and she'd realized she hadn't embellished a single thing. He was gorgeous. Tasty. Perfection.

"We're not going to have a repeat of the elevator, are we? Because I don't have any coffee this time."

An embarrassed twitter escaped her lips. Here she was becoming a sex-obsessed nymphomaniac wanna-be, and his thoughts centered around capturing her vomit.

"I'm fine. I just lost my balance." She hightailed it back to her seat, which was thankfully in first class and sporting a good deal of leg room. On the flip side, it was right next to Damien's seat, which was mortifying and distracting.

He had taken the window seat on boarding, so she had to hover in the aisle while he eased past her. His leg brushed hers and she shivered like a ninny.

"This air-conditioning is too high," she said to cover her movement.

He frowned at the sleeveless dress she was wearing. One she had chosen because it had no waist, which helped for comfort and camouflage.

"Don't you have a sweater or something?"

She shook her head and sat down as he was clicking his seat belt back on. Damien was wearing black pants, sandals, and a white T-shirt with a black stripe. It was made of stretchy fabric that showed her quite clearly he managed to squeeze time at the gym into his busy schedule.

It just wasn't fair that he was so hot and she couldn't do anything about it.

Except sit there with beaded nipples.

Mandy looked up from fastening her own seat belt and realized Damien's eyes were pinned on her chest. The chest with the beaded nipples.

His expression was inscrutable, but he said, "You need a blanket," and pressed the button for the flight attendant.

Oh, dear, God.

She was mortified.

Yet her uncooperative body was gleefully warming up from the inside out, reacting to being so close to a virile man.

Virile? Where the hell had that word come from? Mandy crossed her legs tightly. She was pregnant! The last thing she needed was more virility in her life. Any more virility and she'd be having quadruplets.

The flight attendant smiled at them. "Can I help you?"

"We need a blanket."

What was this "we" business? Of course, he was probably embarrassed and wanted to get her covered up. As the flight attendant searched the overhead compartment for a blanket, Mandy scrunched in her seat toward the aisle, away from Damien. She could smell him, a light masculine cologne intermingling with the scent of fabric softener.

He seemed like the type to be overenthusiastic with the fabric softener. His neatness was legendary around the office. In the bottom door of his desk he kept a dust buster, to suck up the crumbs from his lunch.

"Thank you." She took the blanket being held out to her and peeled it out of the plastic bag.

"Thanks." Damien nodded to the flight attendant.

The woman, attractive and *neat*, smiled at Damien. "You're welcome. Is this your first trip to Punta Cana?"

"Yes." And he smiled back.

He actually smiled. The man who never smiled to Mandy's knowledge, not that she had much, she realized. It wasn't as if she ever saw him, since she was usually hiding behind a cubicle wall or slipping into the copier room when she heard his voice approaching. But he wasn't known for being the life of the party. Yet here he was smiling at the flirty flight attendant with the big breasts and sleek blond hair.

Mandy snapped the blanket open, aware that this woman was probably more Damien's type than she was anyway. Not that she wanted to be his type. She was just hormonal and celibate and plagued by dreams of those stupid, freaky, blue eyes of his.

"Oh, it's gorgeous there. You'll love it."

"I'm sure we will. We're looking forward to it."

Placated, yet simultaneously unnerved by the whole plural pronoun thing, Mandy curled her feet under her legs and snuggled beneath the blanket. Busty Blonde took Damien's not-so-subtle hint and continued on down the aisle.

"She was flirting with you, you know," Mandy said after a minute, unable to keep her mouth shut.

Damien glanced up from his *PC Now* magazine. "Was she?" The question was rhetorical—he clearly knew she'd been sending out flight attendant feelers.

"Yes. And don't feel you have to restrain yourself on my behalf." Well, that sounded incredibly stodgy.

He turned a page and glanced at her. "Don't worry, I don't restrain myself for anyone. If I had wanted to flirt back, I would have. But thank you for your permission."

She'd just crawl under her blanket now.

"Are you feeling better?" he asked, his hand hovering over the seat pocket in front of him, ready to grab the airsick bag. "You still look a little . . . pale."

"I'm British. I'm always pale." Though offended, she realized immediately she had snapped at him, when he was actually being very solicitous. He'd come to check on her in the rest room, got her a blanket. "But thank you. I feel okay now."

He just nodded and slapped his magazine closed. His leg jiggled. "Did they say we could turn on our laptops yet?"

They were twenty minutes in the air and he was already restless.

"No, not yet. I don't think we're at cruising altitude." Only three more hours to go smothered up next to the object of her fantasies.

Maybe if she thought about work, the time would pass quicker. "Mr. Sharpton, what are we going to be doing on this trip, exactly?"

"I think you should probably call me Damien, Mandy. It's the Caribbean, man. Things are casual."

She grabbed her armrest so she wouldn't slide to the floor in shock. He had used an *accent*. He wanted her to call him Damien. The changing air pressure must be affecting his sanity.

But then again, she'd always suspected he had a sense of humor behind his workaholism.

"I won't be able to do as much as I'd like, because the Internet connection will be slow, so I can't connect to the server. But I plan to get caught up on reviewing promotion requests and employee development plans."

"What will I be doing?" And how far away from him

would she be? She couldn't imagine hovering in his hotel room with him.

"Clearing out my e-mails and submitting my expense reports for the last three weeks."

"That won't take me very long. Maybe a day."

"Then I guess you can go to the beach when you're finished."

It was an appealing thought. New York had been gray and cool all spring, and the thought of lying in a chaise lounge and taking a twelve-hour nap sounded like paradise.

"You didn't really need me to come on the trip, did you?" Mandy was curious why he had chosen to take his superfluous secretary when he could have taken a girlfriend or a buddy. Or his mother, though she had a hard time picturing a maternal influence on Damien.

He shrugged. "Maybe not. But think of it as a reward for going two whole months working for me and never once shedding a tear."

Mandy laughed. "I can't picture you making anyone cry. That girl must have been overly sensitive."

"I don't scare you?" he asked, his lip curving up at the corner.

"Not at all." *You intrigue me. You stimulate me. You turn me on.* "I've enjoyed this position."

His eyes locked with hers, and suddenly her words sounded vaguely suggestive. She was acutely aware of how close they were, surrounded on three sides by seats and the window, and of how her breath caught. Her already tender and swollen breasts ached painfully, and that tight pit of longing swirled in her belly and rolled down between her legs until she wanted to twitch.

"I'm pleased with my decision as well."

Then his finger slid up to his mouth, and he bit his fingernail, before yanking it out and looking at it in disgust. "I haven't done that in . . ."

Damien shifted on the seat, whatever comfort and intimacy that had been brewing between them gone in an instant. His shoulders were stiff, expression guarded, words polite. "I suppose I should have asked you if there was a reason you didn't want to take this trip. Like maybe a husband or a boyfriend that doesn't want you gone."

Mandy didn't even try to stifle the snort that flew out of her mouth. "No, don't have either one of those."

And she was grateful for it. If Ben had stuck around and given his half-hearted support to their relationship and their child, it would have been nothing but a burden. The clean break was better, and this baby was hers and hers alone.

"Good." Then he frowned. "I mean, that it wasn't a problem for you to travel."

She smiled and adjusted her blanket, so the whole front of her was covered. "Not a problem at all."

"I didn't think about what it would look like, though. There are rumors running around the office now, and I'm sorry."

"Rumors?" She touched the swelling bubble of her stomach, panic rising up into her throat. "What kind of rumors?"

"Some people seem to think I invited you because we're having an affair."

Damien hadn't meant to bring that up. Ever.

Especially since it didn't look like that thought had occurred to Mandy. At least he figured that's why she was curling her lip back in horror.

"Who thinks that?"

"A friend of mine just mentioned it." And Damien shouldn't have. "It's no big deal," he said, trying to backpedal and reassure her.

Mandy was an enigma to him, a blend of prissy efficiency, sly humor, and intense vulnerability.

Damien was glad she had draped that blanket over her like a tarp, covering every inch of her from neck to ankle. He was ashamed to admit that when she had been shivering with cold, he had been painfully aware of the effect on her chest. He'd gawked at her nipples like a teenage boy with a Victoria's Secret catalog.

It was disturbing, an uncomfortable awareness growing in his body again. Something he'd really and truly thought was dead was rising back to life, no pun intended.

He was horny.

For Mandy.

She licked her lips nervously. "That's a little awkward."

"I'm sorry, I didn't mean to make you uncomfortable in the office." No, he hadn't meant for that to happen. He had just wanted to corner Mandy, trap her into his presence, force her to look him in the eye.

Why, he wasn't sure.

But she was here with him now, and he was sexually attracted to her, and intellectually attracted to her, and he now wanted to pursue both and yet knew he wouldn't, couldn't, because of his past. And he was acutely aware that she was his assistant and this was supposed to be a business trip.

The only person he'd backed into a corner had been himself.

Mandy had soft brown eyes, expressive and poignant, compassion sprinkled in them like the amber flecks around her pupils. "That's okay." She smiled, a sweet, secret, slightly wicked smile that did all kinds of riotous things to his gut. "Besides, they could be thinking worse things about me. I'd rather people envy me than feel sorry for me."

"What makes you think they would envy you an affair with Demon Sharpton?" He'd overheard that moniker one afternoon when he'd stepped into the break room for a cup of coffee. It had mildly irritated him then, but now he didn't care what anyone else called him—he just wanted to know what Mandy thought of him.

She laughed a soft, rich, tinkling sound. Her head tilted toward him, the blanket slipping down to the swell of her breasts. "Oh, come on, Damien, you have to know that they call you Demon Sharpton because you're tough, yes, but also because you don't pay attention to any of the women. It frustrates them."

He liked the way she said his name, her accent giving it a sophistication it had never had before. "Actually I think they call me Demon because asshole doesn't rhyme with Damien."

A startled laugh flew out of her mouth, her lips splitting in a wide, genuine grin. "I don't think that's it at all." Then she studied him, curious, fingers gripping the fuzzy blue edge of the polyester blanket. "Why do you let them think that about you? I don't think you really deserve either appellation."

How could he tell this woman, with her honest and direct eyes, that it was easier to let people think he was an asshole? That it kept people away from him, who would infringe on his time, his friendship, his emotions, drawing him back into entanglements that he no longer had the strength to deal with. There was no way to describe how he'd crawled back out of a raw agony, and the only means to keep the crushing fear at bay, to protect his sanity, was to prevent anyone from getting close to him.

When Jessica had been murdered, he had retreated into a carefully constructed house of cards. If he let people start flicking their fingers at the shaky walls, it was possible it would all fall around him.

So he shrugged. "I don't care what people think."

Two months ago he would have said that and meant it.

But now it felt like he was skirting the edge of truth. He definitely cared what the woman next to him thought.

"Well, bully for you," Mandy said softly with a smile, resting her head on the back of the seat. "If we should all be so mature."

He shifted, turned more fully toward her, disturbing her blanket in the process. Damien twitched it back into place, careful not to touch Mandy's bare arm. "Maybe it's not maturity. Maybe it's arrogance. I'm just a jerk, like everyone says."

If she believed it, she would retreat, leave him alone, stay outside the bitter bubble he lived in. Because if Mandy started to look at him with softness in her eyes, he wasn't sure he was going to be able to resist.

And he had nothing of value inside his soul to offer a woman like her.

But she already was gracing him with a lazy smile and a sweet understanding shining in her eyes. "I don't believe that, Damien Sharpton. I think there's much more to you than meets the eye."

Then hers drifted closed, and in a minute, her breath evened out as she dozed.

His attraction, that interest in her, grew exponentially.

Damien bent over and got out his laptop, careful not to disturb her. Determined to work and push her out of his mind, he reread a report he was working on, proofreading it for errors.

But every few minutes, his gaze scuttled over to Mandy, sleeping peacefully, her pink lips parted on a sigh, her bangs tumbling down over her eyebrows.

Damn it. Damien slammed the lid closed on his computer. It was impossible to type when the thing was rocking back and forth, destabilized by his massive erection.

He let down his tray table and set the laptop on it, but he didn't accomplish a whole lot.

Except give himself whiplash checking Mandy out every five seconds.

This trip had been a huge ass mistake, and if he had to see her in a bikini he was screwed.

The thought sent his tray table bouncing up enthusiastically as his cock swelled.

Chapter 6

Mandy lay in a chaise lounge and flipped through the parenting magazine she had subscribed to eight weeks earlier when she had thought educating herself about pregnancy would actually alleviate stress.

The weightier *Everything Guide to Pregnancy* was collecting dust in her beach bag. She had brought it, knowing she had to read the thing sooner or later so she didn't miss the early signs of labor, or make an ill-informed circumcision decision. But she had discovered something about herself—she was a wimp. She just wanted to sit back and enjoy anticipating her baby—not memorize terms like VBAC and effacement, or create her Delivery Advocacy Plan to take to the hospital like Jamie kept insisting she needed to do.

There was just too much information flooding her brain cells, and she had decided to take a month-by-month approach to things. She would read up to the point she had reached in the baby's gestation and no farther so she didn't collapse under information overload. But she had thought glancing through the magazine wouldn't hurt, since it had cute pictures of chubby babies and funny little essays on parenting.

Besides, she was bored.

Punta Cana was beautiful, a breezy eighty-five degrees and blue sunny skies, not a raindrop in sight. But Damien had been avoiding her, or at least it seemed that way to her. She hadn't seen him since they'd arrived at the hotel forty-eight hours earlier. On her own, she had taken all her meals with total strangers, having been adopted by a nice British couple in their sixties who clearly felt sorry for her.

While they were a couple of dears, and she had gluttoned herself at the amazing buffets the hotel offered—not the least bit worried about unwashed fruit—it wasn't the same as being on holiday with family or friends.

She wasn't comfortable parasailing, speed boating, snorkeling, or scuba diving since she was pregnant. Though she had swum in the ocean a few times, played three games of water volleyball, and one round of shuffleboard. She'd entered an egg race on the beach with other hotel guests and had petted a monkey, perched a parrot on her shoulder, and sat on a donkey.

All of which were delightful, but she was used to being surrounded by friends and coworkers. People to talk to. And as much as she'd tried, the parrot hadn't said a peep. Mandy sipped her virgin daiquiri and wondered for the hundredth time why Damien had brought her on this trip. He didn't need her here, clearly.

Which left her to read an article on the risks of pregnancy when using condoms.

Many pregnancies result from the condom breaking or a hole in the latex, but just as many pregnancies are the result of improper use.

How did one use a condom incorrectly? Stick it on their ear?

Many men try to put the condom on inside out, realize their mistake, and flip it over, thereby inserting the condom with seminal fluid already present directly in the vagina.

Oh, my God.

Ben had been notorious for doing that.

"Well, that explains a thing or two," she said out loud, tempted to fax the article to Ben. At his office.

"Explains what?" Damien asked from right behind her shoulder.

Damn. Mandy jumped in the chair and slapped the magazine closed. Hell, there was a cue-ball-headed baby on the cover, grinning for all he was worth. She flipped it to the back cover, which was a teary-eyed toddler gazing at the mess he'd made on the floor.

She shoved it in her bag. Which left her stomach completely exposed to his view.

Her bare, pregnant stomach, popping up above her bikini bottoms. She raised her knees to de-emphasize the bubble below her belly button.

"Nothing, just muttering to myself." Mandy shielded her eyes from the sun and turned to look back at him. "So you decided to actually leave your room?"

Complex and mysterious woman that she was, she found herself equal parts thrilled and horrified to see him. Or maybe she was just idiotic.

Damien dropped into the chair next to her and kicked his sandals off in the sand. "I figured the guys back at work would give me a hard time if I came home as white as when I left."

"That's true." Mandy tried to command herself not to look at his body, but it was hopeless. Already she was raking up and down him like a starving woman at a feast. Or like a horny pregnant woman having sexual dreams about her boss.

He was sickeningly flawless. Broad chest, a smattering of hair across his well-defined pectorals, a ripped washboard stomach. When he sat back on the lounger, he brought his arms up to cup his head, and Mandy sighed.

Those were the kind of arms a woman just wanted to sink into.

If she weren't pregnant and hiding the fact from her boss.

"Make sure you put on your sunscreen. This sun is extremely powerful. I slathered it on, and I still got burned on my back and shoulders where I couldn't reach." The sun was so hot Mandy had wondered if she were actually cooking her baby in utero.

She had shifted the chair to the shade of a tiki hut and made sure she drank lots of water and took breaks back in her room, so she thought she was safe, but maybe she ought to look it up in *The Everything Guide*. After Damien went away.

"Do you have your sunscreen?" Damien held out his hand. "I'll get your back."

Oh, he did not just say that. Mandy bit her lip. There was just no way she was letting him rub lotion all over her bare back. "Oh, well! I'm in the shade, so I think I'm fine, thanks."

"We don't want your British skin burning." Damien leaned over and started rooting in her beach bag. "Is your sunscreen in here?"

How very like a successful businessman to just take over and stick his fingers where they didn't belong. "No, really . . ." She trailed off when he pulled out her issue of *Baby Talk*.

"What's this?" He glanced curiously at it.

She ripped it from his hands. "Oh, just something I picked up by accident."

Because it was so easy to confuse a big, bald baby face on the cover with the half-naked women always on *Cosmo*.

But she couldn't worry about how ridiculous her lie sounded when he was bound to encounter *The Everything Guide to Pregnancy* in another three seconds. Mandy reached out and snagged her beach bag from him.

"Let me get the sunscreen. You'll never find it, I have tons of crap just rattling around in here." Hand deep in the bag, Mandy felt her cheeks heat. Damien's eyes were shielded behind dark sunglasses, but he looked perplexed. Suspicious.

Palm closing around it, she pulled the tube of sunscreen

out and slapped it into his hand. With a brilliant smile, she tried to distract him. "So, have you been to the buffet for dinner yet? It's absolutely divine."

Damien frowned, and even with the sunglasses shielding his expression, she could tell his gaze had landed on her stomach. Was he putting two and two together—her belly, the magazine . . . Mandy's heart started racing, her palms sweating, her cheeks burning from more than the Caribbean sun.

"I haven't made it to the buffet, but I'm glad you're enjoying it. Lots of desserts?" His words were polite, casual, as he tossed the sunscreen from hand to hand.

Mandy realized with dawning horror just what his words implied. Oh, that was just lovely. He thought she was fat! Two and two in his head hadn't equaled pregnancy. He thought she'd been hitting the dessert table too hard. Allison was right—men didn't notice *anything*.

Except hard nipples.

"Turn around," he said, clearly no idea he had offended her.

Bloody idiot.

She gave him her back. "Yes, the desserts are marvelous. You're going to have to roll me onto the plane."

A breeze kicked her hair across her lip, and she pried the strand off as she heard lotion squirt into Damien's hand.

His chair squeaked as he scooted forward on it. "That's good. You look better than when I first met you. I guess it was the flu, but you looked kind of thin. You seem healthier now."

Fatter. That's what he meant.

Mandy rolled her eyes behind her sunglasses. Then tensed when his hands landed on her shoulders, smooth and cool with lotion. Big hands, confident hands, that glided across her skin with strong strokes, his thumbs skimming along behind his fingers.

Damien had leaned over closer—she could hear his breathing, smell toothpaste and the coconut scent of the sunscreen. "And people think I'm tense. Relax, Mandy."

He had no idea what he was asking of her. If she relaxed, really and truly relaxed, she'd sink in to his touch, sigh and moan and revel in the feeling of a man's strong but gentle hands caressing her.

It was hell being stoic all the time, and she wasn't even doing a very good job of it. And Damien was so gorgeous and competent and broad-shouldered, with those delectable baby blues.

He skimmed her spine, sending a shiver rolling through her and setting her inner thighs burning with desire.

She groaned, a long, low sound of abandonment.

Damien knew he was pushing into dangerous territory. Hell, he'd jumped into a fucking volcano.

His plan to avoid Mandy had just failed. And then some.

After shutting himself in his hotel room for two straight days, working like a fiend, and intermittently wondering what Mandy was doing, and what she was wearing, he'd needed some fresh air. It had been a happy coincidence that ten steps on the beach and he'd found Mandy lying in a chaise lounge, reading a magazine.

Except he supposed it didn't count as a coincidence at all since he had the funny feeling he would have paced up and down the beach like an expectant father until he'd found her.

Even so, he hadn't meant to put his hands on her. That had been an impulse. A stupid one. A head-up-his-ass impulse.

But she had looked so good.

Every imagining he'd had of Mandy wearing a bikini hadn't prepared him for the sight of her stretched out in an army green scrap of nothing bathing suit. He had always pictured Mandy as thin and fragile, probably because she'd had the flu when they first met.

But she wasn't thin and bony and untouchable. She was curvy and lush and delicious, with full breasts straining the tiny triangles and making his mouth water. So he'd pressed an excuse on her to rub his hands all over her back and shoulders.

And she was groaning.

He felt like doing the same.

Instead, he said, "Do you want to go to the buffet together tonight? The room service is really slow, and I need to get out a little anyway."

Her head fell forward. "I'd love to. I'm sure the older couple I've been shadowing would like some time alone. Though they did say I remind them of their daughter Annie, who's off at university. The one they told me in the next breath is something of a screw-up."

Damien chuckled and refilled his hands with lotion. "Lift your hair and I'll get your neck." He leaned forward until his mouth was near her ear, his fingers tracing her clavicle bones. "I owe you an apology. I asked you on this trip impulsively and never considered the inconvenience to you."

That was probably the first time ever that he had admitted a wrong to one of his assistants. But he knew it was true. He was harsh and inflexible sometimes, and thought only of himself.

Mandy's elbows were out as she piled hair in a bundle on her head, and he spoke right over her shoulder. A little push forward and he could skim his lips along her jaw, kiss that dimple in her cheek that appeared when she smiled.

"While I accept your apology, I have to say it's very relaxing, actually, which is something I really needed. I've been under a bit of stress lately."

He paused. "I heard your boss is an ogre."

She laughed. "That's not what I meant. I like working for you, believe it or not. There's just been some personal . . . issues I'm dealing with."

Lord knew he could understand that. But she'd said she

didn't have a boyfriend or a husband, so before rational thought could intrude, he tugged on the tie that held her bikini top in place.

She grabbed the front of the top to hold it against her and made a sound of distress. "What are you doing?"

Taking a dip in that volcano. "I can't get under the strings with the sunscreen." Which was true. But he also wanted to see her bare back, touch all of her, imagine what it would be like to take Mandy as a lover, to undress her like this in heightened anticipation, both of them breathing hard and wound tight with sexual interest.

Sort of like he was right now. He moved his hands over the whole of her back, kneading her muscles with his thumbs.

"Oh, okay," she said, sounding a little unnerved. "But be careful. I don't have the sangfroid of some of these women strolling around topless. I'd prefer to keep my breasts an alluring secret."

That they were.

With no excuse to linger, he retied her strings with sticky fingers. "There, all set to fry."

Mandy turned to him and held her hand out. "Your turn."

He settled back in his chair. "Turn for what?"

"Back and shoulders. Face front, Damien, so I can put the sunscreen on you."

What? No way in hell he was letting her touch him. He'd need a bucket of ice from the beach bar poured down his shorts first. "I'm fine. I don't need sunscreen."

She shot him a look of disbelief. "You're a very difficult man, you know."

And this was news? "I know."

"You're not supposed to admit that."

"Why not?"

"Because it's rude or something. I don't know." Mandy

set her feet on the sand and reached for the sunscreen he'd dropped on her beach towel.

"I thought it was mature to admit my flaws."

"Not when that flaw is being difficult." She squirted a great white glob of sunscreen on her hand. "Turn around."

"You don't have to. I can get it." Just the thought of her touching him made him a little desperate. His feelings for her were unexplainable and unwanted, but they were there. Since he was not in as firm of control as he would like, it was possible she would guess he was attracted to her.

Which would be the end of the world as he knew it.

"Turn around. Even demons need sunscreen in the Caribbean." And she grabbed both of his shoulders and tried to twist him.

Their knees bumped, her breasts hovered close to his chest, and he didn't know whether to laugh or cry. It was torturous to want her and know he couldn't have her. Until Mandy, his body had been sexually dormant, and while it had woken up raring to go, nothing else had changed. His heart was still frozen.

"All right, all right." He hooked his leg over the chaise longue and spun away from her. "Now who's being difficult?"

Damien expected Mandy's touch to be soft and gentle. He'd misread her again. Her strokes were bold, sensual, the lotion making a squishing sound between her fingers as she moved across his back methodically.

"It's not being difficult when you're right. And I caught you just in the nick of time—your shoulders are pink already."

"I've only been out here for ten minutes." Damien fought the urge to close his eyes and sigh. He had forgotten how good it felt to have a woman so close, hovering behind him, warm and alive and concerned for him. To smell her, to have her hair brush against him.

"What's this? A tattoo? Why, Mr. Sharpton, I'm shocked." Her voice was teasing.

Damien stiffened. He only had one tattoo and he did not want to discuss . . .

"Jess. Who's Jess?"

Pain kicked him in the gut, pain he thought he'd buried down deep under a layer of work and exhaustion. What could he say? Jess had been his wife. His beautiful, successful wife, and she had been murdered. How was that for a little light, lounging-in-the-sun conversation?

Since the tattoo was on his upper arm, he rarely looked at it and could effectively ignore that Jessica's name was scrawled on his skin. Branding her to him forever, the physical manifestation of what was interwoven in his soul. Jessica had laughed that day he'd come home with it, her blond hair falling over his chest as she had inspected it. It had amused her, pleased her that he had taken such a dramatic way to display his feelings.

What I love about you, Damien, is the way you love me.

How many times had she said that?

He had lost himself in her all those years ago, and had never found a way back out.

"A woman," he said. "She was a woman."

Mandy's fingers slowed. Her voice cooled. "Is this woman still in your life?"

God, if she only knew how much Jessica was still in his life. Damien dug his toes into the sand. "No. No, she hasn't been for a long time."

"Then you should get her name turned into something else. A celtic cross, or flowers. No, flowers are too feminine . . . maybe barbed wire, or you could switch Jess to Jesus."

Damien felt the tightness in his chest lessening as Mandy spoke. She was doing the unimaginable—talking about Jess with a flippant, irreverent attitude. But she didn't know the whole truth, and for some reason, hearing her joke about his tattoo eased the peach pit that had lodged in his throat.

"It could say 'Jesus is my home boy.' "

A startled laugh burst out of his mouth, surprising him. "That doesn't really sound like my style." And it sounded downright hilarious in Mandy's British accent.

Her fingers strayed to his stomach, and she wiped back and forth. "Extra sunscreen."

His muscles clenched, a jolt of sexual awareness ripping through him.

But Mandy stood up. "Oh, look, they're starting beach bingo. Come on, let's play."

She patted his shoulder and started down the beach.

And he didn't even resist.

Chapter 7

Damien was kicking ass at beach bingo. Mandy watched him with growing amusement. She held her card in her lap, the beans they'd been given as markers rolling around, no longer on the numbers that had been called.

The first time she'd upset her whole card, she had asked Damien to read her the numbers he had. It had aggravated him, since he hadn't been able to hear the new numbers as they were called with her distracting him.

So the second time she'd spilled her beans, she had just leaned over and shifted his markers around so she could see the numbers. Only in doing that, she had got in the way of him seeing his board, and he'd got bingo just seconds behind another hotel guest.

He'd been ticked off. Mandy didn't understand why, since he'd won twice already, but Damien was nothing if not competitive. Now he had his card set on the ground, his feet pinning it so the wind wouldn't take off with it. His knee went up and down in agitation, and his hand hovered over the card with a bean at the ready.

Mandy sometimes wished she had an ounce of competitiveness in her, but it had never surfaced. She liked to do things she enjoyed and didn't really care about the outcome as long as she had fun. Which probably explained why her toy shop had never turned a profit.

The games coordinator sat at a table calling the numbers. With a smile, he pulled the next ball out.

"Eight. Ocho. Huit."

Before he was even finished with the French translation, Damien was on his feet. "Bingo!"

There was some good-natured grumbling from the half a dozen women in their seventies playing, while Damien strutted to the table to collect his latest prize pack. Sitting at Mandy's feet were already three bottles of rum, two T-shirts, a piece of Dominican artwork, a model of a sailboat, and a necklace made out of shells. She couldn't even begin to imagine why he needed any more booty.

At least the bingo caller had said that was the last game. Mandy was enjoying herself, but she was also getting hungry. The buffet should have opened for dinner, and since Damien already thought she had a pastries pouch, she might as well indulge herself.

Damien collected his prize, then to her surprise, turned and passed the two bottles of rum and the T-shirt out to the ladies who had been playing. He came back over to Mandy, retrieved the rest of the winnings, and finished doling them out, until everyone had received something.

The ladies laughed, beamed, gave him cheek kisses, and called him "blue eyes."

He kept a bottle of rum and the shell necklace, which he undid the clasp on as he stood in front of her. "Lift your hair, Mandy."

She did, and he put the necklace around her neck, hooked the clasp, and stood back, inspecting the way it lay on her chest. "Thank you, Damien," she said, a little stunned, a little touched, and a little worried.

The way he looked right now, serious yet happy, good-looking and generous, she had a feeling her dreams about him might not revolve around just sex anymore.

"Perfect," he said. His eyes locked with hers. "Beautiful."

She had wrapped a sarong around her waist, but hadn't pulled on a shirt, and the necklace hovered above her cleavage, cool on her warm skin. Without meaning to, her fingers trailed across the shells as she stared deep into his ocean blue eyes, and she couldn't think of a single thing to say.

The bingo women didn't suffer from the same problem. "Hold on to this one, honey. He's a keeper."

"That is one hot look he's sending her."

"If I were thirty years younger . . ."

"You'd still be old enough to be his mother."

The speaker was eighty if she was a day, wearing a straw hat that probably weighed more than its owner, and Mandy and Damien both laughed, the moment broken. But Mandy still knew that something was happening, something that shouldn't. Something that had no place in her life now that she was going to be a mother, with huge responsibilities.

She was falling for Damien.

Which meant she should beat a hasty retreat, eat dinner alone in her room, and pray for a dreamless night of sleep.

Then he smiled and held out his hand. "Ready for dinner?"

"Absolutely. Let's do it."

Now there was the way to hang tough.

Damien wished he could blame it on the rum, but the truth was he hadn't swallowed a drop. He'd had ice water with his dinner and enough food for three people.

Which didn't explain why he was feeling so incredibly relaxed, mellow, why he had kicked off his shoes, rolled his pants up, and was letting the sand fall over his feet.

"It's such a gorgeous evening," Mandy said, staring out at the waves hitting the beach.

She was gorgeous. After bingo, they'd separated to change for dinner, and Mandy had put her hair up into a little twist on top of her head, soft, wispy tendrils falling around her face. She wore a coral-colored sundress, and the silly little necklace he'd won was resting between the two straps.

New York seemed a million miles and a lifetime away. There was nothing but soft island music, the crash of the waves, a balmy breeze, and Mandy.

"I still can't believe they brought the whole buffet down to the beach. It's amazing."

She was amazing. She had chatted with him throughout a long and leisurely dinner. They had talked about her childhood, her distant father, and her overbearing mother, and he had realized from her stories that Mandy had been given lots of material things growing up, but she had craved her parents' attention more than anything. It made him want to put a call through to England and inform them they were idiots for neglecting their intelligent and compassionate daughter.

"My mother would be horrified at eating on the beach. 'Think of the bugs!' she'd say," Mandy said with a laugh. " 'The germs! The sand. That soup probably has a tablespoon of sand instead of salt in it.' " She shook her head. "It's not civilized enough for her."

"She doesn't like nature?"

"She likes nature when it's been controlled. In a proper English garden."

Damien sipped his water. "My mom would love it here. She hates Chicago winters. They're hoping to move to Florida when my dad retires next year."

He should call his own parents, see how they were. He hadn't talked to them since Christmas. And they had never neglected him, far from it. Their house had been a happy one, with lots of love and laughter.

"You're from Chicago?"

He nodded, suddenly shocked at the overwhelming sense of homesickness that swept over him. He hadn't been back since, well, since he'd left. "Born and raised. Just a regular kid, in a middle class suburb, Dad's an engineer, Mom a homemaker. I had a brother, a dog, and a passion for baseball."

Mandy smiled at him, slow, relaxed, her finger wiping a stray bit of whipped cream off her dessert plate. "What happened to that regular kid? The brother, the dog, baseball?"

That boy had wanted to pitch for the White Sox, marry a pretty girl, move into a rambling house down the block from his parents in Beverly, and have a couple of boys of his own. Damien remembered the dreams, but wasn't sure he even knew how to relate to them anymore. That's not who he was at thirty-three. Life had taken him to New York, where he was very successful, lived in an apartment building with a doorman, and worked twenty hours a day.

He had very few friends, never saw his family, and had long ago given up the idea of ever having children.

This was why he never got introspective. It was damn depressing.

"The brother lives in Seattle and I never see him. The dog's long gone, and there's no time in my schedule for baseball."

Instead of looking at him in disgust and going to seek better company, Mandy licked the cream off her finger and shot him a wicked look. "I'm in charge of your schedule. Maybe next week you'll find baseball penciled in for Saturday at one o'clock. The Yankees are playing."

"You would, wouldn't you?" His assistant was efficient, he'd give her that.

"Yep. I have access to your credit card."

He laughed in spite of himself. "Get two tickets then. You and me."

"You got it."

And at that moment, it occurred to him that he was sitting back in his chair, completely relaxed, and not one thought about his laptop lying idle in his room had crossed his mind.

He was on vacation and it didn't hurt.

Wonders never cease.

"Walk with me." He stood up and tossed his napkin on the table. There were a hundred people around, dancing to the live band, eating their dinners at the dozens of candlelit tables set up on the sand. Crowds didn't bother him—he usually liked to get lost in an anonymous crowd—but here, tonight, he wanted to be alone with Mandy.

He had changed his mind about his assistant. He no longer wanted to avoid her. He wanted to kiss her.

To taste those full pink lips and draw her into his arms, hand in her soft wavy hair. To absorb her feeling, her scent, take her all into him and remember what it was like to know passion, pure tactile pleasure.

Damien stuck his feet back in his sandals, but Mandy shook the sand off hers and put them in her bag. "Where are we going?"

"Nowhere. Just walking." He gazed at the horizon. "I've forgotten how to do that."

Every step he took had a purpose, every thought in his head task oriented. He didn't walk for pleasure, he didn't indulge in daydreaming.

But as the sun started to sink and the palm trees danced in the breeze, he wanted to walk and do nothing, be nothing, pretend that he was normal, a whole human being, who could have a beautiful woman at his side.

Mandy put her arm through his, leaning on him a little as they started to walk. He liked the feeling, like she trusted him. Like she wanted to touch him.

"Are you happy, Damien?"

The question caught him off guard, made him give a snort. He wasn't even sure what happiness was, or that it existed. He believed in hard knocks; he believed in hard work, but happiness? It was nothing but a faint, fading memory.

They were walking past beach vendors who hawked their

T-shirts and jewelry and artwork from their makeshift shacks. Damien was saved from answering by an aggressive salesman calling out, "Señorita! Hola . . . I give you good price, come see. Pretty bracelet for a pretty woman."

Mandy shook her head with a smile. "No, thank you."

"Señor is cheap, huh?" he asked with a sly grin at Damien.

Mandy laughed and waved as they walked on past.

"You didn't even defend me," Damien said in mock protest. "I am not cheap."

"Well, I don't think you are, but I'm really not entirely sure, having never seen you shopping. But you're not going to distract me from my original question." Her fingers pressed into his flesh. "Are you happy?"

Damien stopped walking and looked down at her, at the warm expression in her mocha brown eyes. She had a dusting of freckles across the bridge of her nose that he wanted to kiss. "Why does it matter to you, Mandy?"

"Because I like you," she said simply, and it stirred to life embers he had thought were long burned out.

He started walking again, eager to move past the vendors, to where the sun and the ocean met with nothing but beach between them. He ached inside and out, with the physical need to bury himself inside Mandy, to seek pleasure and oblivion in that tender sensual give and take of sex with someone he respected, admired, was a bit in awe of.

"I'm content," he told her, figuring that was close enough to the truth. "Or at least I was until I met you."

"What did I do?" she whispered.

"You made me see that I'm lonely . . ." Damien stopped, took Mandy's hand in his, turned her to him. They were only a few feet past the noise and laughter of the vendors, but he didn't care. "I can't—don't want—a relationship. But Mandy, I find you very attractive, and I would really like to kiss you right now."

Of course, he wanted to have sex with her under the

nearest tiki hut, but he figured he should ease her into the idea.

Start with a kiss, *then* move to wild sex on the beach.

Mandy swallowed a bucketful of saliva. Whoa, boy. This was unexpected.

Or maybe it wasn't.

They had spent the evening talking, laughing, relaxing, and in Damien she saw some of the same loneliness, the same fears that seemed to have taken up permanent residence in her.

She thought, perhaps, Damien Sharpton wasn't so much a cruel, heartless man as he was a wounded man, scarred inside where no one could see it. Except her.

And she wanted to hold him, be held in return, in a mutual clasp of comfort.

But he was her boss, and she was keeping a big secret from him, and this was a sandy beach far away from home where reality was skewed and where mistakes could be made.

"Damien, I find you very attractive as well. Both physically and as a person. So I'm very much afraid that a kiss would lead to something else, and would that really be such a good . . ."

Mandy lost complete track of her thought as a fluttering sensation moved across her abdomen. "What on earth?" Heart racing, she placed her hands over her stomach and felt it again. The very first movements of her baby.

Oh, my God, it was incredible, absolutely amazing. She reached out and clutched Damien's linen shirt with her free hand, suddenly light-headed.

"Are you going to throw up again?" Damien grabbed her elbows, looking left and right as if seeking help.

Mandy laughed. She was going to be a mother. There was a *child* growing inside her, and she/he was swimming laps back and forth from the feel of it. An almost overwhelming surge of love stole over her for this baby, and she wanted to share such a perfect moment with someone. Had to explain to another person that her whole world was shifting and morphing and she was settling into a wondrous kind of excitement over those changes.

"I'm not going to be sick." She grabbed Damien's hand and laid it flat on her abdomen. "Can you feel it, Damien? The baby's moving."

"The baby?" he squawked, eyes the size of dinner plates. "What baby?"

Now he looked like the one capable of tossing his tea and toast. "My baby. The one I'm having in approximately twenty-three weeks."

His mouth moved, but nothing came out. His gaze dropped to her stomach, where his hand was pressed over the coral sundress. Mandy put her hand over his, so he wouldn't pull back. She wanted someone to feel the same miracle she was experiencing. Maybe it was too early for someone else to feel the movements, but if it wasn't . . .

There was a quick push outward, as if the baby had jettisoned off a springboard, and Mandy broke into a smile as awareness dawned on Damien's face.

"Holy shit," was his opinion, and he looked a little as though he'd walked into a wall after drinking a fifth of gin, but at the same time his thumb stole over her belly in a little soft stroke.

"That's amazing." His eyes locked with hers, and she saw the same wonder in them that she felt. "I actually felt it."

Tears of joy blurred her vision. "I think I just fell completely in love with my baby."

"Your baby," he repeated softly, before pulling his hand back and rubbing his forehead. "Your baby." He shook his head. "Want to tell me exactly how that is possible?"

Then he quickly held his hand up. "No, wait, that's not what I mean. I don't need a detailed description of conception. But . . . can I ask . . . who's the father? Where is he?"

Mandy wiped a tear off her eyelash and knew she needed to explain everything to Damien. This wasn't a secret she could keep any longer, not when she knew Damien the way she did now. Not when this mutual attraction was undulating between them.

"I was seeing a man for six months. He misused a condom, and when I turned up pregnant, suggested I terminate. When I refused, he offered me five thousand dollars to have my baby and never bother him again. He has two grown sons who are a disappointment to him. He didn't want to bring up another child, only to have it let him down." Mandy was still horrified by Ben's reaction. She had thought she'd known him, but clearly she had been completely wrong.

"Asshole," was Damien's vehement opinion.

"Yes." She nodded. That about summed it up.

Damien took a step to the right, then back. His hands went on his hips. "The flu you had . . . it was morning sickness, wasn't it?"

She nodded. It didn't surprise her he had worked that out already. Damien was an intelligent man, a quick thinker. It was how he was so successful.

"No wonder I didn't catch any germs from you then. I kept waiting to come down with the flu. I sure in the hell can't catch what you have." He shook his head and gave an ironic laugh. "Is this why you've avoided me? You didn't want me to know?"

His finger went into his mouth and he chewed on a corner of the nail.

Mandy wanted to explain herself, wanted to take away the harshness that had crept into his face. "I need this job. I need the health insurance and I need the nine-to-five hours so that day care arrangements will be easier. I didn't think that the Damien Sharpton I'd been told about would hire a pregnant woman." And she hoped like hell Demon Sharpton wouldn't fire a pregnant woman.

But she didn't believe he would, despite the tension in his shoulders. She wouldn't have told him if she had.

"You're probably right." Damien glanced at his finger and dropped it. "Why the fuck do I keep biting my nails?"

She hoped that was a rhetorical question.

The beach had darkened, and his face was pale against the dark sky. His voice softened. "So why did you tell me now, Mandy?"

"Because I wanted to be honest with you." She took a step closer to him, skirting the bag she'd dropped in the sand. "And because when I felt the baby move, I needed to share it with someone, and I think that you're a man who can appreciate what I'm experiencing. Was I wrong?"

She didn't want to be wrong. She didn't want to think that her impulsiveness in telling him had been a poor choice. She had told herself now that she was going to be a mum, she had to leave impulsiveness behind. But something had told her to tell him, and she just didn't want to regret it, not now when she was feeling so humbled and in awe of the life growing inside her.

"You should be wrong." Damien looked over her shoulder toward the water. He sighed. "There are reasons why you should be very wrong."

He looked down at her, closed the space between them. Her heart started to pound faster, harder, when his hand cupped her cheek.

"But you're not wrong."

She closed her eyes, turned her nose and mouth toward his hand. She could smell the salty tang of his flesh, feel the rough callus of his thumb stroking over her. Without thinking, she pressed her lips into the moist hollow of his hand.

"Mandy." His voice was hoarse, quiet. Intense.

"Yes?"

But he didn't speak, and his hand dropped. Her eyes flew

open only to see that he was closing in on her, his nose inches from hers, his mouth a hairbreadth away, his shoulders descending toward hers. She only had time to suck in her breath as anticipation spiked between her thighs, made her breasts tingle.

Then he was kissing her, an honest-to-goodness, lips everywhere, tongue-teasing, knee-wobbling kiss. Excitement exploded throughout her body in little spastic lightning bolts of desire.

Mandy dipped her head back, opening her mouth, marveling at the taste and texture of him, so firm, so wet, so eager, so different, and yet exactly what she should have expected. Damien was in control, but beneath the surface of the kiss, beneath his dominating impatience, skittered an edgy vulnerability that was just as appealing as his confidence and skill.

"Ooohhh," she murmured when his lips moved to her jaw, her neck. Her body felt different, more sensitive, quicker to react, and she wasn't sure if it was Damien or the pregnancy, or a blissful combination of the two.

His thigh shifted, surrounding her with his heat, and he cut off her moan with another kiss that left her clinging to him like seaweed. Mandy could hear the excited little rush of both their breath, the pants, the moans, the shift from casual exploration to urgent questing.

She ground herself against him, then was shocked that she did. Even more so by the obvious dampness in her knickers and the eager kick of satisfaction at feeling Damien's thick erection nudging her.

"You taste so good, so damn good," he said in a hot whisper, thumbs rolling her sundress straps toward her shoulders.

"Damien, what the hell are we doing?" Then she yelped when he brushed her nipple. "Bugger it, that feels good."

She was certain her nipples had never been quite so *enthusiastic* in her whole life. Just what she needed. She was single and pregnant and her nipples had suddenly become supersensitive sluts looking for action.

"We're kissing each other. We're touching each other. And we're going to go back to your room or mine, doesn't matter, and we're going to spend the night having hot, wet sex."

Chapter 8

Damien watched Mandy's eyes shoot up to her bangs, a strangled gasp coming out of her mouth. Okay, so maybe he could have phrased that a little more sensitively. But he hadn't had sex in three years, and he needed to get to someplace private before he tossed her onto the sand.

When Jessica had died, he hadn't thought he'd ever feel a sexual stirring or attraction to another woman. And then later, when his body had betrayed him, and wanted in an eager, shameful, lustful way, and he might have been tempted to go out and seek some quick company, he hadn't been able to because they were watching every move he made. Picking a girl up for a one-night stand wouldn't have worked to his advantage in the courtroom.

Then eventually, he had lost those angry physical urges, until he'd forgotten a time when he'd ever thought of sex as a wonderful, intimate, fulfilling experience.

He remembered now.

Mandy had stirred every one of those feelings back up into a tornado of intensity and want, and he had to have her. He just had to, or the very last vestiges of his soul and sanity would crumple away from him.

"But you're my boss, Damien, and I'm, well, I'm having a baby." Even in the dark, he could see her eyes were dilated with pleasure and anticipation, but she was worried. Concerned about the future.

He didn't give a damn about the future. There was only now and the two of them.

"Correct me if any of my assumptions are wrong, okay?"

She didn't hesitate, just nodded.

"I'm attracted to you and you're attracted to me. We're both a little lonely, but neither of us can get involved with anyone right now. You need me. You want me. I need you tonight, too." Perhaps more than he was willing to admit. "I want you. Very, very much. And you shared a special moment with me."

Damien gently laid his hand on her slightly rounded stomach. He had been about knocked off his feet by the strong jerk he'd felt before. And while he was shocked to find out Mandy was having a baby, it had explained a lot of oddities, and if anything, had made her all the more attractive in his eyes.

She wanted to be a good mother. She loved her child. She had rejected that schmuck's offer for money and was doing this on her own. She had risked the wrath of Demon Sharpton to secure her child's future.

It told him everything he needed to know about her.

"Spend the night with me, Mandy. Just while we're here, in Punta Cana, and nothing else matters. Let's enjoy each other. Let's appreciate *life.*"

There was a long pause where she seemed to be weighing his words, and while he waited to feel the agony of rejection, the letdown of being told to go to hell, he buried his head in her neck and ran his lips over the soft flesh.

"I'll spend the night with you, Damien," she said quietly.

Relief sang through him. Taking his tongue over the shells of the necklace she was wearing, he held her for a second. Just held her.

"That is, if you don't think it's unseemly for a mother-to-be to act this way." Her words were teasing, but there was a level of seriousness to the question, too.

Damien stood up and shook his head. "Not at all. I think it's damn sexy. I can show you my erection if you need proof."

She laughed as he bent over and picked up her beach bag. "Let's wait until we're in the room for that, shall we?"

"But first we have to stop by the hotel store. Unless you have condoms in your room." He didn't want her to worry that he wouldn't use one since she was pregnant. He had no intention of making her uncomfortable.

She covered her face with her hand. "No, I don't. God, I think I'm blushing. This is just so unbelievable."

"But in such a good way." Damien put his hand on the small of Mandy's back and herded her in the direction of the hotel shop.

Good thing it was a short walk, because now that he had been given the green light by Mandy, he was more than a little eager. He was on fucking fire.

Mandy hung back in the store, hovering over by the imported magazines displayed both in English and Spanish, her cheeks a charming pink. Damien didn't feel any embarrassment whatsoever. He strode over to the counter and asked the clerk, "Where are the condoms?"

Why waste even five minutes looking for them?

The man, in his late twenties, grinned at Damien and pointed behind him. "Individual or a box?"

"Box." No sense in having to repeat this shopping expedition if things went according to plan.

The clerk slapped the box down on the counter, and Damien studied the busty Hispanic woman in a bikini on the front. The carton was bright yellow, the bikini a violent orange, and while the label was in English, the small script was in Spanish. He hoped like hell these weren't novelty condoms. He wasn't wearing anything with parrots on it.

"Would you like some Mamajuana, too? Good stuff." The man pointed to a bottle of what looked like alcohol, shelved next to the rum.

"What is it?" Not that he had any intention of getting drunk. He wanted to remember every second of this.

"You drink it. We call it Dominican Viagra." The clerk winked. "Helps you last, if you know what I mean. If this doesn't work, they say you should just go and kill yourself."

Did he look like he needed Viagra? What the hell. He was so hard he could moonlight as a woodpecker. Damien shook his head. "I don't need any help, thanks." He handed over the six hundred pesos for the condoms, which he shoved in his pocket, and turned to find Mandy. She was biting her lip, arms over her chest, staring vacantly at a display of T-shirts.

"Have fun!" the clerk yelled with a knowing grin.

And people thought New Yorkers were rude.

Fortunately, he'd forgotten how to blush. But Mandy looked like she'd spent too long in the sun, so he took her hand and hustled her outside to the quiet walkway that lead to the main lobby.

And kissed her eagerly.

"Damien," she protested, trying to pull back. "There are people around."

"No, there aren't. Not a single one." The path was deserted, everyone still down at the buffet, and it was lush with foliage, and thick with humidity in the glow of faux gas lamps.

But she was still darting her eyes around, hands pressed on his chest to hold him at bay. So Damien dropped his mouth to her forehead and gave her a soft kiss. "My room is in the first building on the right."

"Then it's closer than mine. I'm by the adults-only pool." But she didn't move in the direction he had pointed to. She worried her lip, and Damien watched her, waited for her to say what was on her mind. "I just want you to understand that I don't usually . . . I don't sleep around. I thought Ben really cared about me, and well, I've never really fancied one-night stands. But that's all this can be, because I can't get involved with anyone until I've sorted out my own life."

Damien brushed a hair back that had caught on her lip. "This isn't a one-night stand. It's not just about sex. It's about being together, enjoying each other, if only for a few hours." It was about loosening the suffocating chains of loneliness and reaching out for something simple and uncomplicated. "But I'm not looking for a relationship either."

He couldn't believe he was about to admit this, but he wanted her to understand, wanted her to know what this—she—meant to him. "I haven't been with a woman in three years."

"You haven't been in a relationship in three years?"

"Yes, but I also haven't had sex in three years."

Understanding dawned in her eyes. "Oh. Oh, my." She stroked his forearm. "Since Jess?"

He nodded, not willing to say any more. "That's been a conscious choice I've made, and now I'm making the conscious choice to change that. Let me have you tonight, Mandy."

There was no way she was going to say no. He could read the acquiescence in her eyes, the way she leaned toward him, stroked his arms and opened her mouth. Her breasts pressed against him as she tilted her head to the side and gave a small, sweet sigh.

"Oh, I'm not a bloody idiot, Damien. I have every intention of doing this—I just needed to make sure we were clear on what it was, and that you don't think I'm some sort of swinger who sleeps with her boss in the Caribbean on every job she takes."

He raised an eyebrow. "That definitely wasn't on your resumé."

She gave a soft laugh and wet her lips, making him want to suck on both her lip and her tongue, taking turns. "What if I don't meet your expectations? Three years is a long time to wait. I'd hate to be a disappointment."

That was a joke. He'd be lucky if he got a full five seconds in her before he exploded. "As long as you don't have some sort of objection to oral sex, we'll be fine. I have it in my head that I'd really like to taste you."

Her breathing quickened. "Funny, that. I had a dream you were doing that very thing to me, and I was really quite enjoying it."

Damien's groin tightened. What the hell were they doing standing here then?

"You know, you're usually much more efficient than this. Move it, Mandy. Before I drop your sundress here on the sidewalk." And he reached for her zipper.

Mandy had taken Damien's threat seriously, and a quick two minutes later they were in his room, her beach bag tumbling to the floor as she reached for the buttons on his linen shirt.

She'd seen the way he looked in his swim trunks that afternoon and she wanted to touch that broad chest. She wanted to explore his hard flesh, make him tremble with want. She wanted to draw this all out and enjoy every blasted second of it since she was facing a future of celibacy.

Damien's own hands were busy unzipping the back of her dress. But whereas she was fumbling, overeager, nervous, he was quiet, studied, intent. Goose bumps rose on her flesh as his fingers trailed over her back. His room was at the end of the hall, remote, the sounds of the resort buffered by palm trees and flowering plants. The whirr of the ceiling fan and the uneven tempo of their breathing were the only sounds in the room.

All her doubts, all her concerns, fear about how she should behave and how he might react to her pregnancy, her body the way it was now, had all evaporated when Damien told her he hadn't been with a woman in three years. She'd seen it then, what he had been telling her. That they both needed each other, just here, just now, to touch and taste and push on each other in uncomplicated pleasure.

She wanted that. She wanted him.

Buttons free, she spread his shirt and sighed as the palms of her hands caressed hard, warm muscle. "You have a lovely chest."

His lip quirked up. "What a coincidence. I was thinking the same thing about you."

Mandy glanced down and saw that with the zipper undone, her dress had slipped a bit, only to come to a crashing halt at her cleavage. Nothing could get past her newly blossoming breasts, and her plump flesh was bursting out of the top of her strapless bra.

"This isn't my natural state, you know," she told him, pushing his shirtsleeves down to his wrists. "Every day I wake up to find they're a bit bigger, like I've taken an air pump to them."

Damien's thumb ran over the swell above her bra. "I like the end result."

"Yes, well, easy for you to say." Mandy gripped his wrist as his thumb brushed lower and lower, skirting her nipple. She gave a sound of disappointment. "But at this rate, I fully expect one day to roll over and have them clap."

He laughed, expression relaxed and amused. "I love your sense of humor."

She was about to tell him that back in England, at The Wycombe Abbey School for Girls, she'd been quite the comedic thespian, but she only had time to open her mouth before he ripped her dress down to her waist, and she promptly forgot how to speak.

Or breathe, when his head descended to her chest and his tongue traced above the rim of her overburdened bra. Back and forth it went, as if it was on a leisurely stroll in the park, and Mandy shivered, appreciating fully how much more sensitive her breasts were now. Torn between wanting to just enjoy his teasing tongue and urging him to dispense with her bra and head south to her nipple, Mandy gripped his wrists and squeezed.

Damien lifted his head, and Mandy expected him to shove her dress down, strip himself, and slide right into her standing up.

Or maybe that was just wishful thinking.

But she had expected Damien to be urgent, to take charge, to rush through to the release they were both seeking.

He was taking charge, yes, but he wasn't interested in rushing. Which had its pros and cons.

As she tugged his shirt off and dropped it to the floor, Damien pulled the clip out of her hair. He stroked in it and smiled. "I love your hair. It's just like you. Sort of free, with a mind of its own, but always in control."

Was that the way he saw her? Mandy thought that was just a lovely way to describe her, even if she felt control was the last thing she possessed. Unable to resist touching him, she smoothed out his dark eyebrows, traced his cheeks, brushed along his lips in a caress that was too intimate, but felt so, so right here with Damien. His lips pressed in a kiss over her fingers and she smiled, knowing she felt as raw and vulnerable as he looked.

"If you think I'm in control, you're a sandwich short of a picnic," she whispered to him. "But thank you for that."

He drew her fingertip into his mouth and sucked, sending a rush of heat through her body. Her nipples pushed painfully against her bra, and Mandy leaned closer to him, pulling his scent of night breeze, sand, and male muskiness into her nostrils.

"Of course you're in control. You're an awesome assistant."

When she pulled her finger back, he followed it, until his mouth was brushing along her jaw. Mandy's eyes fluttered closed. "Should that be my title? Awesome Assistant? I can post a sign on my cubicle."

He kissed the corner of her mouth, such a light teasing touch that she shivered. "How about Asshole's Awesome Assistant? Or ASS for short?"

She laughed, their breath mingling together as his lips hovered above hers, his nose alongside hers, forehead brushing hers. "You're not an asshole at all, but you're a very funny man when you want to be."

If anyone would have told her two months ago that Damien was a man she could banter with, be relaxed and completely abandoned with, she would have laughed herself sick. And goodness knew, she hadn't needed any more of that.

But it was all so easy, so right, so comfortable with Damien, that she was taking, but she was giving just as much. He made her feel sexy, she made him laugh, and they were both the better this night for it.

His answer was to stop the torturous teasing hover over her mouth and kiss her, a full open kiss that had her wrapping her arms around his neck to get closer. Mandy loved the way he kissed, as though he had nothing to lose, nothing to prove, like he just wanted her more than anything he'd tasted before.

Then his tongue found hers, with hot, wet urgency and Mandy wanted more. She pressed her breasts against his bare chest and ransacked his short hair with her fingers, pulling back to catch her breath and moan. It wasn't enough, not when she needed, had to have all of him over her, inside her.

Her body pulsed and throbbed, ached and suffered, as he kissed her again and again, a delicious promise that felt blissfully good but was never enough to fulfill the hunger coursing through her.

"Damien." His hands weren't even exploring, but were just resting on her back while he kissed her, and Mandy wanted more, more, more, with an intensity that shocked her and set her hands shaking.

"Yes?" He stopped doing everything, stepping back to look at her in question.

Mandy yanked her dress down over her hips and let it drop to the floor. "For a man who threatened to unzip me outside on the pavement, you don't seem all that interested in getting me naked now."

"Oh, I am," he said, his pale blue eyes darkening in the soft glow of the bedside lamp he'd left on as he looked her up and down. "You have no idea how interested I am. But I'm savoring this."

The warm breeze from the ceiling fan fluttered over her as she stood in her bra and panties, her breasts full and tingling from his inspection, her thighs shifting together restlessly. "Don't savor for too long."

His head slowly went back and forth, eyes not meeting hers but still studying her body with revelry. "Forever wouldn't be long enough to look at you. You're beautiful."

And Mandy's heart squeezed and her breath caught, and at that moment, she would have given him anything he wanted, suspecting that of the two of them, he was the one who actually needed this more.

But she needed, too. Desperately. So she held her breasts with one hand, unpopped the bra hook with the other, then let it join her dress on the floor.

Damien's jaw clenched. He swallowed hard.

Mandy waited, her nipples hardening, her fingers splayed across the front of her hips. She waited, while he stared and stared and her panties grew damper and damper, and her fingers itched to move lower and her breasts ached to be touched and her eyes fell into slumberous half slits.

Then finally, when she thought she would scream or cry

or whimper or puddle on the floor in a drenched mass of sexual longing, he moved.

And cupped both of her breasts, while his mouth closed around her nipple and sucked hard.

Okay, that was worth the wait. "Oh!" she said, unable to think of a better word to sum up the feeling that she was going to die of pleasure.

He pulled back, not releasing her nipple until the last second so it gave a wet, sucking pop. "Mmmm," was Damien's opinion as he switched from right to left.

She would have to second that. This time he plucked, then sucked, making her toes curl on the hard ceramic tile.

His thigh shifted, pressing against her swollen clitoris, which was damn cruel in her opinion. She moaned softly, her fingers peeling down the waistband of her panties, ready to be naked so she could then get him naked and they could be naked together, which would clearly be the best possible outcome of all of this.

But he stilled her hands. Frustrated, she shifted them to the button on his pants, but he held her hands firmly against his hard abdomen, preventing all movement, while he continued to lave his tongue across her nipple.

"Damn it, Damien, I want us naked." Mandy jerked at her hands, but he was stronger than she was.

"It's not time for that yet."

"What's it time for?" Besides death by excess desire? Mandy was a healthy woman and had enjoyed the few adult relationships she'd had. She'd thought she'd known what lust was like. She'd thought she'd understood urgency, the rush of sexual longing.

She had been stupid.

The way Damien made her feel, with so very little effort, made those previous experiences pale into bland. Like salsa without the jalapeno. On the Mexican menu of sex, Damien was four and a half chili peppers, full of flavor and heat.

He lifted his head from her chest, leaving her nipples wet and aching. "It's time for you to lie down on my bed, so I can spread your legs and taste every inch of you. Then start all over and do it again."

Mandy sucked back her drool.

Make that five chili peppers. If he got any hotter, her eyes were going to water.

Chapter 9

Damien readjusted his cock in his pants, hoping to give it more room but unwilling to let it out.

Let free, who knew what it might do.

Tear down walls at the very least, like the dick that destroyed Punta Cana.

That was how desperate he felt, how painfully he throbbed, and how much his body ached for release. So he was keeping it in his pants so he wasn't finished before they even got started.

It wasn't that he'd forgotten, exactly, what a naked woman looked like. But he hadn't realized how much he had missed this—the hot kisses, the shaky fingers undoing buttons, the damp prickles along his flesh, the heavy timbre of their breathing.

Mandy stood in front of him in nothing but a white pair of panties, and even those served to fuel his desire. Because he could see the outline of her sex, see where her curls were pressing into the satin, see a tiny wet spot that proved her need for him was as great as his need for her.

Damien brushed his thumbs over her nipples, enjoying the soft groan she gave. Her breasts were full and curvy, and her skin had a rosy tint to it. She was lush and firm and radiating health, life, sexuality.

But she wasn't moving. He lightly pinched her nipple. "Lie down, Mandy. Now."

Her hand closed over his, and she removed his finger from her breast, like she couldn't take the touching anymore. "Yes, sir. Right away, sir. And would you like some coffee as well?"

She tossed a grin over her shoulder as she turned and walked to the bed, a definite sway in her hips, her panties drooping so that he could see the swell of her backside, the dip between her cheeks.

He gave a snort. It still shocked him that she teased him so easily, with no concern for the consequences. He had erected so many walls around himself, built his hard, cold reputation to the point where no one would dare toss out a joke at his expense. It was appealing that Mandy didn't treat him like the victim, or the guilty, or the heartless cynic, but just like a man. A friend. A lover.

"Very funny, wise ass. But if you're thinking of stand-up, don't quit your day job."

As Damien followed her to the bed, Mandy crawled up on top of the yellow floral bedspread, giving him a heart-attack-inspiring shot of her backside.

"I have no intention of quitting my day job. My boss and I are very compatible." Mandy lay down and rolled onto her back, arms above her head. She smiled and lowered her knees until she was displayed all before him, delicious and sensual.

Damn it. Damien swallowed hard. Sweat trickled down his back, his fingers itched to touch, his tongue felt thick, a buzzing rang in his ears. "When we get back to New York, we go back to the way it was. But for now, we're going to enjoy each other."

Her knees dropped open. "Enjoy me, Damien."

With fucking pleasure. He reached forward, took the two strings on either side of her panties, and ripped them with one hard jerk.

"Ohmigod!" she said, staring down at him in shock. "You destroyed my knickers."

With just an index finger, he hooked the white satin and pulled the remnants away from her, baring her caramel curls to him. "Knickers are easy enough to come by." And he tossed them over his shoulder.

Knees on the bed, Damien leaned down and kissed her inner thigh, right, then left, nuzzling his nose into her firm flesh and breathing the salty scent of her perspiration, and the sweetness of her arousal. He brushed a kiss on the damp hair, below her clitoris, his mouth pressing into the give of her sex. Mandy jerked below him, a hissing sound pushing through her teeth.

He pulled back a little, shifted until he was comfortably resting on his elbows, cozily ensconced between her legs. Then he spread her folds and took a long lick over her pink, swollen flesh.

Damien narrowed his eyes, fingers squeezing into her thighs as her taste exploded on his tongue. He heard her groan, felt her legs shift restlessly on either side of him. His blood rushed, his heart pounded, and his control frayed dangerously as he buried his tongue inside her. She surrounded him, hot, quivering, a damp rush flooding over him as she reacted to his invasion, his thrusting deep parody of sex.

"St-op," she said, back arching on the bed.

"Why?" he asked as he pulled back and ran the pads of his thumbs over her plump swollen folds, up and down, up and down, enjoying the soft give, the way she squirmed and mewled in distress, the way her legs spread farther and farther in invitation.

"Damien . . . I'm too close. I can't . . . stop."

"Too close to what?" he asked with forced indifference. The thrill, the satisfaction of pleasing her, raced through him, urging him to take this slow, no matter how deep he ached.

And this was a pleasure all in and of itself. He had never been so aroused in his entire life, and he didn't think it was the result of three years' abstinence. It was Mandy. Her intelligence, her humor, her beauty, her pure unrestrained responses to him. The naked honesty on her face as she looked down at him and said, "I'm too close to an orgasm. And I don't want to yet."

Her heels dug into the bed as she tried to shift up and out of his way.

Damien dropped his weight down on her legs, anchoring her on the lumpy mattress. "Why not?" He kissed her clitoris. "Two orgasms are better than one."

She swore, twitched to try and free herself, and he almost laughed.

"I never have more than one, so I'd like to delay it as long as possible, if you don't mind."

He did mind. He wanted her to come now. He wanted her to come later. He wanted her to come again and again until they both forgot who they were and where they came from and why they couldn't share a future like normal people could.

Dragging the tip of his finger across her moisture, down between her cheeks and back up again, he flicked his tongue around her clitoris in a teasing little circle. "I do mind. Come for me, Mandy. Please."

Swallowing hard, he plunged his finger into her softness. She gave a cry of shock that dissolved into a ragged moan. Hearing her spurred him on, made him want to, need to, hear more, hear her burst in that ultimate pleasure.

As he stroked into her, he dropped his mouth down onto her clitoris and sucked the tight pink button. Mandy jerked up, then froze half sitting as she shattered. Her hands slapped at his head, searching for a hold, as her orgasm set her muscles clenching around his fingers and her clitoris tightening.

For a long moment, she convulsed in release, and Damien held her, still stroking.

Then her groan trailed off into a curse.

"Oh, damn it!" she said with a cry of frustration. "I told you not to do that." Her fingers curled in his hair and jerked his head back and forth with a violence that both amused him and turned him on. "God! This is all your fault."

Damien wiped his mouth and tried to feel shame, but it just wasn't there. "I'm sorry. But I couldn't help myself." He sat up and reached for the button on his pants. "I can't help this either."

Still feeling shattered and more than a little miffed at her lack of control, Mandy lifted her head at the tone in Damien's voice. He was dispensing with his trousers.

Fine. Whatever. It didn't matter in the least to her. He had ruined it all by forcing the orgasm issue after she had specifically made a point to explain to him that she didn't achieve that more than once per sitting, and now she was feeling languid and sleepy and not the least bit interested in . . .

His erection nudged her. "Oh!" she moaned, then slapped a hand over her mouth. *No moaning, Mandy*. It would go to his head.

"Feel good?" he asked as he pulled back.

"Actually, it's rather unpleasant," she said, even as she lifted her backside in an encouraging offering. Damn, it was so hard to stick to her principles when he was tickling his finger there.

He gave a low laugh as he dug a condom out of his pants pocket and opened the package. "I'm really sorry. Do you think you could suffer a little more unpleasantness for my sake? Just two minutes, tops. And next time, I promise to give your requests the attention they deserve."

Bereft without either his finger or his penis, she decided that was prettily said and she could forgive him for forcing shattering pleasure on her. After all, it wasn't his fault she was an easy mark, and she didn't doubt that it would feel good to have him slip inside her, imbed himself deep in her body.

Mandy felt aftershocks of excitement fissure through her thighs. "All right. Two minutes. Tops." She tried for an insufferable sigh, but couldn't keep the corner of her mouth from lifting.

With a laugh, he said, "Ogre. Next you'll have me in tears."

He nuzzled his nose along her thigh, then skimmed his lips over the slight bump of her belly with a tenderness that made her throat tighten. He was momentarily distracted by her breasts, spending a good minute or two lavishing attention with his tongue on each one while she tried not to go cross-eyed. Then he moved to the curve of her neck, and finally, to her mouth.

Damien kissed her deeply, openly, while his hands brushed her hair back from her face. Then he murmured against her lips. "Thank you. I truly appreciate your generosity. I promise to make the next two minutes as painless as possible for you."

"Do get on with it," she said, though the effect of using her mother's voice when addressing the maid was ruined by the groan she collapsed into at the end.

He was nudging her again, his pupils dilated, eyes glazed with passion, and Mandy exhaled a shaky breath. It felt so torturously good, the tip of his erection resting just inside her swollen damp flesh, and she involuntarily rocked her hips toward him.

Now he was the one swearing. She could tell Damien was clamped on tightly to his control, easing himself deeper inside her one slow steely inch at a time. It had been three years for him, and yet he held himself back, sweat beading on his forehead, shoulders straining, neck muscles bulging, corded sinew and throbbing veins.

She didn't understand, couldn't think why he didn't just plunge inside her like they both wanted him to, and her fingers snaked past his waist and settled on his rock-hard backside. Slowly, slowly he filled her until she was squirming and aching and pleading with him. "Damien, please . . ."

But he ignored her, sucking on the swell of her breast above her nipple as he rested inside her, only half buried. "I'm savoring again, that's all."

Well, he needed to stop. Mandy grabbed his bum and shoved down, at the same time she rammed her hips up toward him. She may not be as strong as him, but she had surprise and determination on her side. The thrust sent them colliding together, and he filled her fully, stretching her sensitive muscles and giving rise to the speculation that maybe she could have another orgasm.

Bloody hell, that felt good.

Her body was taut everywhere, tingling and swollen, and she used her inner muscles to clench on to him, afraid he'd leave.

"Mandy, oh, damn, honey." His eyes were closed, a shudder rolling over him.

She knew the feeling. But after a long drawn-out second that felt like half her life, Mandy started to worry that he wasn't going to do anything. That he was just going to sit there in her, like a parked car.

He was a complex man, who clearly had some issues in a past relationship, and he had more willpower than she could ever hope for, but now wasn't the time for him to be exercising it. It was time for him to let it go, to allow himself pleasure.

"Damien, darling, aren't you going to make love to me?"

He wanted to. God knew he wanted to. But Damien was afraid that if he moved, he would go careening into an orgasm that would embarrass the hell out of him. He was afraid that if he let go, if he unleashed all the passion he'd been withholding for three years, that other, uglier emotions might rise along with it. He was afraid that if he moved, and it was over, then it would be, well, over. This was it.

But Mandy's soft, coaxing words nudged him out of his indecision.

The way she felt, wrapped around him, under him, her body open for his, hot and slick, and the way her lips parted on a pant and her eyes glazed over convinced him. He'd risk it.

With a groan, he pulled back as a precursor to gently sliding into her, but Mandy dug her nails into his ass and cried out, "No, don't leave!"

Mandy did some female trick that had her muscles tightening, holding him in place like she refused to give his cock up. His mouth went dry, blood thundering in his head, and he decided he didn't give a damn about staying in control. He'd already gone this far, he'd already let his body feel passion again, he might as well take it all the way.

He slammed into her and forced a groan out of both of them. Mandy's eyes rolled back in her head.

"I'm not going anywhere," he said through gritted teeth.

When he stroked again, he had to close his eyes. Jesus, she felt so good. So hot, so giving, so close around him, holding on and milking his cock with her tight body, agony and ecstasy intermingling in his mouth like a potent mixed drink. He felt drunk on pleasure.

"Fantastic," she murmured, her heels kicking him in the backs of his thighs as he moved over her, and she made no attempt to meet his erratic rhythm. Some strokes were quick and short, others slow and deep, and he didn't know what in the hell he was doing, he just wanted to feel her every which way. But he forced himself to rein back in, get a grip on himself, and he found a spot that felt just right, so perfect that he had to keep hitting it over and over.

Mandy seemed to like it, too, since it had him pressing against her clitoris, and she gripped the bedspread and gasped. It spurred Damien on, made him pump harder, until he forced himself to an abrupt stop. Legs trembling as he held himself on the edge of orgasm, sweat running down into his eyes, the dim room brighter, the sounds of the fan sharper as he hovered in the high of anticipation.

The sound of frustration she gave was nothing short of a scream. "What the hell are you doing?"

The outrage on her face made him chuckle, even as his body screamed its own protest with quivering jerks inside her. "I told you only two minutes. I think I went over."

Her brown eyes went wide with shock. Then she pinched his waist, hard. "Oh, my God. Finish me now, Damien, or I won't be responsible for my actions."

Oh, he would finish her. And himself in the process.

Bracing one hand on the wall over her head and the other on the bed, Damien gave one, two last strokes. As Mandy cried out and bucked behind him as she came, he let it all go and poured himself into her with a muffled roar.

He pulsed and throbbed on and on in a delicious surrender that sent a rapturous shudder through him. And when his moans petered off and his legs relaxed and a great exhalation of air shot out of his lungs, Damien felt empty of everything for the first time in three years.

Anger, frustration, pain—it all washed away and he was just left feeling very, very satisfied.

Chapter 10

Mandy breathed in the warm night air from Damien's balcony and gave a lusty sigh of contentment.

"Do you want something to drink? I'm going to raid the minibar." Damien stood in the doorway, wearing his pants and a sardonic smile.

Damn, he was really quite fabulous. Mandy was feeling pleased with the whole world, but especially with Damien. He had no idea how much it meant to her that now, when she was feeling scared and lonely and unattractive, he had chosen her to end his celibacy.

And he'd done such a nice job of it, too, my goodness.

Her body still felt flushed and relaxed from that second orgasm, and she crossed her ankles as she leaned over the railing, in her dress but with nothing underneath it. "I am thirsty, but minibars are notoriously expensive, Damien. I'd feel guilty drinking an eight-dollar bottle of water, even if work is paying for it."

"The minibar is free, Mandy. The trip is all-inclusive, which includes the minibar."

That got her attention. "You must be joking."

"No."

"Damn, I've been ignoring that bag of chocies then for no reason. You'd better bring them to me, quick."

"Chocies?"

"The chocolates." Mandy pulled back a little, away from the railing bar pressing her stomach. She knew the baby was nicely cushioned, but she still rubbed a protective hand over the bump. "I've been eyeing them for two days, telling myself that since they probably cost twelve dollars and my backside doesn't need chocolate anyway, I should resist them. But forget it now, I want them."

She'd hardly gained any weight, thanks to the morning sickness. One little bag of chocolates wouldn't hurt. They weren't bad for the baby, just not good for the baby. And she was on holiday and entitled to indulge.

Damien reappeared with water and the chocolates. She was definitely indulging, and in more than the chocolates.

Strange, she didn't feel the slightest bit guilty or ashamed of herself on either account.

He sat down on the plastic deck chair and popped the top off one of the waters. He handed it to her, then opened the little box of chocolates and held them out for her to make a selection.

She took one that looked like a caramel filled and settled into the chair next to him, scooting it closer so she could rest her feet on his thighs. "Do you mind?" she asked, licking the edge of the chocolate.

Shaking his head, he dropped his hand on her ankle, caressing her bare skin. Making sure her dress was tucked under her so she wasn't flashing Damien or anyone walking by on the path below, she sighed and relaxed back into her chair.

"Comfy?" he asked. His pants were still cuffed a little from their walk on the beach, and he looked sexy and rumpled, his bare chest gleaming a bit in the muted shadows of the balcony.

"Very comfy. I feel boneless." She popped the whole candy in her mouth and closed her eyes in appreciation. "Oh, that's good."

He was massaging the bottom of her foot, and Mandy

decided nothing could get better than this. A half-naked, gorgeous man rubbing her feet while she floated in chocolate and post-orgasm endorphins. "How about you? Are you comfy?" she murmured, her voice sounding throaty and sensual even to her own ears.

"Very." His mouth was smiling, but his eyes were serious. "I haven't been this relaxed in a long time."

She was about to ask him to tell her, to let her share that burden, to confess what caused those deep shadows in his eyes, what drew him to work so hard all the time. But he startled her by asking, "When's the baby due?"

His fingers roamed up her leg as if he were going to touch her stomach, but he stopped at her knee. Mandy wished he would touch her belly and wasn't sure why. But she seemed to be feeling a lot of strange things and wasn't sure why.

"October eighteenth. Give or take." It seemed so far away, yet just around the corner, and she was so unprepared, so nervous.

"And everything's okay? The doctor did one of those ultrasound things?"

Taking a sip of water, she reached for the box of chocolates resting in his lap. She wanted—no, needed—another one. "It's a bit early for an ultrasound. If a woman is healthy, they only like to do one at about eighteen to twenty weeks so I haven't had mine yet. But the doctor has reassured me every step of the way that I'm healthy and the baby is progressing normally."

He stroked lightly across her kneecap. "I'm glad to hear it." His voice was thoughtful, his head turned away from her as he watched the ocean. "I think it would terrify me to know I had a kid on the way, but you seem really in control."

God, if he only knew. She actually laughed. "Damien, I am absolutely terrified, trust me. I never expected to be having a baby this soon in life, and there are all these books and manuals and rules about how to do this. I have a huge textbook sitting in my beach bag that I'm trying to convince myself to read, but whenever I pick it up I have a panic attack. It's overwhelming."

He smiled. "If you approach motherhood the way you do your job, you'll have that kid whipped into shape in no time."

The laugh she knew he wanted stuck in her throat. She hated the way she felt so uncertain, so needy, but she couldn't stop herself from asking, "Am I good at my job? Truly?"

The water bottle he'd had poised at his lips descended back into his lap. "Are you serious? You're awesome at it. You're my ASS, remember? Asshole's awesome assistant, that's you."

"Thank you." She nibbled at a nut in the center of the nugget she held. "It seems I have some self-esteem issues I was never aware of. I always thought I hadn't got into an office job because that's what my father did and I didn't want to lose myself in a career the way he did. That I wanted to be free to be creative, pursue my own interests, set my hours, and live according to my own terms."

Mandy sighed, realizing something she should have a long time ago. "But I'm just a hypocrite. If I really disapproved of my parents' lifestyle, of their focus on money, I would have cut myself off from their checkbooks. But I haven't. I've been living off of them all these years while I proved that I didn't need a high-powered job to be happy. It's silly, really. All I've proved is that I do need my parents and that I was afraid to follow in Daddy's footsteps because I was afraid to fail. I'm twenty-six years old and I'm lazy."

A snort wasn't exactly the response she expected to that heartfelt confession. "What a bunch of bullshit, Mandy. You aren't lazy at all. You ran your own toy store for three years. How many hours did you put into that business? Eighty hours a week, minimum, would be my guess, when you add in ordering stock, managing payroll, and scheduling and handling the taxes."

She chewed her lip. "Maybe, but I never turned a profit."

"Not for lack of effort. Maybe it was just the wrong business. But that doesn't mean that you're a sponge."

"But now I'm having a baby and I have to be responsible, go for security over what interests me."

"And you are."

That was true. She was. She'd given up the shop, and it didn't even bother her. She'd do whatever was needed to ensure her baby was happy and healthy and well provided for.

"And you made the incredibly brilliant decision to work for me." He winked at her.

That pulled a laugh out of her. Damien looked wicked beautiful winking. She shifted a little in the chair; her thighs started to feel warm. "You'll never get rid of me, you know. I like this job and I'm keeping it, and you can be as insufferable and demanding and bossy as you like and I won't quit."

"Damn. I'll have to cross 'be insufferable to Mandy' off my calendar for next week."

"Beast." She slapped at his arm and laughed. "Don't be absurd."

"That's one adjective no one has ever applied to me."

While he sipped his drink, she stared at him, wanting to ask, but knowing she shouldn't. If he wanted to tell her, he would. But his tattoo was dark on his skin, and she couldn't help but say, "So, what happened? To Jess?"

There had to be a compelling reason for a man as sensual as Damien to go three years without sex, and to bury himself in his work.

For a long moment, she thought he wouldn't answer her. Then he turned and met her gaze. "She died."

"Oh!" Somehow that possibility had never occurred to her. She'd thought maybe Jess had been unfaithful or something, but this was far, far worse. "Oh, Damien, I'm so sorry. I shouldn't have pried."

But Damien patted her leg like she was a child he was comforting. "You know, it should matter. It always has before. But right here, right now, with you, it's okay. Really. But I don't want to talk about Jessica, if you don't mind. She's always in my head, my thoughts, my heart, all the time, and I don't want her here with us."

Fine by her. Mandy really wasn't interested in a mental ménage à trois either. But she was burning with curiosity and maybe, deep inside, where she was ashamed to admit it, a seed of jealousy. This woman, Damien had loved her, with a passion so deep that he still suffered over her death three years later and had chosen not to take another woman to his bed.

But Mandy brushed the ungracious feelings aside. She wasn't looking for love. And she was the one who had inspired Damien to break his celibacy. For now, that was enough. Though part of her was pleased to know that she had been right about Damien. No matter the rough edges, he was a good man, just a wounded one.

She nodded. "Thank you, by the way. I've been feeling a bit sorry for myself, you know. Ben dumped me so soundly, and I haven't exactly been glowing with this pregnancy, and any future relationships look doubtful. I'm not the kind of woman who will be parading men through my child's life. I don't plan on being a nun, of course, but I'm going to be very, very cautious once this child is born with who I date. I can't afford to make any mistakes when it will affect my baby, too."

Mandy rolled a chocolate between her thumb and forefinger and stared at him, hoping he would understand, really, truly understand. "But you've made me feel attractive again."

"You are attractive. Inside and out." He shook his head ruefully. "You have no idea how much . . ."

She thought he'd planned to say something else, but he clamped his lips shut. Stuffing the chocolate in her mouth, she glanced at the half-eaten box. "I'm going to regret eating all these, aren't I? And come next week I'm probably going to regret sleeping with my boss, too."

Damien set her feet off of him and onto the floor. "Don't ever regret that. I don't plan to."

He shot her a look so hot, she glanced down to see if her clothes had burst into flames. The chocolate melted in her mouth and her nipples puckered.

Damien scooted forward in his chair. "In fact, I was thinking of leaning over and licking that chocolate off the corner of your lip. Then I'm going to take your dress off and make love to you all over again, and trust me, I don't plan on ever regretting that."

Her breath hitched and her hands pressed into her thighs. Somehow she thought this night was going to be worth any sort of regrets she might have later.

Damien moved forward, and with unnerving accuracy, his tongue flicked out and grabbed a piece of chocolate from the corner of her mouth. "Delicious," he said.

No, she wasn't going to regret any of this.

Chapter 11

Damien slid his tongue from one side of Mandy's lip to the other and closed his eyes.

Unbelievable. Everything about her and this night was unbelievable.

But Mandy was his box of chocolates. He wanted her and he couldn't resist her and he was going to eat all of her.

He should be done for the night, depleted and ready to send her on her way back to her room so he could get some work done. But he didn't give a damn about software that didn't work or customer demands or the training he wanted to schedule for June.

All he could think about was that Mandy wasn't wearing any underwear or a bra under that very thin sundress.

And the way she treated him was so novel, so alluring, that he didn't want this night to end and he didn't want to retreat back into himself. Mandy sat with him, talked with him, with a trust and a frankness, her expression honest and open. Yet she expected nothing of him.

No hoops to jump through, no promises to make, no lavish gifts, no handing her his bleeding heart for her to own.

They were almost something like friends.

Except with one key difference.

Damien pushed his tongue between her lips and met the wet heat of her mouth as she sighed with pleasure. He wanted to capture that sound, keep it, hold it with him to reflect on later, when the world tilted back on its axis and he was alone with his apartment, his remote control, and his rampant destructive thoughts.

Nails moved along his scalp as she tugged him closer, the deep, questing kiss kicking up his need a notch. He pulled away so he could stand up, take her back into the room where it was private. He wanted to take that dress off and explore her body all over again. This time he was going to map her every inch like goddamn Lewis and Clark.

But Mandy had different plans. She was grasping at his fly, making desperate little jerks at the button, her teeth grazing along his shoulder with nips.

Fuck, yeah, that felt good.

But he wanted to take it slow. Explore. Soft, gentle loving to show her he appreciated and respected her. He took her hands.

She ripped them away. "If you want to stop me, you'll have to tie me up."

Oh, my God. There was an image. And he was a sick bastard for picturing a helpless pregnant woman tied up while he licked her from the bottom up.

"I want in your trousers. Now." She tore the button out of the hole so viciously it dangled from its thread, useless.

Okay, then. Maybe she wasn't so helpless after all. "Jesus." He held his hands out in surrender, hoping she didn't rack him when she tried to unzip over his hard-on. "Go for it, honey."

He certainly liked a woman who knew what she wanted, even more so when it was him. "But don't you want to go in the room before we become oceanside entertainment?"

Since her mouth was on his nipple, sucking lightly, and her hand was dragging his zipper down, he was thinking she wasn't too concerned about getting caught. But what he was feeling, what they were sharing, hell, it was private.

And he was having trouble thinking, breathing, resisting

her. Another second and she was going to be dipping her fingers right over his . . .

Damien groaned. Damn, she had paused with her hand right over his cock. He throbbed, swelling harder into the palm of her hand, and she gave an encouraging squeeze that had him reaching for the chair, her, anything to hold him up and to keep from falling over onto her and begging.

"I suppose we could go inside," she murmured, letting go of him so suddenly and stepping away, he almost pitched backward over the railing into the bushes below.

He might have whimpered. But before he could even recover his balance, Mandy was passing through the door, her arms twisted behind her back like she had an itch in an unreachable spot. Damien stepped toward her, his undone pants sliding down his hips, intent on scratching whatever itch she had. With his tongue.

But her arms settled back at her sides, and he realized she had been unzipping her dress. It fell to the floor with a soft thump, and Mandy glanced back at him over her naked shoulder.

Damien's vision blurred, his tongue suddenly three sizes too big. Damn, his grandmother was right. She had always told him if he stared at a naked woman, he'd go blind. At twelve, he'd scoffed, sure she was just trying to scare him off girls. But now he had to rethink things. Mandy was so astonishingly beautiful it seemed actually possible he could lose his sight if he looked too long.

"Thank you, God," he said, voice hoarse, throat tight.

She turned, a wicked little smile on her face as she reached for his crotch. "Are you praying?"

"Yes, I think I am." The swivel she'd done had been too swift, he hadn't gotten a good view of the front of her, but he was compensated by her sidling right up to him with full skin-on-skin contact.

Her breasts crushed against him as she bent down a little and he shuddered, stealing up to cup the fullness of her flesh, test its weight, stroke over her nipple. Her flesh was hot, her hair corkscrewing in the ever-present humidity, and she smelled so seductive, like chocolate and desire and coconut sunscreen.

"Oh, babe," he said on a satisfied sigh, skimming his lips over her shoulder as she edged his pants down his thighs. "You don't know how good this is for me."

"Tell me." Mandy reached into his boxer briefs and cupped his erection.

He sucked in his breath. "Very, very good. If it feels any better you'll be feeling it in your hand."

"Oh!" Her hand jerked on him, and when she glanced up at him, her cheeks were pink.

"Too crude? Sorry, sorry." *Just don't stop, holy hell.* She was holding him lightly, almost absentmindedly.

He ground his teeth, part frustration and part excitement that he was going to learn all the things Mandy liked. He looked forward to finding all the ways to arouse her, all the hot spots he could stroke or kiss or suck until she was mindless, screaming his name.

But first she was going to make *him* scream. Her fingers brushed over him again, a nothing little touch of torture.

"Hmmm?"

"I embarrassed you by being too forthcoming, no pun intended." Oh, dear God, if she didn't move her hand or do something with it, he was going to grab and grind it against him, and give away that he was losing control, letting his emotions and needs gush over and drive him.

"Oh, Damien, no." She shook her head, wetting her bottom lip. "I was embarrassed because I had a sudden desperate desire to lay you on the bed and climb on you, and do, well, you know, to . . ." Her voice dropped to a whisper. "*Ride* you."

Yee-haw. Damien's hand shot out, grabbing hers, and pressed them both against his erection, rocking a little to ease his suffering. "Do it."

"But then I started thinking that I've never really been the sort who got into that, and it always makes me feel rather like I'm a tightrope walker being gawked at and liable to fall off at any given moment. And really, should I be entertaining these sorts of thoughts at all? It's shocking."

What was shocking was that she could stand there forming complete sentences. He was sure he couldn't even recite the alphabet anymore.

"Just do it," he repeated, practically growling.

Their hands were stroking in tandem over him now, and he wasn't sure who was creating the movement, but he wasn't going to worry about details.

Mandy nodded. "I had just come to that same conclusion. This holiday is about sensation and freedom and going with instinct. What feels good. And you feel so good, I have to feel you under me."

Damien exercised the extreme willpower he had learned in the last three years and yanked himself away from her. With one swift motion, he dropped his pants and boxer shorts and stepped toward the bed, groping for the condoms he'd left on the nightstand.

Mandy didn't wait for him to lie down. She attacked him, hands everywhere, lips racing frantically, legs tripping up with his until he fell flat on his back. Good to see he wasn't the only one who had utterly lost control of the situation.

He wasn't thinking, wasn't even sure he was conscious, afraid that this wasn't real, yet at the same time steeped in the certainty that this was happening, it existed, and it was fabulous and powerful and the most amazing experience of his life.

Grabbing her waist so she didn't tumble down onto him, Damien gazed up at her, trying to decide lips or breasts first to take with his mouth, when Mandy sat up, legs on either side of his.

And spread herself with her fingers, aligned herself with his cock, and dropped down onto it.

The girl didn't mess around.

He'd always known she was efficient.

It was the hormones. It had to be. Mandy shuddered over Damien, afraid to move, shocked at her aggressive behavior, stunned at how swollen she felt, how her body clasped around his hardness and tingled.

Never had she experienced anything like this, a total surrender to anything but how her body felt, a desperate urgent need to take.

Damien thrust up into her, stretching her, and she gripped the bed sheets, swallowing hard. Looking down at him, his pale illusive blue eyes locked on her with agonized pleasure and aching vulnerability, she groaned.

It wasn't pregnancy hormones—it was Damien. It was the way he looked at her, the way he wanted her, the way he *needed* her, that had her spreading her knees apart so she could take him in farther.

Normally she didn't like to be on top—the ballet lessons Mother had forced upon her were useless for the coordination required to move up and down on a man and look sexy at the same time. She figured she usually looked more as if she was in the throes of an epileptic seizure.

But Damien was just going to have to get past it.

Mandy wiggled a little to brace herself better, leaned over and kissed Damien, and took a deep breath.

He looked amused, his hands tightening on her bottom. "Show me your stuff, cowgirl."

With pleasure. "Just remember, you asked for it." She lifted, until only the tip of him remained inside her.

His eyes had narrowed, and he wet his bottom lip. "Oh, I'm asking all right. I can even beg if you want."

When she sank down on him, they both groaned. "No begging required," she panted.

"Good, because I've lost the ability to speak." He squeezed his eyes shut while his fingers convulsed on her hips.

She knew the feeling. All her energy was focused on not whimpering as she moved up and down, up and down, finding a slow, delicious rhythm that sent shots of pleasure clear through to her toes.

"Oh, yeah, baby," he said, eyes popping open to watch her with flared nostrils. "That's it, you've got it."

"I do, don't I?" She did. She'd found the perfect pace, the perfect spot, and for this, right now, right here, the perfect man.

It was that thought, the sheer surprise of it, that had her widening her eyes and pausing. Damien reached between them and strummed his thumb over her clitoris.

"Damien!" She rolled her eyes back and skittered over into an orgasm. It was a smooth, drawn-out, wave after wave of ecstasy, her inner muscles clenching on to him still imbedded deep in her.

"Aah," she whimpered, relaxing her hold on the bed, and tossing her hair out of her face.

Ready to slide off of him and collapse in a puddle of gratitude at his feet, Mandy's head snapped back when Damien ground her hips down onto him.

"Just give me two minutes," he said, thrusting with short, hard bursts that set off aftershocks in her body.

She tried to *tsk,* but it came out a breathy sigh. "That's what you said last time."

"This time I mean it."

And apparently he did, because after two more pounding thrusts, he pressed his lips together and paused. Then exploded in her, the condom inflating a little as he filled it.

"Oh, my," she said, reaching up to push her damp hair back.

"Oh, fuck, yes," he said with a sigh, collapsing his head back onto the bed.

Legs wobbly, Mandy lost her balance trying to untangle her curls and pitched forward onto his chest. Yes, Mother had wasted all those hundreds of pounds on ballet.

Damien caught her before she could slam her nose into his, or break his teeth. "Hey, easy now. You're baking a bun, remember? Got to be careful."

He eased out of her and settled her gently on his chest, caressing along her spine, and Mandy had the stupid overwhelming urge to cry. This was so right, yet so wrong. Damien was her boss, a Caribbean fling, and yet he had more concern for her unborn child than the baby's father.

And when he pressed a kiss on the top of her head as she snuggled into his hard chest, she did start to cry. Her child was never going to have a father, and when they got back to New York, this wonderful intimacy with Damien would be gone.

Embarrassed, she buried her face in his downy hair and tried to suck the sobs back, hold her shoulders still so he wouldn't know.

But of course he did. "Are you crying?" He sounded terrified.

"Hormones. It's nothing."

Making shushing sounds, he kissed her again, body tense beneath her. "Do you want a chocolate?"

That drew a startled laugh out of her, and she lifted her head to give him a wobbly smile. "No, thank you. I'm fine really, though you get points for a brilliant suggestion."

He searched her face, tucking her hair behind her ear. "No regrets, right?"

"No. None." Without thinking, her fingers trailed over his lips, and he kissed the tips. "A few months ago my roommate Jamie brought a psychic to our apartment. At the time, I might have been pregnant but didn't know it, or was on the verge of conceiving. This man, who was a bit of a loon, by the way, told me when he looked at me, he saw pastries. Sweet, sticky things."

Damien's eyebrows shot up.

"I thought it was ridiculous, but then I did get pregnant, and hearing you call the baby a bun, I just had the thought, that well, maybe this is the way things were supposed to happen."

Lying a little on her side, she touched the swell of her stomach. "Maybe I was meant to have this baby just like this, and it's not an accident at all. Maybe I was meant to give up the shop and come work for you."

No matter her feelings on Ben, she wouldn't go back and give up her relationship with him, because he had given her this child, unwittingly or not. A child she wanted more than anything, ever.

And she wouldn't give up this night with Damien.

The lamplight set his face in the shadows. "I'm not sure I believe in fate or destiny, Mandy, but all I know is that I'm really damn glad you're here with me."

"So am I, Damien." She laid her head back down on his chest and felt him relax one slow breath at a time.

Her thoughts emptied one by one, her body replete and satisfied, her skin sticky in the hot night air.

They lay still, together, until her eyes started to drift and she knew she was in danger of falling asleep. "I guess I should head back to my room," she murmured, to be polite and give him an out if he didn't want her there.

"Stay," he said, shifting a little so she oozed off his chest and down onto the bed. "Sleep with me, Mandy."

"Okay." Tucking her hands under her chin and turning her nose away from the tickling hairs on Damien's arm, the word was barely out of her mouth before she was asleep.

Chapter 12

Damien stared at the ceiling, watching an insect flutter ecstatically around the light on the ceiling fan.

He hadn't given a whole lot of thought to Mandy's baby.

Sure, he'd felt that odd sensation of her stomach spasming beneath his hand.

Yes, he could see the small bump growing below her belly button. And he appreciated her breasts, which were full and tender, but he'd never seen them before her pregnancy, so most of the changes in her body meant nothing to him.

Intellectually, he'd seen the worry on her face on the beach, the hurt that dickhead Ben had offered her money to leave him alone. He'd heard her talk about her fears, her need for day care, her desire to be a good mother.

But he hadn't really thought the whole thing through. In a few months Mandy would be walking around looking like she'd swallowed a basketball, then she would have a baby in one of those chest parachutes women used to carry their babies around, and her whole world would revolve around that child.

He'd known, but he hadn't gotten it, and he still wasn't sure he did. But when she had started to tumble forward onto him, some instinct he hadn't even known he'd had had leapt to the surface and reminded him she was carting around precious cargo.

Mandy slept deeply next to him, her ankles crossed, legs drawn up, her breath warming his arm, and he understood her fears. Suddenly he was terrified.

What the hell had he done here? He had slept with a pregnant woman. A *mother*.

Way to be uncomplicated.

He couldn't have just found an acquaintance willing to have a carefree night of fun. No, after three years of abstinence, he went and had sex with a woman pregnant with another man's child. How did they say dumb ass in Spanish?

Damien shifted on the bed, curling his hand behind his head. He supposed he could have slept with another woman, someone confident and independent, who just wanted commitment-free sex. He'd had a few offers like that in the last couple of years and had turned them down.

That wasn't what he wanted.

What he wanted was someone to talk to, someone who would understand why he needed what he did, someone to just hold for a little while. Someone who would make him laugh, while knowing they couldn't have a relationship.

Someone he could be deeply attracted to.

That was why he'd slept with Mandy.

That was why he'd do it again.

And her baby was part of the package, part of what drew him to her, the love and worry in her brown eyes.

Damien sat up, drummed his finger on his knee. He couldn't sleep. Nothing new there. He usually only slept four hours a night, then once a month or so collapsed in a twenty-four-hour coma where he slept straight through a Saturday. The first few times it had happened, he'd scared himself. But he'd learned it was a system that worked for him. He couldn't sleep during the week, not when his mind was busy and he would lie there hour after hour thinking, seeing, feeling.

So he'd learned to drop into bed only when he couldn't

keep his eyes open anymore; then once a month he caught up on his sleep. Big improvement from the days when he hadn't been able to sleep at all because of the nightmares, because of the guilt, because of the feeling that he had failed miserably.

In the first weeks after Jessica had been found, raped and strangled in an alley, he couldn't close his eyes without seeing the agony of her, once so vivacious and confident, lying in that morgue. Then the police had decided he was the prime suspect. They had thought he could have done *that* to Jessica, his wife. The pain had eaten him from the inside out, leaving him a jittery insomniac, hovering on the edge of insanity.

He was better now.

But never whole. Never again.

Damien got out of bed, glancing down at Mandy as she sighed in her sleep and turned her head in the other direction on the pillow.

He couldn't have a relationship with Mandy, but he was so glad they had this, here, tonight. With her teasing smile, Damien thought she'd taken a part of him buried deep inside under a layer of avoidance and had started to help him heal.

Grabbing his boxer briefs off the floor, he pulled them on and grimaced as his feet stuck to the tile floor because of the humidity. He pulled a soft drink out of the minibar and popped the top off. He thought it was cool they had Coke in glass bottles, like he'd had as a kid.

Taking a swig, he plopped on the chair at the round table holding all his work papers, notes, and his computer.

He could work.

But after five minutes, he admitted his concentration was off. He stood up, stretched his sore leg muscles, wondering why sex always seemed to use muscles that the gym could never touch. He straightened the table, picked up Mandy's dress and folded it. Tossed her torn panties in the trash, indulging in a fantasy of buying her a new pair. Sheer, low cut, hot pink.

He'd never been a pink kind of guy, but the idea of seeing Mandy's soft mound behind sassy pink had him hard.

"Damn. Enough already," he told his erection.

He picked up Mandy's beach bag to set it on the table, marveling at how heavy the thing was. "Jesus. She got sand bricks in here?" He took a peek. Sunscreen, sunglasses, her wallet, and a really thick book.

"*The Everything Guide to Pregnancy.*" He pulled it out and glanced at the cover. Some woman was grinning, which she really shouldn't have been considering the ugly floral dress she was wearing.

Thumbing through it, he decided to read Month Four, which was where he thought Mandy was. Sitting back down, he put his feet on the chair opposite him and glanced at the drawn picture of a woman at sixteen weeks gestation. "That's a freak out." There was an alien sucking its thumb in that woman's stomach.

"What you may be feeling . . . fatigue, constipation, breast enlargement, nosebleeds, mood swings, weepiness." Well, he could attest to the weepiness.

There was advice on exercise, diet, and tests the doctor would be performing. "Measuring the height of the fundus? What the hell is that?" Suddenly getting a little nervous that there was a whole lot more to this pregnancy thing than he had thought, he used the index to look up Sexual Intercourse.

Thumbing back to page one hundred and twelve, he realized it might have been a smart idea to read this *before* he'd dipped his wick twice. Two paragraphs in, he was shifting uncomfortably reading about engorgement of genitals and colostrum leaking from breasts and bleeding of the cervix.

"If this happens, you may want to avoid deep penetration?" Damien felt a sweat breaking out all over his body.

He'd deep penetrated, he was sure of it. "A fear that the baby is 'watching' you is normal, but unfounded, as is the fear of 'bumping' the baby."

"Oh, my God!" That had never even occurred to him. He glanced over at Mandy, still naked. He'd read the baby already had eyes, and the image of Junior cringing as Damien's you-know-what came hurtling toward him was horrifying and graphic.

He sucked down his Coke and turned the page.

"If air is forced into the vagina during oral sex, it can cause an embolism and prove deadly to mother and fetus. Oral sex is safe as long as you're careful not to blow any air into the vagina."

Damien reread it twice to make sure he'd gotten it straight. He bit his fingernail and tried to remember if he'd blown into her vagina. What constituted blowing? His tongue had been in her, plunging, licking. And maybe air would go along with his tongue on the way in, but it wasn't like he'd pursed his lips and whistled "Yankee Doodle" into her crotch. What the hell did they mean? Fucking A.

"I could have killed her!"

Rubbing his forehead, he closed the book, flipped it to the front, and opened it at page one. He'd be better off just reading the whole damn thing.

Mandy woke up naked with Damien's hand resting on her bum. It was just about a perfect way to start the day.

Except she had to use the loo.

Rolling onto her back with a sigh, she was planning on easing herself away from Damien's sleeping form and taking care of business. She jumped a little when she saw he was wide awake. Staring at her.

"Good morning," she said with a smile, brushing her fingers over his chest.

"Hi." Damien gave her a warm kiss. On the forehead.

Mandy wet her lips, leaning toward him, but he made no

move to touch her. She decided she'd have to initiate a proper good morning. She didn't want him to feel awkward about the night before, and she didn't want things to end so quickly. They had a whole day and a half left before they had to go back to New York and she wanted to make good use of them.

Damien stiffened as she started wandering lower, fingers fanning out in feathery touches. Stiff was good. She was disappointed to find he was wearing briefs, but wasn't about to let that deter her. Only she looked up again and found he was still wearing that same odd stare, a sort of reverent gaze of awe that was damned unnerving and not in the least bit sexual.

"What?" she asked, shifting a little under his scrutiny.

"Hmmm?" His hand touched her hip, but lightly, as though he was afraid she might deflate like a souffle.

"Why are you looking at me like I'm the Madonna? And I don't mean the one who kissed Britney Spears with tongue." He was scaring her, the intensity in his blue eyes searching and expectant.

"I just think you look beautiful." His hand slid over onto her stomach, and he stroked softly. "I can't believe the baby is five inches big. That seems so little, yet at the same time so huge, considering it's growing inside you."

Mandy dropped her hand from the front of his briefs. He wasn't thinking about sex. He was thinking about her *baby*. Good God.

"Five inches?" she said, not sure what to say. This wasn't a conversation she'd pictured having with Damien.

"I know, it's unbelievable." He shook his head. "And it has eyes and can suck its thumb and has fully formed sexual organs. It's a boy or a girl already, a real live human being." His thumb went over her belly. "Right there. Amazing."

Had he slipped in the shower and hit his head? Something had obviously happened while she'd been sleeping, and whatever it was, he had lost his mind as a result. He shouldn't be looking at her like that. He couldn't. Their relationship couldn't go there.

"How do you know all that?" She didn't think fetal development was knowledge Damien had just picked up along the way. And they were facts he hadn't seemed to know the night before.

"I read the book in your beach bag. Very informative."

"You read *The Everything Guide to Pregnancy*?" She gaped at him, shocked at the idea of Damien Sharpton, workaholic businessman, thumbing through the Labor and Delivery chapter. "The whole thing? When?"

"While you were sleeping." He frowned. "Hey, do you think I blew into your vagina?"

"*What?*" Mandy felt all the blood leave her face. "What the hell are you talking about?"

"It says in the book blowing into the vagina during oral sex can cause an embolism and is dangerous. I don't think I blew any air, but what do you think? Did it feel like air was going into you?"

Mandy blinked. No one had ever discussed her vagina with such a cavalier attitude before, and she didn't like it in the least. It felt uncomfortably as if she was at the OB/GYN, not lying in bed naked with her lover.

"I forgot to turn on my vaginal air pressure gauge," she snapped. "I don't know! I was too focused on not losing my mind to worry about physics."

He looked hurt, the idiot. "Well, I didn't know . . . I'm sorry, Mandy. I didn't mean to do anything harmful to you or the baby."

Oh, damn. His hand was stroking on her again, and she felt like the biggest bitch for yelling at him. "I know that. Of course you wouldn't hurt me. But you startled me, and frankly, I haven't read that chapter in the book so I have no bloody idea what you're talking about."

Which was rather distressing to realize that she was walking around making choices for herself and her baby without having the facts straight first. What was the matter with her? Who was she to think she could raise a child and not make a disaster out of it?

"I'm sure it's fine. We just won't have oral sex again. And when you go to your next prenatal appointment, you can ask the doctor about it. Oh, and we should avoid deep penetration or having you on your back for long periods of sex." He nodded, as though this all made perfect sense to him and that this wasn't an incredibly bizarre conversation for a man to be having with his knocked-up secretary.

"I have to use the loo." She shoved on his chest so he would back up. All thoughts of sensual good-morning sex were gone, shot into orbit by his vaginal-blowing fears.

"I'm starving," he said, obviously not picking up on her tension as he sat up and moved to the edge of the bed. "Do you want to grab some breakfast? Then I should probably get some work done for a couple of hours."

"That's fine. I'll shower while you're working." And read the damn *Everything Guide to* goddamn *Pregnancy.*

She didn't want to make any more mistakes. She didn't want Damien, who wasn't even the baby's father, to have a better sense of what was happening to her body and baby than she did.

And most of all, she wanted to know why along with all the other sacrifices she had to make, she couldn't even be allowed the pleasure of having Damien eat her out.

Chapter 13

Showered, dressed in a bikini, and armed with information, Mandy went off in search of Damien around lunchtime.

He had completely freaked her out, on so many levels, with his behavior that morning. He had brought back to the surface her doubts about her abilities as a mother, made her feel guilt for ignoring the textbook she really should have read two months ago, and he'd worried her that maybe she had done something sexual she shouldn't have.

What kind of mother was she? She should be knitting booties like a proper mum, not having sex with her boss.

Unfortunately, being naked with Damien seemed much more appealing than laboring her way through the creation of a yarn sock.

Then added to all of that was the confusion over watching Damien Sharpton focusing in on her child. She supposed he wasn't acting completely out of person, since he seemed to have taken a divide-and-conquer approach to her pregnancy. He had devoured all the information available to him, now was prepared to do everything by the book, literally.

He had sent her into the shower with admonishments

about the water temperature not exceeding one hundred twenty degrees.

Like she even knew what that was just by turning the taps. She had never quite mastered the whole Celsius/ Fahrenheit conversion.

But no matter if the behavior fit Damien's aggressive, assertive personality, it was unnerving. And his concern, no matter how thoughtful, coupled with the way he had opened up to her the night before, made her feel a strange, confusing longing that she had no business feeling.

They needed to keep this simple. They needed to keep this about sex.

But it was so hard when Damien had become her friend on this trip. He had shown her parts of him that were hidden from everyone else. She saw the humor and the caring and the worry. The loneliness.

He had made her feel so relaxed, so sexy, so capable. He didn't doubt her abilities to raise her child. He didn't look at her and see nothing but poor choices. Damn it, he liked her, respected her, trusted her, and that was so appealing.

And now he wanted to look after her unborn baby.

It couldn't happen. She couldn't let him in like that, couldn't learn to lean on him, get used to him being in her life. He had said he didn't want a relationship and she believed him. He hadn't healed from his wife's death, and his heart wasn't his to give away, even if she were looking for that, which she wasn't.

Was she? Mandy halted in the hallway outside Damien's room, startled by her thoughts.

No, of course she wasn't. She was still hurt and dealing with Ben's rejection, and most importantly of all, she needed to focus on her job and her baby. There was no time for a relationship in her life, and it would only be a needless distraction. Plus she never wanted her child to become attached to a man who wasn't its father and who could leave at any time. Bad enough Mandy would have to explain someday that the child's biological father had no interest in seeing her or him. She couldn't create a situation where her child could be rejected a second time.

So it had to be about sex, and nothing more.

That had been fabulous between them, so what in the hell was wrong with just leaving it at that?

Annoyed that Damien had complicated things, she pounded hard on his door.

"Come in," he called.

Mandy flung open the door, determined to seduce him into a nooner. She'd spent the entire morning reading the *Everything Guide,* and there was absolutely no reason why they couldn't be as sexually active as she wanted to. The book had even encouraged it as a way to keep you relaxed and alleviate stress.

Damien was sitting at the table trying to work on his laptop, a gigantic hamper taking up most of the space and leaving him dangling precariously on the edge.

"What is that?"

"I don't know." His fingers flew over the keyboard. "It's for you. The front desk had it when I went to check messages and send a fax. It came on the flight from Heathrow."

Mandy went to the table and leaned to read the label. Right in front of Damien. Dangling her breasts in front of him like really big carrots. It wasn't subtle, but she had only two days to work with.

He made a strange coughing noise.

She would have turned to check on the promising sound, but the behemoth package was from her mother. Mandy laughed in comprehension. "Oh, for heaven's sake, it's from my mother." She untied the bow on top and let down the cellophane wrap. "It's a food hamper from Fortnum and Mason."

She lifted the lid as Damien shoved his chair back and stood up. He peered over her shoulder. "Food hamper?"

"Yes." She grinned at him and pulled out some strawberry jam and Darjeeling tea. "Hungry?" There were biscuit tins and a variety of cheeses, crackers, marmalade, and lemon curd. Her stomach rumbled in anticipation. "Mother is worried I'll starve or eat bad fruit in this heathen tropical country."

"She sent this from London? I can only imagine what that must have cost." Damien shook a tin. "Chocolate cookies. Good stuff."

"Cost is no object when Mother thinks she's right." But for the first time, Mandy saw beyond her mother's desire to maintain strict control over every aspect of her life. "But you know, I think I finally understand. A mother's fears aren't always rational, but they're born of love. I don't think I've ever appreciated just how my mother feels about me until right now."

Damn it, she was going to get weepy. Just when she was trying to prove to Damien that her pregnancy was irrelevant to their relationship, she went and turned into a hormonal watering pot.

Damien didn't stop to think about what he was doing. He just wrapped his arms around Mandy and pulled her into his chest. She gave a little sniffle and sank against him with a sigh.

His heart raced as he held her there, patting her back. He hadn't held a woman like this in so long, hadn't felt he had any comfort to give. And Mandy was so, so different from Jess. His wife had used tears to manipulate, to wrench guilty apologies from him, to gloss over her own transgressions.

Those very thoughts now—unkind, scrutinizing thoughts of Jessica's flaws—made him feel guilty all over again. He hadn't loved her well enough in life, and he couldn't get it right in death either.

Mandy was looking up at him. He could feel the weight of her brown eyes studying him. But he looked over her shoulder as she spoke, unable to bear the openness she was wearing on her face.

"Love, no matter how it's expressed, is still love. We all have flaws, and so our love will be flawed. But that doesn't diminish it."

Damien squeezed her tighter to him, swallowing hard, unable to speak. How did she do that? How did she manage to get inside his head and find his thoughts, anticipate them, refute them, offer him a comfort that he wasn't sure he deserved.

One of the walls of defense towering around his emotions and heart had a good hole in it. About the size of Mandy's foot, where she inadvertently was kicking down the fortress that had protected him for three years.

"I'm not sure I agree with you, Mandy. Just because we're flawed doesn't mean it's okay to let those flaws bleed into our feelings."

"Do you think there is a perfect love, then?"

"No." That he was sure of. And he wasn't even sure there was love.

"I think perfect love is any time you love unconditionally, without selfish intent, without concern for personal gain."

He wanted to scoff. Call her hopelessly naïve and begging to be taken advantage of. But he couldn't. Maybe because he wanted so desperately to believe that she could be right. "And do you think people really do that?"

"I do, Damien. I really do."

Her hands wrapped around his waist, her hair tickling his chin, and he knew that she meant what she said. That she would love her child that way. That she had bits and pieces of her that alone were greater than the sum whole of his soul.

He knew that he didn't deserve whatever she had to offer him.

That he couldn't resist her.

That he wanted to believe.

That he didn't want to be alone anymore.

That while the court had dismissed the charges of murder against him, he had effectively been living in a prison of his own making for the past three years.

And that Mandy was helping him turn the key.

Damien wasn't taking the hint that she wanted to make love to him. Mandy lounged on the bed, the contents of the hamper spread out all around her, stomach happily full, while every trick she tried was ignored.

He was either exceptionally dull witted, or he was choosing to ignore her. Knowing him like she did, she was forced to conclude the latter. Damien was no dummy.

But Mandy had done everything short of a striptease to get his attention. Instead of jumping her bones, he just looked pained. As though he had indigestion.

He hadn't done a thing when she had brushed her chest against him. Hadn't made a move when she'd tossed her hair and given him a smoldering look. Hadn't even blinked when she had spread out lunch on the bed, claiming the balcony was too sunny this time of day.

No, he had pulled up a chair instead of climbing on the bed with her and was sitting there devouring biscuits. If he did have indigestion, it wouldn't surprise her. He'd worked his way through a whole tin, after eating a cheese wedge and an entire cracker sleeve.

"Do you want to go sailing this afternoon?" he asked.

"Sure." Right after they had sex. "I've never been."

She purposely let marmalade dribble from her cracker down onto her chest. Her barely contained in a bikini, newly burgeoning chest. The sticky orange jelly slid down into her ample cleavage. Damien's fist closed, crumbling the cracker he was holding to bits.

But he didn't do a damn thing, not even when she leaned over for a napkin and started delicately blotting herself inches from his nose.

"Oops." She gave him ample opportunity to come to her assistance with his hand or tongue, whichever method he preferred, but he just shoved another hunk of cheese in his mouth.

Exasperated, she dropped the napkin, marmalade still clinging to her breasts. "Damien, I think in your case, too much knowledge is a bad thing."

"What's that supposed to mean?" he asked around a mouthful of Brie.

"You read that pregnancy book and now you see me as some kind of vessel for creation. You've lost all sexual interest in me."

It was gratifying to see his mouth drop completely open, Brie clinging to his tongue, though not as gratifying as him reaching over and untying her top would be.

"You're kidding, right?" He swallowed the cheese.

A cracker crumb clung to the corner of his mouth, and she wanted to lick it away. "Well, maybe I sounded a little overdramatic, but no, I'm not kidding. I dropped marmalade on my breasts and you didn't even blink!"

"You did that on purpose?" He looked shocked.

Hello. Of course she did. "Yes. I was trying to entice you, for all the good it did me."

Damien rubbed his forehead and laughed, his shoulders shaking. "Oh, my God, you're killing me. You know that? Here I've been trying my damnedest not to touch you all day and you've been trying to *entice* me? I've only got so much self-control, Mandy, and you're coming close to using mine up."

Why was he laughing? Why was he resisting her? "I've

missed something . . . Why can't you touch me? I don't want you to resist. I want you to get on this bed with me and shag."

He stopped laughing and gave a strangled groan.

"You don't find me attractive anymore, do you?" She didn't mean to say that, but it slipped out. She didn't want to sound needy or emotional, but she was puzzled and hurt that he didn't seem to want her anymore. When they got back to New York he was supposed to stop wanting her.

But here in Punta Cana he could want and he could have all he wanted.

Damien lifted the napkin off his lap and tossed it on the bed. He pointed to his pants. "Does it look like I find you unattractive? I almost bit my tongue off when that jelly slathered over your chest."

He had an erection, which the napkin had masked. It was a big one. Her breath came faster, her body tingling with awareness. "What am I missing here? Why can't we have sex?"

"I want you so much, Mandy, that it shocks me. I mean, you're pregnant, you're going to be a mother—I should treat you with respect. But all I can think about is how luscious you are, how good you taste, and how much I want to be inside you. That makes me a pig. I'm racking up perversion points on the sexual scoreboard here."

Thank God, he wanted her. "That's a lovely sentiment, and I'm glad you feel the need to respect me, but there is absolutely nothing wrong with being sexually attracted to a pregnant woman." At least she hoped there wasn't, considering he hadn't been the one to impregnate her.

"Oh, I know that. Trust me, if anything, it makes me more attracted to you. But the thing is, there is still a baby inside you, and that needs to be taken into consideration." Jaw clenched, eyes burning with desire, he balled his hands into fists. "I just don't think I can trust myself if I get near you. I don't think I can stop myself from doing things we shouldn't." He looked at her, desperate.

"I want to deep penetrate, Mandy."

Have mercy and then some. Inner thighs burning, Mandy undid the ties to her bikini top and ripped it off.

Chapter 14

Why him? What had he done to deserve the hell that his life was? Damien groaned out loud in ecstasy and torment when Mandy tore off her black bikini top and let it fall in the open hamper at the foot of the bed.

This just wasn't fair. Struck dumb, he could only stare as she trailed her fingers between her breasts, in the sticky jelly remnants. It would be sweet, he knew. It would be warm from her heated flesh. He would be able to smell her, the tangy saltiness of her skin intermingling with the fruity spread and the warm musk of her desire.

"Mandy." He pleaded for her to understand. He dug his nails into his legs through the fabric of his shorts, hoping pain would keep him from leaping on her.

Her thumb brushed over one nipple, and he became paralyzed. Incapable of movement of any kind. Frozen in panic and overwhelming lust.

"Damien, I read the book this morning." While she spoke, her fingers went up and down, up and down between her breasts, luring his gaze. "What it said was that at the end of your pregnancy, there may be slight bleeding after intercourse, and if that is the case you might want to avoid deep penetration. Otherwise, as long as it's comfortable for the mother, it's completely safe."

He could barely concentrate on her words when oh-soslyly her touch shifted to the right and she was stroking the swell of her breast, the full curve underneath, her head turning to the side a little as she made contact with her nipple.

Even with his tongue too large for his mouth, he forced words out. "It seems like we should err on the side of caution." Though he was starting to think her arguments were pretty damn persuasive.

She was breathing now with that sound he loved—the little gasp of pleasure slipping out now and again, the deep jagged edge to each breath she pulled in, her mouth open in invitation.

"Absolutely, I agree. So if anything feels uncomfortable, I'll just tell you to stop."

Well, that was good enough for him.

Damien grabbed the jar of jelly with a growl and leaned over the bed. Knee in a plate of crackers, he slapped a big heaping handful of the sticky orange goo over her right breast and bent down for a taste.

"Oh, Damien, yes!" she cried when his tongue touched the tip of her nipple.

The taste of the fruit spread mixed with the taste of her skin and crashed with the sound of her calling out his name and gave him a heady rush of pleasure. He sucked the bud into his mouth, hard.

Her cry dissolved into a low groan.

For a man who had thought himself pretty much devoid of all sexual feelings three months ago, he was pretty damned turned on. Swirling his tongue around her nipple to clean up clinging bits of jelly, he reached into the jar with an index finger and hauled out another scoop.

She pulled in her breath. "What are you going to do with that?"

Moving away from her breast, he teased his finger back and forth in front of her, jelly sliding down his knuckle, a dollop still resting on the tip. When he skirted past her nipple, Mandy let out a soft cry of disappointment. She had thrust her breasts out toward him in invitation, full and plump, her taut nipples a deep pink, the one still shiny and wet from his mouth.

Teasing himself as well as her, he asked, "Oh, did you want it here?" He hovered over one nipple.

"It doesn't matter to me," she said, employing that clipped secretarial voice of hers. "Whatever works best for you."

"How generous of you." His body was tense, his skin hot and tight, blood rushing through his head with a sexual buzz. "Maybe I will put it here, then."

Coming a half inch from contact, he pulled his finger back. "Or maybe not."

She groaned, and he gave a low laugh. "Are you hungry, Mandy?" He stared into her rich brown eyes and wanted her to understand, wanted her to feel the same urgency and longing. "I am. I'm very, very hungry."

He smeared the jelly on her bottom lip from side to side. The tip of her tongue came out and flicked across his finger. The burn in his gut increased, and he snatched his finger back, out of her reach.

Replacing his finger with his mouth, he kissed her, licking at her lips, teasing his tongue into her until they were both covered in sugar and sweet fruit, passion, and the taste of each other. His hands dug in her hair as he drew her in closer, and her bare breasts brushed across his button-up shirt. Wanting to feel her against him, he used one hand to laboriously undo each button on his shirt, while he nipped and ate at her mouth.

When he got the shirt apart and her chest collided with his, they both groaned. "You feel so good, Mandy. So perfect."

Her head tipped back and he took the opportunity to suckle her neck.

"Damien, it's so different with you. So much more . . . intense. That sounds ridiculous, doesn't it?"

"No." Not at all. "I was thinking the same thing."

His knees were crunching around in crackers and cheese, and he shifted, needing more.

"Lie back." Even as his hands were easing her down, he realized that was wrong. "Shit, we're not supposed to do that." He pulled her back up, immediately feeling guilty for forgetting and flinging her around like a rag doll. "Sorry."

Mandy touched his cheek. "Don't do that. Don't apologize for something like that. This is new for both of us and we're trying to learn how to adjust. The book did say after the fourth month I shouldn't lie on my back for long periods of time, like sleeping. I don't think this counts, but if it makes you more comfortable we can just try a different position."

He loved how she was so matter-of-fact about what they were doing. They were lovers, having sex, and no sense in tiptoeing around that.

She was wiggling out of his arms. "The book encouraged couples to experiment with new ways of making love."

The only problem with that was they weren't a couple. They were something that was getting more and more complex and harder to define. Not willing to dwell on that too long, Damien was about to suggest they lie down on their sides and see where that went. Before he could open his mouth, Mandy turned and crawled toward the pillows, peeling down her bikini bottoms.

He was about to protest that he would have liked to have done the peeling down of those, when she went up on all fours.

"Though they did suggest coming from behind as a good one. Would that interest you?" And she stuck her perky little ass in the air toward him.

Holy hell. Damien closed his eyes and counted to five before he could answer. Everything ached with longing. Even his teeth wanted her. His ears were turned on.

She had no idea. Absolutely no fucking idea what she did to him. "Yes, that interests me."

Yanking his shirt and pants off and tossing them in the hamper along with Mandy's bikini bottoms, he shoved the cracker mess right off the side of the bed. He'd give the maid an extra large tip. Then he put one hand on Mandy's pale backside and moved right alongside her.

Thighs touching hers, he stroked her smooth skin, enjoying the curve of her heart-shaped ass, the arch of her spine rising gracefully to her neck. Goose bumps rose under his touch, and she gave a sweet, low sigh.

"I think this will work."

"Oh, this will definitely work." Damien leaned over and kissed her shoulder, his fingers trailing between her legs, his erection pressing into her hard and urgent.

And what he thought might work would be them. Him and Mandy. Together. Not just here, but there, too. Back in New York.

The thought startled him so much, kicked him in the gut and head and everything in between, that he forgot where he was going with his hand and let his finger pause right where the swell of her bottom met her inner thighs.

Resting on her forearms, Mandy was wet with anticipation, swollen with longing, tilted back as far as she could without snapping her spine in two, and Damien had stopped. His finger hovered over her crotch like a hummingbird with a flower. He was supposed to be dipping into her bloody nectar, and he wasn't doing a damn thing.

"Damien?" She felt ridiculous with her bum in the air, arms forward, as if she was paying homage to the mattress.

This could get very embarrassing in a moment or two.

"Mandy," he whispered behind her, voice hoarse and raw.

Then when she would have been satisfied with just his finger, he came in with the big guns. Or gun. He slid inside her with one quick thrust that tore the breath right out of her.

"Oh, my." She kneaded the sheet and swallowed hard as he filled her.

"Is this okay? You're comfortable?"

"Oh, yes." She closed her eyes, head resting on her forearm, and shuddered. "I'm fine, thanks. Never been better, really."

Then she decided talking was going to have to wait.

She was going to be much too busy having an orgasm to form words.

Especially since he started moving with tight just-right movements, his hands on her waist, firm and hard and masculine. She loved his control, the way he rolled his desire in and out at will, the way his emotions loosened when he was with her like this.

He was taller and more muscular than Ben, but it wasn't just physical features that made Ben seem small in comparison. It was Damien's presence. His aggressive, vibrant approach, his confidence, yet secret hidden depths attracted her to him in a way she never had been to another man.

If Ben was a biscuit, Damien was a Danish. Cool, sweet, complicated and very, very irresistible.

Too much Danish wasn't good for her.

But she was on holiday and it was okay to indulge. She would resist the temptation when she got home and thought through the consequences of overnibbling.

Damien's fingers snaked around and cupped her breasts. He stroked in and out of her as he played with her nipples, and Mandy let go of her thoughts and gave in to the ecstasy of his body in hers.

As she tumbled into an orgasm, blurting out the obvious, "Don't stop, I'm coming," Damien swore.

Then her own cries of pleasure were drowned out by his as he let go and poured himself into her. She felt the spasm of his body, felt the jerk of his hand on her breast, felt the heat of his skin pressed against hers.

And as she heard his groan, mingling with hers, her eyes closed, Mandy knew this wasn't just sex.

This was something much more, and it scared the bloody hell out of her at the same time it exhilarated.

Chapter 15

"Tell me we never have to go back," Mandy said as she lay on the bow of the sailboat.

Damien tilted the sail and watched her sun herself, looking relaxed and beautiful, arm flung over her eyes. He had the urge to suggest they toss over their lives back in New York and sail off in the vast ocean and never look back. Pretend the real world didn't exist and that they could just have each other, idyllic days in the sun, and nights spent making love.

But Damien was no dreamer.

And even the ocean wasn't calm every day.

"Maybe it will be warm when we get back tomorrow." He scanned the horizon and told himself he didn't care.

That it didn't matter to him that this was the end of his time with Mandy.

But his heart wasn't quite as frozen as he'd thought, and it ached, a feeling he had meant to avoid for the rest of his life. It was a good thing they were leaving in the morning. Any longer and that ache might compel him to an action he would regret.

"That's no consolation," she said, turning from her side to her back, wearing another little nothing of a yellow bikini. She had told him the two-piece she owned made her feel like her growing stomach was more evident. That the bikini was better camouflage, since it drew the eye upward.

Whatever the reason, he found it hard to concentrate when she was half naked.

She sighed. "It will probably be raining. And I have no clothes that fit. And Caroline Davidson who works in accounting is my roommate. She happens to be getting married next month and I'm a bridesmaid, which is ridiculous. I tried to bow out gracefully, pointing out that my dress no longer fits, but Caroline wouldn't hear of it. So I have an appointment to have the dress altered next week, though I don't see how they can alter it unless they cut a hole in the middle."

Damien eyed her stomach and laughed. "You're exaggerating. Most people have bigger stomachs than that after Thanksgiving dinner."

She opened one eye and peeked from under her arm. "I'm whining, aren't I?"

"A little."

She gave a rueful smile. "Well, can't you whine a little, too? That would make me feel better. What is waiting to attack you when you get back?"

"I'm going to Boston at the end of the week for a customer briefing. And I have a meeting on Wednesday with the software developers. But that's all normal stuff." He grinned when she curled her lip in disgust, obviously unimpressed. "I have a dentist appointment. Does that help?"

"No." She ran her hand idly over her stomach. "I have an ultrasound scheduled in a few weeks and I have to drink three glasses of water before I go, and they won't let me go to the loo until the test is done. I've heard it's just *agony.*"

"I have to get a crown. That's agonizing, too," he protested. It wasn't something he was looking forward to.

"Aren't you kind of young for a crown? How old are you anyway?" Mandy looked at him suspiciously, like he was forty-five and trying to hide it.

"Thirty-three. And I have a sweet tooth that gets me into

trouble." He smiled at her and adjusted the sail so they would turn around and start back to the shore. "Didn't you notice how many cookies I ate at lunch?"

"I did make note of that." Then she shrieked when a spray of ocean water soaked the front of her from hair to thighs. "That's cold!"

Damien laughed as she sat up shaking herself. "It is not cold. It's seventy-five-degree water."

Mandy didn't like his answer. She leaned over and tossed a handful of water in his direction before he realized what she was doing. Warm water hit his face and bare chest.

Damien blinked and shook his head so the water scattered. "Definitely warm."

She laughed. "You idiot."

"What? What did I do?" He leaned toward her, thinking it would be a really great idea to kiss her right now.

Mandy must have thought he was going to splash her or some other form of retribution because she quickly scooted backward. "No, don't!"

Only her laughter cut out when she lost her balance and rocked precariously. Damien shot his arms out and grabbed her before she tumbled over the side of the boat. "Careful now."

He settled her onto his lap, away from the edge, and took a deep breath to slow down his racing heart. She'd scared the shit out of him for a split second there.

"You rescued me," she said, her chocolate brown eyes melting as she looked at him.

He had a funny feeling that the opposite was true. She had rescued him. As she dusted her lips over his, and her bottom pressed into his thighs, her breasts firm and warm on his chest, Damien held her to him.

"It was nothing." And if he kept telling himself that, maybe he'd believe it.

Mandy pulled back and raised her eyebrows suggestively. "Ever done it on a boat?"

"No." Damien gave in to the pleasure of caressing her backside, but refrained from anything else. "And I'm not going to today either, since we're fifty feet from shore."

Mandy looked over her shoulder at the beach and let out a sigh. "Oh, damn. That's really a shame."

Her mournful expression made him laugh. "What do you want to do now? We could play water volleyball, or go for a donkey ride on the beach. Or we could go back to my room, and I could lick you all over and make you come. I'll let you decide."

Moistening her lips, she smiled, a slow, sensual smile. "As fond as I am of donkeys, I'll choose the third option."

The boat hit the sand, and they lurched to a stop. Mandy's ass smashed into his erection. "Good choice," he said through clenched teeth.

The plane was quiet, the sun-soaked passengers lethargic. A Julia Roberts movie was playing on the TV monitors, but Mandy hadn't bothered to plug in her headphones. She was content to just lean on Damien's arm, a blanket wrapped over her.

A little different than the trip down. Then she had been avoiding Damien. Now she didn't want to let him go, knowing this was it. Their last few hours together. But they weren't talking about that. Damien was telling her about his apartment and the renovations he was making to it, taking down some walls to open up the space.

She was content to just listen to him, interjecting an occasional comment or thought, but mostly she just wanted to feel his nearness, the rumble in his chest as he spoke, the rise and fall of his breathing. The way he squeezed her waist to emphasize a point as he talked.

"Where will you live after the baby is born?" he asked.

"Since Caroline's getting married and moving to the Upper East Side, I'll have the room to myself. And Jamie and Allison swear they don't mind sharing an apartment with a baby, but I don't know. It seems like a lot to ask of them, with all the mess and the noise. We'll see how it goes after the baby is born."

"They must be good friends."

"They are. The best." Mandy stifled a yawn, ready for a nap. She was getting addicted to the midday naps she'd been taking on this trip. "I met Jamie in my shop when she was looking for a gift for her niece. She needed another roommate, and we hit it off. That was three years ago. Jamie and Allison went to NYU together, and Allison went to high school in Connecticut with Caroline, so they've all known each other awhile. I was the latecomer to the group and yet I feel like we've been friends forever.

"You'll like them," she said without thinking, sleepy.

"I doubt I'll ever meet Jamie and Allison, Mandy."

That jerked her out of her semislumberous state. His words were a harsh reminder of what the rules for their relationship were. Rule number one—there was no relationship.

"You're right." She gave a forced laugh. "I don't know what I was thinking. I'm just tired."

She could feel the force of his stare on her, but she refused to look up at him. She didn't want him to see the neediness she knew would be reflected in her eyes. They couldn't get involved, she knew that. And if he changed his mind, she might not be able to resist changing hers.

But she had to resist. This was not the time for her to embroil herself in another relationship with a man when she had a baby to think about.

She knew that. She did. But knowing it and liking it were two different things.

"If we could . . ." Damien kissed the top of her head. "I want you, Mandy, I do. Very much. But I can't . . . and I want more for you than I can give you."

He sounded so anguished, she couldn't bear it. She turned and looked up at him, taking his chin with her hand.

"Hey, hey, it's all right, Damien. I understand. This is what we agreed on, and this is the right thing to do. But I'm so very glad we had this time together, and the only thing I regret is that it has to end."

If he said it didn't have to end, Mandy seriously doubted she could say no to him at that moment. He was looking at her so intensely, as though he wanted to see inside her soul, his grip on her tightening.

But he just said, "No regrets. Just good memories, and that's more than I expected."

Somehow that didn't seem like enough.

Chapter 16

Damien set his suitcase down inside the front door of his apartment and let the quiet settle over him. No ocean. No Caribbean music. No Mandy.

He lived on the twenty-seventh floor to avoid some of the usual noises of the city, so the only things he could hear were the hum of his refrigerator and taxi horns honking down below on Eighty-fifth Street.

He wanted to throw something. He wanted to lift his suitcase and toss it right out the window of his living room.

Everything had been fine. He had been living his life, in a narrow, stilted kind of way, that was true, but he had been coping. He hadn't *felt* anything.

Now he wanted what he couldn't have.

Damien picked up the cordless phone by his kitchen table and hit the "on" button. No voice mail messages waited for him. He had been gone five days and he didn't have a single fucking phone message. This was what had happened to him. No one knew where he was, no one cared.

He had nothing.

Hurtling his keys on the counter, he dug in his pocket for his wallet. He flipped it open and pulled out the picture he kept in the back. The one of Jess leaning over his shoulder, her long hair tumbling down his chest. Her eyes were laughing at the camera as she posed, looking perfectly pretty the way she always had. The expression on his face was different than hers. He looked graspingly happy, like he was in ecstasy, and terrified it would disappear.

Well, it had, but not the way he'd always expected. In the back of his head, he had always assumed Jessica would leave him someday. He couldn't keep her happy, and they had always swung from blissful calm to outbursts of discontent—weeks where she would mope around and he would do everything short of kissing her ass to get her to smile again. But never had he expected that night when Jess had gotten angry with him and run off with her friends, as she did on a regular basis, that she would wind up dead.

The picture was fading now that it was five years old.

But the guilt he always felt was just as fresh as it had been years ago when he'd realized that he wasn't strong enough, man enough, smart enough, to love Jessica the way she needed to be loved.

Yet for the first time ever, Jessica's voice, her smell, her touch, was drowned out by another woman.

And he knew that was the ultimate betrayal of his dead wife.

Mandy was grateful Jamie had been walking into the apartment building at the same time as she'd been getting out of the cab she'd shared with Damien from LaGuardia. It had given her the option to wave away Damien's offer to carry her suitcase up and avoid more awkward goodbyes.

Jamie, bless her, had been oblivious, giving Mandy a big hug and grabbing her suitcase straightaway, chattering about the spring storm they were expecting as she waved Damien off with a smile. Mandy had managed her own tepid smile before letting Jamie lead her into the building. Damien hadn't smiled at all.

"You look so awesome, Mandy! The weather must have agreed with you."

The weather or the sex. One of the two. "I do feel much better."

"Good. Hey, let's order some takeout and you can tell us all about it."

"Super." This was the downside to having roommates. When you wanted to be alone and just have a good crying jag, they were there. Not that she had any right to be crying. There had been no surprises from Damien, and she hadn't wanted any.

Maybe she was just tired.

Maybe it was hormones.

Mandy opened their apartment door and stepped inside, shivering a little. Sixty degrees and sunny was okay, but she had adjusted pretty quickly to running about in a bathing suit.

Caroline was on the couch, her glasses on her nose as she studied some papers in her hand. "Mandy! You look great. How was the trip?" Caroline looked behind her at Jamie and curled her lip. "But first I have to warn you, Ben was here."

Oh, God. Mandy wrapped her arms around herself and groaned. "When?" She was looking forward to putting her feet up, eating herself sick, and sleeping straight through to tomorrow. She did not want to think about Ben.

Caroline tossed down what she was holding and lifted her glasses off. "Just ten minutes ago." Her disapproval was obvious. "I told him you were just getting back from the Caribbean and would call him tomorrow, but he said he'd wait. He went across the street to the deli. He probably saw you come in and he'll be here any minute."

"Damn!" Mandy ran over to the mirror hanging in the hall. "I'm a wreck! I have plane hair."

"Who cares what you look like?" Jamie sniffed. "I think he has a lot of nerve just showing up here without even calling first. Where has he been for the last three months?"

While that was true, it didn't negate the need to look good when she saw him again. Obviously Caroline understood her plight better as she was whipping a comb and lipstick out of her purse on the coffee table.

Mandy had just patted, powdered, and finished puckering when someone knocked on the door. She was glad she was wearing a sundress and heels. "Do I look pregnant?" she asked as Jamie went to answer the door.

"No," Caroline said.

"Good." She wasn't sure why it mattered, but she didn't want Ben to see her as a pregnant woman. She didn't want to see how he would react.

After letting Ben in, Jamie and Caroline discreetly took themselves off down the hall, and Mandy was left staring at the man who had fathered her baby.

She felt surprisingly little.

She didn't remember him being quite so short, or his blond hair quite so thin on top. "Hello, Ben. How are you?"

"Mandy." He came forward and kissed her cheek. "I'm fine, thanks. And I have to say, pregnancy agrees with you. You look fantastic."

Well, it was something. She couldn't help but grit her teeth, though. Had he been hoping she would look like hell as she pined over him?

"Thank you." She stared at him expectantly. There had to be a point to this little visit, and she didn't feel like being courteous in the meantime. Any feelings she had ever had for his politeness, his stability, his kindness, had all evaporated when he had told her he had no intention of ever seeing his child.

"Can I sit down?" Ben was wearing neatly pressed navy slacks and a white golf shirt. He patted his pocket and smiled awkwardly, almost as if he were nervous.

"Ben." She sighed. Sleeping was sounding more and more appealing. "I just got home from a business trip. I've been on a plane for over three hours and stood in line at customs for almost two. I'm tired. What do you want?"

"My son just graduated from Fordham this past weekend."

A pain started behind her eyes. That son was her child's half brother and her baby would never even know him. "Give him my congratulations then." She almost laughed at the inanity of her comment, but her mother had taught her manners, if anything.

"I will. And seeing him, well, it got me thinking. You're having my child."

Was that supposed to be a newsflash? Mandy decided her feet hurt too much to stand anymore. She sank onto the couch and kicked off her sandals. "That's my understanding, yes."

"And I thought I ought to check on you, see how you are. See if you need anything." He cleared his throat and looked at her.

Was she supposed to understand what the hell he wanted? Because it wasn't getting through to her. "I'm doing quite well. I have a new job, with good benefits." Though the biggest benefit—Damien in her bed—was no longer available. "I'm feeling better now that the morning sickness has passed, and the doctor says everything is progressing normally. I don't really need anything right now." Except for him to go home so she could lie on her bed and give large melancholy sighs as she thought about her boss.

"We could get back together," he blurted suddenly, ramming his hand into his pocket. "Pick up where we left off."

Mandy closed her eyes and prayed she would not strangle the father of her unborn child. Searching for every shred of decency she possessed, she spoke slowly so she wouldn't start cursing at him. "I don't think that's possible, Ben. I don't have the feelings for you I once did."

"I'm not suggesting we live together or anything." He hastened to make qualifications to his statement as if she hadn't even spoken. "I don't think either of us is ready for that. But I want to be in our child's life. And yours. We've a permanent bond now, Mandy."

That's what she was afraid of. "I won't deny our child its father if you want to be involved."

Ben came toward her and smiled, sitting next to her on the couch. "I knew you'd be a sport about this, Mandy. I just needed time to get used to the idea. You can understand that."

Oh, she could understand it all right. But unlike him, she hadn't been given the option of ignoring the situation for three months. She turned, her patience entirely used up, when she saw that Ben was leaning toward her.

Oh, dear God, he was going to kiss her. She stood hastily up, bumping Ben's nose with her arm. "I'm really done up, Ben. Why don't you call me in a few days when you've thought out exactly what it is you want."

"I know what I want. You and our child." His gaze went to her chest as he stood up next to her. "You've changed since I saw you last. You look bloody fantastic, Mandy."

If he tried to touch her breast she was going to scream. "Ben!"

"What?" He looked genuinely surprised, which meant he hadn't been listening to a word she'd said. "I care about you, Mandy. We were together for six months, and I thought you'd be happy now that I've come to my senses. A child needs both parents."

That was true. It was absolutely true. Yet she suddenly felt like crying. "Ben, please just give me some space. I'm really tired. Please."

She wondered what would happen to his face if she told him that she'd just got back from having sex with her boss. Would he turn purple? Would his face just slide right off onto her hardwood floors? Would he suffer an apoplexy? It seemed safer not to find out right at the moment.

"All right, of course." He touched her elbow, the picture

of concern. "You can call me at home or at the office any-time, you know that. My ex-wife is throwing a graduation party for Nick on Saturday, but other than that I'm free."

She nodded. "I'll be in touch." It didn't matter that she'd be perfectly happy to never see Ben again. He was this baby's biological father and there was no way around that. If he wanted to be a father, a real father, she couldn't deny him or her baby that relationship.

But that didn't include her. There was no way she could rekindle whatever feelings she'd had for Ben. Not after his abandonment.

Not after Damien.

Ben let himself out, and Caroline and Jamie burst from the bedroom to find her clutching her stomach, tears rolling down her cheeks.

"Are you okay?" Jamie grabbed her hands and led her to the couch.

"Of all the nerve," Caroline proclaimed. "Where exactly does he think he's been for the last three months?"

Mandy started to cry harder.

Jamie clucked. "Oh, honey, don't cry. It will all work out."

"He's not worth it," Caroline assured her.

Mandy shook her head. "It's not that."

"What is it?" Jamie wiped the tears off her cheeks with the bell sleeves of her prairie top.

"I had sex with Damien Sharpton!"

Caroline's jaw dropped. Jamie looked confused. "Just now?"

"Well, not in the taxi! When we were in Punta Cana."

"But you're pregnant with Ben's baby and . . . oh, shit." Jamie's hand went over her mouth.

"Exactly. Oh, shit." Mandy felt a headache coming on.

Damien was having sushi with Rob on Monday and try-ing not to be a brusque jerk. He didn't think he was suc-ceeding.

"Man, I thought going to the Caribbean would loosen you up. You're tighter than when you left." Rob poked his chopstick at Damien. "Told you you should have slept with your assistant."

"Fuck off." Damien adjusted his tie and chewed his maki. He had spent an absolutely hellish weekend shut up in his apartment trying to work, with very little result. All he could think about was Mandy. Mandy and her baby. Mandy and him.

He hadn't seen her at work that morning, but then he hadn't expected to. She was good at avoiding him when she wanted to.

Rob shook his head. "You know something? You make it really hard to like you sometimes."

Damien thought Rob was joking, but when Rob looked at him, he had disgust on his face. "What do you mean?"

Only he knew what Rob probably meant, and Rob was right, but maybe for the first time, he needed to hear it said out loud.

"I mean you're so busy feeling sorry for yourself, you treat everyone else like shit."

Chest tightening, he set his own chopsticks down on his sushi plate. "You think I'm feeling sorry for myself? That's fine for you to say. You weren't the one who was charged with raping and strangling your wife. You're not the one whose marriage was dissected for a grand jury, and whose wife's attributes and flaws were picked apart and discussed as if she had never been a human being."

He never did that. He never spoke about Jess like that out loud. He never talked about the arrest, the charges, the feeling that he might as well be dead like Jess. He had felt empty, soulless, when they had charged him with her murder. And only marginally less so when the grand jury had voted not to indict him.

But the reins of his tight control slipped through his fingers at Rob's accusation. He felt anger, hot and bright. He couldn't have anything he wanted, and yet his only friend had the balls to accuse him of feeling sorry for himself?

"Look, Damien, I know you've been through some serious stuff. But I've known you since we were kids. We've got a lot of history, and you're just not the same guy anymore."

No shit. When had Rob figured that out? Damien had known it for a long time. "Of course not. I can't be the same stupid kid I was, the one who thought my dad was as strong as a superhero and that my mom was the perfect woman. I can't be the same stupid twenty-two-year-old who met Jessica and thought I'd be happy and in love for the rest of my life."

Rob shook his head. "If I could go back to that day at the lake, the day you and I cut out of work at the bank early to hit the beach, I would. I'd throw the football the other way so it wouldn't hit Jessica's friend . . . what was her name?"

"Patty." Damien's maki churned in his gut. He remembered that day with agony. Patty had been a flirty little thing, who had zeroed in on Rob after he'd beaned her with the football on accident. Jessica had been more aloof. It had taken Damien the whole afternoon to convince her to give him her phone number.

"Even though she was a hot little thing and we had a fun weekend together, I wish I'd never met Patty so you had never met Jessica. Because ten years later she's still fucking with you."

"She's not fucking with me. She died. That wasn't her fault."

But Rob gave a sound of exasperation. "It's not her fault she was murdered, of course not, and I wouldn't wish that on any woman. I'm damn sorry that happened to her, I really am. But apart from all of that, before that, you have to recognize that Jessica was just a bitch, Damien. She was a bitch the day we met her and she was a bitch every day after that. She played you for all you were worth."

Damien's face went cold. He sat very, very still, thinking

it was a good thing they were sitting in a restaurant, because he felt like pounding Rob. It was wrong to say those things about Jessica. "That's my wife you're talking about."

Rob's voice was low, urgent, his hand gripping the table. "I know that. And maybe you'll never talk to me again after today, but I have to say this. I can't stand watching you die a little day by day, becoming this person I don't know. You're miserable. Tell me this—when you think of Jessica, are your memories happy?"

No. The answer was in his head before he could consider it. Of course he had some pleasant memories of Jessica. He had loved her, in his own youthful, flawed way, and there had been some fun times. They had been married, they'd lived together, they'd made love. But something had always been wrong between the two of them, and they both had known it. He was always insecure that she would throw in the towel on their relationship, and smart woman that she was, Jessica had always used that to her advantage.

"That doesn't change the fact that she was killed." Something he had never really dealt with. He knew what had been done to her in excruciating detail thanks to his grand jury indictment, but he hadn't dealt with any of that. He had rammed it into a dark, hidden corner of his head to prevent him from losing his mind.

"No, no it doesn't." Rob ran his fingers through his hair. "But you need to let go of your relationship, don't you think? Don't you deserve a chance to be happy?"

But Jessica had never been happy. Running the tip of his finger over a stray grain of rice on the table, Damien told the truth. "I don't know. I don't know if I deserve anything."

"If you could have anything you wanted, what would it be?"

Mandy. And her baby. The realization didn't surprise him at all. The knowledge had been creeping in for days. He cared about Mandy, he worried about her and the baby, he wanted to protect them. "A family. I would want a family." But he was broken, inside, and couldn't expect any woman to take that on.

"Your mother asks my mother about you all the time, you know. She wants to know if I've seen you, how you're doing, if you're dating. I tell my mom I don't know, because I don't. I don't know you. Maybe that's a good place to start—talk to the people who actually still like you."

Damien snorted, feeling something deep inside of him that was almost like hope. It was such an alien feeling he wasn't sure he understood it right. But Rob made sense. He didn't know how to lay Jessica to rest, but he could reach out to the people he loved, let them know he did care, that he would try to dig inside and find the parts of him he'd thought were gone. Parts that Mandy had proven still existed.

"Are you going to charge me for this psychobabble?" But he slapped Rob on the back to show he was kidding.

Rob gave a grin, but his eyes were searching. "No, but you have to buy lunch."

"I can do that. And Rob, you pushed your luck with calling Jessica a bitch, but I'm still talking to you. And thanks for still talking to me after all these years."

That was as gushy as he was willing to get, but Rob seemed to get the message.

He picked up his chopsticks again. "That's what friends are for."

Damien decided it felt good to have a friend again. And maybe, if he couldn't offer Mandy a real relationship, he could be her friend.

Chapter 17

If Damien sent her one more link on the benefits of breastfeeding, Mandy was going to shove a breast pump up his nose.

This was not how she had envisioned the first two weeks back to work after Punta Cana. Frankly, she had been concerned that Damien would be overtly sexual to her, shooting her hot glances and brushing body parts along hers so that she was in a constant state of arousal.

She had worried that if he was suggestive in any way to her, she would crumble like a cookie and leap into bed with him, forgetting all her concerns.

She needn't have worried.

Damien was being as sexual as a bath mat.

No, he wasn't interested in her at all. But he was fascinated by her pregnancy. He had purchased his own copy of *The Everything Guide to Pregnancy*, along with a half a dozen other books, which she had seen on his desk, and he quoted from them quite frequently in the deluge of e-mails he sent her every day.

She had seen him in person only once, and that had been a mistake on her part. She'd been sneaking in some phone messages to put on his desk, and he'd caught her on the way out. But what could have been awkward, or sensual, had seemed to her just rather friendly. He had been big smiles and all kind concern.

It was infuriating.

And now she was in her cubicle, trying to banish all thoughts of him from her head, when she saw in her inbox she had three e-mails from Damien.

With a sigh, she tucked her feet under her rolling chair and clicked the first one. She was wearing a tight stretchy maternity top, and it kept riding up and exposing her stomach. Tugging it down for the twelfth time, she glanced through Damien's message.

This looks cool. And there was a link for a cot that turned into a toddler bed, then an adult full bed.

"Oh, my God." She brushed her hair back. He was checking out baby furniture for her. It wasn't at all obvious to her how they had reached this point in their relationship.

But it was a rather pretty cot. Damien had good taste. It was a sleigh bed. Glossy, rich wood, dressed up with a pink lace ruffled comforter. Then Mandy saw the price and gasped. It was two thousand dollars. She didn't have two thousand dollars.

By the time she had paid off her debts from the shop, paid closing costs, and had invested five hundred dollars in maternity clothes, she had only enough left over for a nest egg. Money for emergencies. Rent money for when she was on her six weeks without pay maternity leave. Not money for buying two-thousand-dollar baby beds.

If she had to, she'd ask her parents for the money, of course, but the thought made her wince.

Then there was Ben. She wasn't quite sure what to do with him, or how to maneuver her way through their new relationship as parents-to-be who weren't dating. Could she ask him to split the cost of the furnishings? Was that tacky? Was it too much, too little?

Ben had called several times, suggesting they go to dinner and talk, but she had been putting him off. It wasn't something she could do indefinitely, but she found she couldn't think about Ben without getting angry over his initial offer of money to relinquish his responsibilities. It wouldn't serve either of them if they met and she was angry, so she felt as though she needed to work through that before she saw him.

Not to mention, she had the sneaking suspicion he wanted to leap right back into bed with her, which was not going to happen.

Sighing, she clicked on Damien's next e-mail. It was a link to childbirth classes at the hospital.

Have you signed up yet? Most seem to last six to eight weeks and suggest starting at twenty-eight to thirty weeks gestation.

She almost wanted to laugh. If she didn't know how to categorize Ben, she sure in the hell didn't know what to do with Damien.

And while she knew they couldn't renew their physical relationship, and that it wasn't practical that they could be friends when he was her boss and she was pregnant with another man's child, they had slept together. She thought about Damien nonstop. She cared about him a great deal, which she could admit when she was feeling honest. And she worried that he needed something more than she had been able to give him.

He needed to relax, not work so hard. He needed a distraction, and not one that was her baby. Because that was driving her batty.

His final e-mail was actually work related, of all things, and Mandy was typing a response to his inquiry when her instant message window popped up. She knew it was Damien before she even read it because of the ring tone she had set up exclusively for him.

Have you thought of any names?

Names for what?

She lost the thread of what she'd been typing in the

e-mail and sighed with frustration. Maybe she needed more sleep. Her ability to do two things at once seemed to have disappeared lately.

The baby.

Of course. Why didn't she think of that? It made perfect sense for her to discuss naming her child with her male boss. She debated telling him she hadn't thought of any, but she did want to put out feelers about a couple of names. Somehow it seemed more natural to do that with Damien than it did with Ben, which was completely wrong, but it was too late to fix that.

I was thinking about Cecilia for a girl and Simon for a boy.

Her heart swelled a little at the thought of giving a name to her child. Giving him or her an identity.

I don't know . . . those sound very British.

All the good feelings she'd been having fled.

I am British!

"Bloody idiot."

Mandy's groan of frustration was so loud that the woman in the cubicle next to her peered around at her. "You okay?"

"Yes, I'm just thinking that my boss is insane." What on earth made Damien wonder at eleven A.M. on a Tuesday more than four months from her due date what she was going to name her baby? And then criticize her choice.

The woman next door laughed. "All bosses are insane, but I've heard yours is the worst."

That brought Mandy up short. "Oh, he's not so bad as all that."

He wasn't bad at all, in fact. Damien was at least asking—that was more than she could say for Ben. He seemed more concerned with investigating her new breasts than wondering about their child. Maybe she wasn't being fair to him, but then again, maybe she wasn't being fair to Damien.

I was thinking that Rebecca is a nice name.

Did he now? And who the hell had asked him? Pursing her lips together, Mandy clicked the "close" button to get rid of the offensive window.

She was done with that conversation.

Unfortunately, she couldn't get rid of her thoughts about Damien as easily as that window. Especially when the tickets she'd ordered for the Saturday Yankees game showed up in her mail at the office.

She had bought them in a moment of weakness, thinking that Damien really needed to pursue outside interests. At the time, she had been secretly hoping those outside interests would involve her and how many sexual positions they could try, but she realized now that was exactly the wrong thing to do.

She'd told herself all along that she couldn't get involved with Damien, long term or short term. She had a child and Ben to contend with. But that didn't stop her from repeatedly entertaining making love to Damien again.

So she had ordered the tickets as a reminder to him of their time together. But Damien seemed completely over his attraction to her, given all the energy he'd put into pursuing her since their return.

Which was none. He hadn't once even tried to see her in person, yet he'd obviously spent hours surfing the Internet looking up baby furniture and birthing classes.

The tickets shouldn't go to waste, but she didn't think she could spend an afternoon listening to Damien extol the virtues of breastfeeding.

As far as she knew, Rob Turner was Damien's only friend in the office. She'd take the tickets to him and suggest he invite Damien. If she gave the tickets directly to Damien, she had no doubt he would stick them in his fastidious drawer and never use them.

Rob was hanging up his phone when she knocked on his

open door. He looked at her curiously. "Mandy, isn't it? Come on in."

"Thanks." Feeling a bit ridiculous, she slapped the envelope with the tickets in her hand. "I was wondering if you're busy Saturday. I've got tickets for the Yankees game and I thought you might like to go."

His eyebrows shot straight up. "Does Damien know? Because I kind of thought you and he . . ."

Mandy stared at him for a second, not sure what he meant. Then she felt her face flush. "Oh, God! I didn't mean you and me. I meant you and Damien."

Rob laughed, but she wasn't feeling very funny at the moment.

"Oh, okay. But what a disappointment for me." He winked at her.

Embarrassed, she rambled on. "If I give the tickets to Damien, he won't go. He'll just come up with some excuse and work the whole day. So I thought if you dragged him there, at least he'd get out a bit."

That little speech had been way too revealing, given the fact that Rob's grin fell right off his handsome face. "It sounds like you know Damien pretty well."

She shrugged.

"Why don't you go with him? Given the way he talks about you, he'd rather be with you than me."

She would not ask, she would not ask . . .

"He talks about me?"

Rob nodded. "He's mentioned you quite a bit. And though he hasn't said anything specific, I get the feeling something happened between the two of you in Punta Cana. And if that's the case, I'm happy for both of you. Damien needs someone in his life."

Rob leaned back, tipping his whole chair off the ground. He had a stress ball in his hand, and he tossed it up in the air.

"I'm pregnant," she blurted, because sooner or later people were going to figure it out, and given the whispers she'd heard from some of the other secretaries, they were already wise to her situation. It was getting hard to hide. And she wanted Rob to stop his thoughts there, because she didn't want any rumors swirling about her and Damien. Nor did she want Rob suggesting to Damien that they could have a future together.

Rob's stress ball plummeted to his desk. His feet hit the floor hard. "Are you serious?" He glanced at her stomach. "Well, hell, that's the best damn thing that could have happened to Damien."

Mandy clenched her teeth. Damn it, she was making a complete muck of this. "It's not his."

His eyes narrowed. "Come again?"

"Damien isn't the father." And for the first time, she was willing to admit that she almost wished he were.

"Are you sure?"

"Yes!" What did she look like?

Rob sighed. "Oh. All right. I'll take the tickets then." He held out his hand. "It's a damn shame though. I thought you might be the woman who could finally get through to Damien."

"He doesn't see me that way." She was still hurt and seething over that. "He thinks I'm a good assistant, and he's curious about the baby. That's all there is between us."

His hand closed around one end of the envelope she held out to him. "You're wrong. He's attracted to you and trying to pretend he isn't. You're the first woman I've seen him have any interest in since Jess."

Mandy dropped the envelope with the tickets. "You care about him."

Rob nodded. "I've known Damien all my life. You should have seen him before. He was a great guy."

"He still is," she whispered.

And she meant it.

Chapter 18

Damien had walked all over the eighteenth floor looking for Mandy and couldn't find her. He paused in front of the reception desk and clenched his fists. He wasn't going back to his office until he found her.

He had gone to the baseball game on Saturday with Rob, thinking it was nice to hang with his old friend, something he hadn't done in a long time. Halfway through Rob had confessed Mandy had given him the tickets. He wasn't sure how he felt about that.

Clearly Mandy was thinking about him, but she was ignoring him. He spent half his workdays trying to run her to ground in her cubicle and the other half trying to engage her in conversation with him via e-mail or instant messaging.

Her responses were polite but brusque.

It was driving him insane. He had to see her. He had to talk to her. He had to make love to her.

He no longer cared if he wasn't capable of having a relationship with Mandy. He had to take whatever she was willing to give, and if that was just sex, so be it.

Their little decision on the plane back from Punta Cana to leave it alone, at just good memories, had been either stupidly naïve or just plain crazy.

"Can I help you, Mr. Sharpton?" The receptionist stared

at him nervously from behind an enormous fake floral arrangement sitting on the desk.

He could barely see her around the damn thing. Shoving the meadow-in-a-vase over, he asked, "Have you seen Mandy Keeling?"

She dropped her pen, and her lip trembled. Damn, without meaning to he was glaring at her ogrelike. He tried to smooth out his features as she shook her head.

"I haven't seen her. But I could call . . ."

Damien cut her off with his hand in the air, because right at that moment he spotted Mandy coming out of the rest room. "Never mind."

It had been twenty-two long and lousy days since he'd seen Mandy, except for that split second in his office doorway when she had scurried away from him.

Now as she walked toward him, he swallowed hard. She looked incredible. Her hair was loose, falling past her chin in those waves he loved, and she was wearing a sundress. The coral one she'd had on in Punta Cana. He figured she was wearing the dress because it had no waist, but he could tell with one glance that her stomach had popped out even farther.

Her breasts were bigger, too, if that were possible.

Something happened inside of him. Everything shifted and cracked and splintered, and he took a deep breath.

"Mandy."

She looked up at him, her hand still in the purse where she'd been digging for something.

Her mouth opened in surprise, and a smile flitted across her face. But then she glanced at the receptionist and tucked her hair behind her ear nervously. "Mr. Sharpton? Did you need me?"

That was a loaded question. "Yes. In my office. Now."

He turned just in time to see the receptionist wincing. When she saw him looking at her, she dropped her gaze to the desk and grabbed a pad of paper. She coughed.

Rubbing the palm of his hand into the middle of his forehead, Damien sighed.

"Do I need anything from my desk?" Mandy started down the hall.

"No." Even he could hear how harsh his voice sounded.

She glanced at him in surprise, but she didn't look inclined to wince or cry or tremble.

When they got into the office, he closed the door, and she turned to look at him in question. "What did you need?"

He ignored the question. "You look good. Sexy. I have such great memories of pulling that dress down over your breasts."

Her expression went from astonished to cautious. "What are you doing, Damien? I thought we weren't going to continue in that . . . vein."

"I tried, babe, I really did. But the last three weeks just haven't been right. I miss you."

And in case she didn't get the message, he stepped up to her, completely invading all of her personal space, and pulled her into his arms.

"Damien . . ."

She dragged his name out so long, it practically took a minute to say it.

Brushing her hair off her cheek, he kissed her forehead. Her eyelid. Her temple, her jaw. "Why have you been avoiding me?"

"That's what we agreed to do. That's what we need to do."

But even as she spoke, her arms were twining around his neck. "And you haven't exactly been coming on to me. You're more concerned about the baby than me."

Breathing deeply, he tugged her closer. He'd been an idiot to think he could just give her up. "That's just not true. I've been going crazy wanting you, and I thought at least if we were friends, I could look out for you, still be in your life." All his thinking, all his logic of the past three weeks, seemed stupid and irrelevant now.

Damien tugged the neckline of her dress down an inch so he could see her impressive cleavage. Nuzzling there, he heard her sigh. "Tell me again why we can't keep doing what we were doing in Punta Cana?"

"Because I'm having a baby and I need to get my life sorted out. I need to find a place to live, make sure my job is secure, find day care. I need to figure out how I'm going to pay for two-thousand-dollar pieces of baby furniture."

He kept kissing, moving from right to left, tasting her sweet flesh. "Anything else?"

"Ben showed up at my apartment wanting to get back together."

That gave him pause. He hovered over her chest and asked carefully, "And did you say yes or no?"

"Of course I said no! After what he did, and after what you and I shared . . . and how could you think I would be letting you kiss me right now if I'd got back together with Ben?"

"Just making sure." He resumed his movements, this time sliding his tongue under the rim of her bra. She tasted absolutely delicious. And he really liked the way she had phrased that . . . *after what you and I shared.*

He felt the same way. It had been something special. Was something special. Could continue to be that way.

"So Ben took a hike?"

"Well, not exactly." When he stopped and lifted his head, she pushed him back down to her breast. "He wants to be in the baby's life. It's all very awkward right now. Which is why you and I can't do this."

"Any other reasons we can't do this?" Damien peeled back one cup of the bra and flicked his tongue over her nipple.

Her words were breathless. "You're not over losing Jess. You said yourself you can't be in a relationship, and you certainly don't want me with all my baggage."

The things she said all made sense. None of the reasoning had changed. She was pregnant. He was an emotional mess.

But none of it mattered. It really didn't.

He would figure out the future later. Right now he just knew he needed to have Mandy in his life.

When he pulled her nipple into his mouth and sucked, she gasped. "So, aren't you going to stop?"

He shook his head and spoke over her flesh. "No."

"Really, Damien, it's the middle of the day. We're in your office . . ."

She did have a point. He let go, brushing his lips back and forth on her shiny nipple one last time. "So have dinner with me tonight."

"I have a fitting for my bridesmaid dress tonight. Caroline's wedding is in three weeks."

"Lunch tomorrow, then."

"I have an appointment for my ultrasound on my lunch hour."

Fixing her bra back over her breast, he asked, "Where?"

"At the Downtown Women's Health Clinic—Broadway and Prince Street—at one o'clock."

"Dinner tomorrow night, then? We'll celebrate your healthy baby."

"Is that all we'll be doing?" She adjusted the front of her dress and looked at him in question.

"I'm really hoping you'll agree to come back to my place so I can make love to you all night long. But if not, I'll settle for dinner."

His heart pounded and his cock throbbed as he waited for her answer. It meant a lot to him, more than he was willing to admit.

Something was happening to him, and he wasn't quite sure what it was. The way he felt about Mandy was much stronger than . . .

"I'll make sure I bring my toothbrush."

Relief flooded through him. Relief that Mandy wanted to spend the night with him, and relief that he didn't have to admit to himself that he cared for Mandy way beyond like.

He had sworn never to love anyone again.

He wouldn't, couldn't, do that now.

And if he was lying to himself, there was no one to know but him.

Her bladder was going to burst. Mandy shifted in the waiting room chair and tried not to imagine her muscles suddenly giving way and wetting her pants right here in full view of twenty people.

If they didn't call her name soon she was going to do something drastic. What, she didn't know. Screaming seemed overdone. Going to the loo in defiance seemed like a bad plan since they would just make her reschedule her ultrasound. Which left her no options but to sit in silence and suffer, praying her bladder was resilient.

It would probably be a lot easier to handle if she had someone to complain to. But she had turned down Jamie and Caroline's offer to accompany her. Even Allison had offered, though she'd looked a bit reluctant, which made it all the more sweet. Mandy knew Allison didn't like anything that smacked of nature, including biological functions.

Mandy hadn't wanted to bother any of them, and also didn't want the situation to be awkward, since Ben had insisted he wanted to attend. She could barely handle him on her own. She didn't think she wanted to chitchat through the tension as her overprotective friends glared at Ben.

Only Ben was a no-show. He was thirty minutes late, and unless he'd got lost or stuck in traffic, there was no reason he shouldn't be there. Even if he was running late, he could call her mobile phone and tell her. The temptation to ring him was great, but she resisted it. She would not nag him or guilt him into participation in her pregnancy.

This had been his bloody idea to be involved. His idea to come to the ultrasound. And here she was sitting by herself.

On the verge of wetting her low-rise Old Navy maternity pants.

Not to mention that she was anxious—terrified that the test would show something wrong with the baby.

She grabbed the magazine next to her on the table and flipped through it to distract herself. It was a news magazine and showed graphic images of bodies littering the ground as workers shifted through earthquake rubble. Lovely.

Someone sat down in the chair next to her. Tossing the magazine, Mandy looked up to smile politely.

It was Damien.

Wearing his suit, carrying the jacket, tie perfectly straight, looking gorgeous and masculine and very, very close.

"Hi," he said, his shoulder brushing hers, and he took her hand, stroked it. "They didn't call you in yet?"

Mandy shook her head. "What are you doing here?" She needed to tell him to leave. It wasn't a good idea for him to be here. Anyone could see them together, get the wrong idea. Or worse, she herself might get the wrong idea.

"I just thought you might want some company. In case it's good news or in case it's not-so-good news."

Now damn it, just when she decided she should really send him packing, he had to go and say something lovely. His touch was reassuring, gentle, and she wondered how it was that he could so easily read into her fears and doubts and sympathize with them, ease them. Maybe it was because he had known pain, understood fear.

"It's going to be good news, right, Damien?"

"Of course it is." He kissed her forehead, then smiled. "How's your bladder?"

"At capacity."

"Mandy Keeling?" A technician stood in the open door with a file folder in her hand.

Thank God. "Yes." Mandy stood up and walked gingerly toward the door, afraid she might be sloshing.

"Dad can come, too." The technician smiled at her and gestured Damien forward. "I'm sure he doesn't want to miss the show."

Now would be a good time to explain that Damien wasn't the father, but she really didn't feel like getting into it with the woman. Besides, she wanted someone with her. She wanted Damien with her.

"Do you want to come?" She turned back to him.

He was already standing and walking toward her. She'd take that as a yes. Mandy glanced at her watch. "I thought you had a one o'clock conference call. It's twelve-thirty already."

"I moved it to tomorrow."

"Right in here." The technician stopped and let them move ahead of her into a darkened room. "My name is Cheryl, and I'll be doing your scan. It takes about ten minutes, and then you'll get to go to the rest room. I'll give you some pictures of the baby and you'll be on your way. The results get faxed upstairs to your doctor. This is your first baby, right?"

"Yes," Damien said.

Mandy frowned at him. "I think she was talking to me."

Cheryl laughed. "Okay, lie on your back on the table and roll down the waistband of your pants."

"You're doing a transabdominal exam, correct?" Damien asked.

Mandy kicked her sandals off and stared at him. She was going to have to wrest that damn pregnancy book out of his hands.

"Yes." Cheryl busied herself with her equipment.

Mandy climbed onto the table feeling whatever small amount of grace she'd possessed had disappeared. And she was only half through her pregnancy. Damien's hand grabbed her elbow and he helped her down.

She pulled up her sky blue stretchy top and peeled down her black pants an inch or two, staring at the ceiling and grabbing a couple of deep breaths. Everything was going to be normal and she was going to see her baby.

Damien's fingers on her stomach startled her. "I think you have to pull your pants down farther."

If he started tugging down her pants she was going to smack him. But Cheryl was already shoving them down and tucking a towel into her underwear. Not very dignified, but the technician explained it would keep the gel from getting on her clothes.

"How does the test work?" Mandy asked.

"The instrument records echoes of sound waves as they bounce off the baby and translates them into pictures on the screen."

Only that came from Damien, not the technician.

"Are you in the medical field?" Cheryl asked as she squirted the cool gel all over Mandy's stomach.

"No, he's a software executive with a desk full of baby books," Mandy informed her. That were going to be disappearing mysteriously the next day.

Damien shrugged a little sheepishly. "I like to be well informed."

That was an understatement. But her mild annoyance was forgotten when the wand was placed on her stomach and the first image filled the screen. It was a baby's head, with eyes, nose, and tiny lips.

"Oh, my," she breathed. She reached for Damien, overwhelmed with emotion. "Look at how clear that is."

Damien's fingers squeezed hers. "That's unbelievable."

Damn, she was going to cry. She was going to be one of those blubbery mothers who sniffled every time their child filled its nappy.

"There's definitely only one." Cheryl whipped the wand around.

Mandy ignored the discomfort she felt from the pressure

and stared in amazement as various parts came into view. The spine, a perfect little hand, a foot.

"Everything looks great at first glance."

Cheryl was clicking and freezing and measuring things on the screen while Mandy stared and Damien gave a running commentary.

"Look at that, he's waving at us. Oh, he's flipping around a little, trying to get comfortable, I guess. Whoa, check out the big toe."

"What makes you think it's a he?" Mandy thought they were looking at the bum, but she wasn't entirely sure. "Do you see something I don't?"

Cheryl laughed. "Do you want to know the sex? I can see if I can get a good shot for you."

"Well, I want to know," Damien said before she could even get her mouth open.

She stared at him. Up to this point, she hadn't been concerned with whether it was a boy or a girl, and she wasn't sure she wanted to know. It seemed like a special surprise at the end. "I don't think I want to know."

"She can just tell me and I'll keep it a secret."

Damien seemed to have forgotten one minor little detail. This wasn't his baby. But he looked so enchanted, so excited for her, that she couldn't bring herself to say anything. Maybe it was the emotion of the moment. Maybe it was her appreciation for all he had done for her. But it seemed to her that maybe, just a little bit, she had fallen in love with Damien Sharpton.

"I'm not going to have you know when I don't know." She laughed, picturing Damien trying to keep that a secret. One glance at his desk would unearth a copy of *Raising Girls* or something similar, and she would have the answer whether she wanted it or not.

"So is that a yes or a no?" Cheryl asked.

He looked at her in agony, leg vibrating as he jiggled his foot. "It's up to you."

Oh, yes. She was in love with him. Heart swelling, fingers clutching his, tears stinging her eyes, she nodded. "Tell us."

"It's a girl." Cheryl pointed to the screen. "You can see right here there are definitely no baby boy parts."

A girl. A little girl. Pink blankets and bonnets and lacy dresses.

"A girl," Damien breathed, staring at the screen. "She's perfect. Like her mother."

Maybe that was pushing things a bit, but Mandy wasn't going to protest. She felt a single tear roll out of each eye, and she blinked hard to fight more.

"But what's wrong with the name Rebecca?"

Not the name thing again. Mandy wiped her cheek and laughed in exasperation. "There's nothing wrong with Rebecca. I just happen to like Cecilia."

"That's one of those names that sounds great with your British accent, but just sounds flat when Americans say it." He turned to Cheryl. "Which name do you like better?"

The technician held up her hand. "Whoa. I stay out of discussions like this."

"Damien, we can talk about this later." Much later. Like never.

"We're almost finished here." Cheryl started printing out the photos of the baby. "Due date comes up as October twenty-one according to the size of the fetus."

"Hey, I wanted to ask, could you tell if there was anything wrong like an embolism or anything?" Damien asked Cheryl. "Because before we knew we shouldn't, we had oral sex. Cunnilingus. And I wanted to make sure we didn't inadvertently force air into the vagina."

Mandy almost fell off the table. "Damien!" She was certain that nothing could sound more horrifying than the word cunnilingus when spoken in reference to her. "You did *not* just say that." She didn't dare even glance at Cheryl, afraid she would melt from mortification at the horror she was sure was on the technician's face.

"What? We're all adults here, and I've been really worried about it."

The man had the nerve to stand there looking completely innocent. Looking concerned. Looking professional. As if discussing his cunnilingusing her wasn't something a bit too private for mixed company.

"You have really lost your mind. Next thing I know, you'll probably be stopping people on the street to discuss my hemorrhoids." Mandy took the towel Cheryl was handing her and started wiping her stomach. She winced as she pressed on her overextended bladder.

"You have hemorrhoids?" Damien exclaimed, his face twisting into a grimace.

She should let him think she did. She should promote any sort of gruesome aspect of pregnancy that would get him away from her before they both found themselves in a complicated mess.

But she couldn't do it. She just slapped the towel down, rolled her pants up, and said, "No. No, I don't. But you're getting a bit personal, don't you think?"

Cheryl handed Damien the printed photos and cleared her throat. "As far as your question, I think you'll need to discuss any concerns of that nature with your OB/GYN." Then she looked at Mandy with a smile. "And it's none of my business, but I think it's great to see how involved your husband is in your pregnancy. So many fathers aren't interested at all."

Mandy felt slapped. Her cheeks went hot and she sat up abruptly. Damien wasn't her husband. He wasn't even her baby's father. And he was far more supportive and interested than the man whose DNA was running through her daughter.

"We're all done here. Rest room's the last door on the right. Congratulations on a daughter." Cheryl left them alone.

Mandy pulled her shirt over her sticky stomach and stood up. She felt shaky, hot.

"Damien—"

"I'm sorry," he said at the same time.

"No—"

"I've completely overstepped. None of this is any of my damn business, and instead of just supporting you, I'm pushing you. Embarrassing you. I'm sorry." His lips were pursed, his hand clenching the ultrasound printout at his side. In the dim lighting of the room, she couldn't see his eyes, but she could feel his hurt. Feel him pulling back.

Which she didn't want.

"No. Don't be. I'm the one who should apologize. I'm being ungrateful. Here you've rearranged your schedule and everything."

"I don't want your gratitude." The words were low, but angry.

Mandy stared at him, forgetting about putting her shoes back on, forgetting about her urgent need to use the rest room. When she looked at him, she saw what she hadn't been able to admit to herself. She saw what she wanted. Him. With her. In a forever kind of way.

"What do you want?" she whispered.

"I want what I can't have." His nostrils flared.

"How do you know you can't have it?" She was dangling on the edge of offering it. Throwing all rational actions aside and following her heart.

"Because life doesn't give you what you want, all in one perfect package." He reached out and handed her the photos. "There are no happy endings for me. I can only take, not give."

"You're wrong." Mandy stepped into her shoes, intent on following him as Damien headed for the door. He had to understand how much he had already given her.

"No. What would be wrong would be to selfishly mix

you and your daughter up in the mess that is my life." He grabbed the door handle and turned to her. "You have no idea how truly fucked up I am, Mandy."

"Tell me. Trust me." What she wouldn't give to take away that pain etched on his face.

"And have you see how ugly I really am on the inside? I don't think so."

He walked out of the room.

But Mandy knew right then, right there, that she wasn't going to let him walk away from her as easily as Ben had.

She loved Damien, and he was going to know it.

Chapter 19

Damien rolled his carry-on bag through the hotel lobby and dialed his cousin George on his cell phone.

"Hello?"

"George, it's Damien." Damien headed toward the elevators, tucking the room key into the pocket of his jeans.

There was a long pause. "Well, I'll be damned. Aunt Becky always says you're still alive, but we never believe her anymore."

Damien grimaced. "I'm still alive. And I'm in Chicago." For the first time since the charges had been dropped.

The cab ride from the airport had been surreal, strange. He had expected to feel homesick, to feel pain, to have memories of Jessica bombard him. Instead, he had felt strangely detached. And the feeling wasn't going away.

"No shit? You on business? How long you here for? My mom didn't say anything about you coming to town."

"I haven't told anyone yet." It had been an impulse. He had walked out of that hospital after Mandy's ultrasound appointment, come home and stalked around his apartment for an hour, then had called and booked a flight. It was eight P.M. central time the same day, and he was in Chicago.

That hadn't been in his plans when he'd woken up that morning. But seeing Mandy's baby, it had brought everything up inside of him. It had made him *want*.

It was everything he couldn't have, but something told him it was time to deal with a few issues from his past.

So here he was. "I want to sell my house, George. Can you list it?"

George was a realtor, five years Damien's senior. He had a thriving customer base and was the smooth talker Damien had never been.

"What house?"

The elevator finally opened, and Damien entered. He pushed the tenth-floor button. "The house in Wheaton."

"You still own that?" George sounded amazed.

Oh, yeah, he still owned it. That house had been his gift to Jess, a wedding present. He hadn't been able to afford it at the time, but they had scraped the money together when Jessica had gotten her first post–law school job. He had thought the house was great, a two-story colonial with black shutters and a bunch of flower beds. Jessica had loved the house at first, too, until she realized how much upkeep it took. The flowers he'd loved so much, she had seen as unruly and extra work.

Damien rubbed his eyebrows. "I've been renting the house."

He hadn't been able to deal with it after Jess had died. He'd asked his father to find a tenant, and he'd gotten the hell out. His in-laws had packed up the furniture and were storing it in their basement.

"How long have you had the house? Do you know what condition it's in?" George shifted into professional mode.

"I bought it six years ago. I don't know what condition it's in, but my dad's been keeping an eye on things, and the same couple has been living there for three years. No pets, no kids."

"If it's in good shape, we should be able to get quite a bit more for it now. It was a young house, if I remember it right."

"I don't care what price you get for it as long as I don't lose money, and as long as I don't have to deal with it." That sounded a little more revealing than Damien intended. He quickly added, "So how have you been, George?"

"Hanging in there. Listen, you've got to sign the listing agreement, so why don't you stop out at my house tomorrow, have dinner with us. The wife would love to see you. She always had a crush on you—something about those ugly blue eyes of yours."

Damien snorted as he stepped off on the tenth floor. "Sure, I can do that, though I highly doubt Melanie ever gave one thought to my eyes. But don't go blabbing to your mom that I'm here until I've had a chance to call my mom. I don't want her to find out secondhand."

"Can do. And Damien? It's good to hear from you."

And Damien found that he actually felt the same way.

Mandy didn't know what to think.

Damien had disappeared.

He had walked out of the hospital and hadn't returned to the office. She had gotten a cryptic e-mail from him asking her to cancel all of his appointments for the remainder of the week, as well as their dinner plans, because he was taking care of some business out of town.

Damien never canceled appointments. And it was only Tuesday. Taking three days off in a row was just unheard of for him.

Mandy was worried sick.

"Are you even listening to me?" Ben asked, a hint of irritation creeping into his voice.

"Hmm? Oh, sorry. It's the pregnancy, you know," she lied. "It makes me forgetful and easily distracted." There was one definite plus to being pregnant. She could blame everything on that fact.

Ben had called to explain that he'd been caught up in a

meeting and hadn't been able to get away for the ultrasound. Mandy crunched pretzels and decided she couldn't care less where Ben had been.

"It apparently has also affected your manners. Are you chewing in my ear?"

"Yes. I'm hungry. This is my bedtime snack." Mandy set her feet on the coffee table and sank farther into the sofa cushions. It had been a sweltering day outside, and she was still sweating, even in the air-conditioning. She picked at her tank top.

"I'll keep this brief, then. I just wanted to see how the test had gone."

"Everything's fine. The technician said the baby looks great and I'm due October twenty-one." Mandy picked up the pictures she'd spent all evening leafing through. "I've got pictures of the scan. Do you want me to fax them to you?"

"All right." Ben didn't sound terribly enthusiastic. "But fax them to my apartment, not the office."

"Okay." She popped another pretzel stick in her mouth. "I've been thinking out some names . . . What do you think of Cecilia for a girl?"

"That's pretty. Cecilia Hurst is a nice enough name."

The pretzel felt inflated in her mouth. She hadn't thought to give the baby Ben's last name. "It's a girl. The technician said she's positive of it."

"Oh, well, then. It would have been nice to have another son, but we can't order these things, can we?" Ben gave a little laugh.

Ha ha. Mandy didn't feel the least bit like laughing. Not when she was thinking Rebecca Sharpton would have had a father who wouldn't have cared one whit that she was a girl instead of a boy.

But Cecilia Hurst was going to have a father like Mandy had. Distracted. Loving, but always distant, always disappointed.

It wasn't what she wanted for her daughter, but then *we can't order these things, can we?*

And she wasn't sure she would change things if she could. If she hadn't been pregnant with Ben's child, she never would have met Damien at all. They never would have made love, and she never would have realized that she loved him. Truly, deeply, loved him.

But if fate had played things out the way they were supposed to be, and Beckwith Tripp's prediction for a long, sweet, enriched life had been correct, she didn't see where she was supposed to go from here.

Her bun was baking, but her bloody heart was breaking.

Mandy stuffed another pretzel in her mouth.

Damien shifted the box in his hands and pressed the doorbell. His palms were sweating, and his heart was pounding. He wasn't sure he could do this.

Even though it was only ten in the morning, the sun was beating down on him, and he felt a trickle of sweat run down the back of his T-shirt. He was giving it two more seconds; then he was getting the hell out of there.

The door swung open. Damn.

His father-in-law's greeting died on his lips, and his jaw dropped. "Damien?" He called back over his shoulder. "Susan, you want to come on out here?"

"Hi, Fred. How are you?" The words stuck in his mouth, but Damien forced them out and willed himself not to shuffle on the sidewalk.

"Good, good." Fred stared at him, then shook his head. "Jesus, come on in. Look at me just leaving you standing there. But you gave me a start, kid. Haven't seen hide nor hair of you in three years."

Fred opened the door and gestured for Damien to enter the hall. Damien's hand shook as he stepped forward. Three years ago Jessica's parents had stood by him, believed in his innocence, but he hadn't been sure they would still feel the same way. With time to think, to stew, to miss their daughter, they could have changed their minds, but it didn't appear that was the case.

"You look good," Damien told Fred, taking in his trim gray hair and fit physique. "Retirement must agree with you."

Fred looked back over his shoulder as he led Damien to the living room. "Truthfully, it's boring as hell." His voice dropped to a whisper. "And Susan gets on my damn nerves. Never thought I'd feel that way, but I have to tell you, now that I'm home, she suddenly thinks I give a crap about the new curtains for the kitchen and the petunias for the yard, and the eighteenth pair of sandals she's bought."

"What's that, Fred?" Susan came into the room and stopped short. "Oh, my God." Her hand went over her heart. "Damien." She reached for him, kissed his cheek. "How are you, sweetheart?"

"I'm okay," he said, because it was the closest to the truth. He'd been better. He'd been worse. "You look as lovely as ever, Susan."

She waved her hand and snorted. "Oh, please. I look like a hag. Fred's driving me crazy being home all the time and I have the dark circles under my eyes to prove it."

Fred looked astonished, and Damien found himself smiling. Susan was still a beautiful woman, just like Jessica had been. He set the box down on the end table next to the suede sofa.

"What's in the box, honey?" Susan sat down and patted the seat next to her. "Come sit by me so I can look at you. You look tired, sad. I'd hoped the next time I saw you there would be a smile on your face."

Damien tried to force one, but it fell flat. "I brought you some of Jessica's things . . . her swimming trophies, her yearbooks, and photo albums from college. It really should all come back to you, and I'm sorry it took me so long to do it. I just couldn't go through her stuff."

He wasn't even sure what had possessed him to do it now. But when he'd decided to come to Chicago, he'd pulled out the taped boxes in his closet and had quickly sorted out some things for Jessica's parents. It felt right to give pieces of Jessica back to them.

He had needed to do this, see them.

"Are you sure?" Susan's hand was reaching for the box, but she stopped.

"Yes. These are from before we met. I kept the pictures of Jessica and me."

Susan opened the box, and a half an hour later, Damien was finding that it wasn't as hard as he had imagined to watch Jessica's parents go through her personal possessions. Susan only teared up once, when she found a grade school report card, but for the most part, she and Fred smiled, laughed, reminisced about the items they pulled out.

They had healed. Damien could see it. They missed Jessica, they loved her, but they had accepted their loss and were prepared to focus on the good times.

He wanted to be able to do that, but he wasn't there yet. Wasn't sure he'd ever be.

"So, are you seeing anyone? Is there a special woman in your life?" Susan asked casually, her reading glasses perched on her nose.

"No." He shook his head. There was no explaining his relationship with Mandy. He was her boss, her one-time lover, and he hoped her friend.

"I'm sorry to hear you say that," she said quietly. "I'd hoped by now you would have moved on, found happiness."

"No," he said, because again it was the simplest answer.

"Cutting yourself off from family and friends—not being happy—that's not what Jess would have wanted for you," Susan said, stroking his arm.

That statement gave Damien pause. He ran his finger

over the edge of Jessica's yearbook, squeezing the tip of his finger between the pages until he felt pain. "You think so? Because I was never really sure what Jessica wanted."

Fred gave a laugh. "Ain't that the truth. Our Jess wasn't easy to live with. She took after Susan that way."

Susan smacked his leg. "Watch it."

Damien didn't think it was anything to laugh about, but for the first time ever he allowed himself to think that maybe all their problems hadn't been his alone. Maybe no matter how much he loved her, it never would have been enough to make Jessica happy. They hadn't been right for each other.

Maybe if she hadn't died, they would have gone their separate ways.

Maybe none of that mattered because he was the one alive and she was dead, and hopefully Jessica was at peace.

"Well, I need to take off." Damien stood up. "I haven't even seen my parents yet."

Then he had one more stop to make before he met up with George to sign the listing papers.

He had to visit the tattoo parlor.

Chapter 20

Mandy picked at her chicken Caesar salad and worried. Caroline stared at her as she wiped her lips on a napkin. "You're really worked up over him. You've fallen for Demon Sharpton, haven't you?"

Her head snapped up, and Mandy glanced around the restaurant. They were just across the street from their office and anyone could be listening. That was the last thing in the world she needed, rumors running around the office about her and Damien. Not seeing any secretarial spies, Mandy waved away a fly and dropped her fork. "Is it that obvious?"

"I've never seen you like this." Despite a summer breeze tumbling down Fifty-second as they ate outside, Caroline looked cool and put together.

As usual, Mandy felt as though she'd run an obstacle course on her way to lunch. She was hot, blown, and sticky. And she was certain her deodorant had given way on the elevator down.

"Ben certainly didn't produce this kind of reaction from you. It makes me wonder if there is more to your feelings than you realize."

Oh, she realized them all right. "I'm terrified that he's got into trouble. We had this sort of fight yesterday at the ultrasound." Maybe *fight* was the wrong word, but they'd certainly not left each other in a happy place. "Then he just took off. He never leaves the office like this. And he hasn't even checked his e-mail. Where could he have gone?"

"Maybe he's at home. Maybe he just needed a mental health day." Caroline touched her hair, smoothing it. "Did you know that sixty percent of women and twenty percent of men have called off sick because of a bad hair day?"

Mandy knew without a doubt Damien wasn't a contributor to that statistic. "Damien would not call off sick because his hair looked bad. He would be bleeding out his eyes before he called off work." Which made her wonder if he was in his apartment, bleeding out his eyes.

Her stomach churned. "I don't even know where he lives! Oh, my God. He could be dead."

"If he was dead, he would not have had the forethought to cancel all his appointments first." Caroline took a bite of her Cobb salad. "Why don't you just call his cell phone? You're his secretary. Surely you know his cell number."

Mandy felt a huge sense of relief that she could contact him. "You're right. I have it in my Palm Pilot." She bent over and started digging around in her purse. "How did you know you were in love with Brad, Caroline? Was it this eureka moment?"

"Well, no, not really." Caroline's voice was puzzled. "I just knew that Brad was the man I wanted to spend my life with. I knew we were right for each other. And of course, I love him."

Mandy lifted her head. She stared at Caroline, thinking that somehow her roommate had managed to do it all so nicely and cleanly. She'd met a responsible, attractive man at her previous job, dated, gotten engaged, bought a great apartment with him, and was planning the perfect wedding.

While Mandy was pregnant with one man's child and in love with another.

She'd never thought of herself as a difficult person, but

she sure in the hell wasn't making things easy on herself either.

"Do you mind if I try Damien's cell real quick?"

"No, go ahead."

Mandy dialed Damien's number on her phone and held her breath. After six rings, she was despairing and preparing to leave a rather pathetic sounding message when he answered.

"Damien! Oh, good, I'm so glad you answered."

"Mandy?" His voice sharpened. "Is something wrong?"

Relief and irritation intermingled. "I could ask the same of you! I've been worried sick. Where are you?"

"Chicago. I had some things to take care of." He sucked in his breath quickly.

"Chicago?" Mandy frowned. He'd just winged off to Chicago, canceling their dinner plans, and nothing was actually wrong? She thought she might be angry about that.

"You were worried about me?" He winced, then said, "Oww, damn it, that hurts."

Well, excuse the hell out of her.

"Stop moving," she heard someone say in the background.

"What are you doing?" If it was kinky and involved a woman, she was going to become seriously unpleasant.

"Getting a tattoo."

Oh. That seemed as unlikely as him taking a bad hair day off, but then she remembered the tattoo on his arm. How she had suggested he get it fixed to cover Jess's name—before she had known his wife had died.

"Where?" She wanted to confirm what she suspected. Crumpling her napkin, she waited for his answer.

"Over my old one."

Mandy closed her eyes. She wasn't sure what it meant, but she thought it meant Damien was trying to leave the past behind. That he was trying to move forward.

Please, God, let moving forward include her.

Trying to make light of it, she swallowed hard. "Is it a demon?"

Instead of answering, he gave another wince. "So why were you worried about me?"

"Surely you've figured that out." Probably everyone except Ben had figured it out. She felt she might as well be wearing a sticky note on her forehead announcing it. "It's because I'm in love with you!"

And over the cell phone probably wasn't the best way to tell him that for the first time.

"Shit," he said, and she wasn't sure if he'd been stabbed by a sharp needle or if her love caused him to swear. "You don't mean that, you can't mean that."

Oh, the hell she couldn't.

"I most certainly do mean that." Mandy glanced over at Caroline, who was gaping at her, but now that she'd opened her mouth, she couldn't stop. He had to know, had to understand how much he mattered to her, how wonderful she thought he was.

"I am in love with you, Damien. Completely and totally. So what are you going to do about it?"

There was a pause where her entire future hung in the balance, as traffic on the street shot past her and cigarette smoke from a pedestrian drifted up her nostrils.

Then he said, "I have to go."

Not quite the sentiment she'd been hoping for.

"This is really uncomfortable, Mandy."

Lovely. Her feelings made him uncomfortable. Her face went hot.

"I don't remember this hurting so much the first time I did it."

Even better. She was painful. Her mouth opened but no words came out.

"So let me call you back when I'm done getting the tattoo."

He said goodbye and hung up before she could even say a word. Not that she could think of any. A strange wheezing sound came out of her mouth.

"What did he say?" Caroline was leaning across the table eagerly. "Did he say it back? God, I envy you the courage to just blurt it out like that."

"He said he had to go. He's getting a tattoo and he'll call me back later." It was a small comfort that he'd been talking about a needle and not her when he'd been using words like uncomfortable and painful. On second thought, no it wasn't.

Caroline's lip curled back in astonishment, and Mandy was so certain her face looked exactly the same that she covered her mouth and started to laugh. Air squeezed between her fingers and made a snorting sound.

She had blurted out her feelings for Damien, and he had rushed off the phone. It was so horrible it was almost comical. She had fallen into a country-western song.

Tossing her napkin on her plate, she said, "Gee, I'm so pleased I called him. Now I only need to be mortified instead of worried."

It was one in the morning when Damien's plane landed at LaGuardia. By the time he had waited in the cab line and ridden through the tunnel, it was two when he pulled up in front of Mandy's building in the Village. He had been planning on picking her up there for the dinner plans they'd had the night before.

The plans he had canceled on her after he'd walked out of the hospital.

And now she'd told him she loved him.

Biting his fingernail, he climbed out with his carry-on and paid the driver.

She couldn't mean it. She couldn't possibly.

He wasn't worthy of her love.

Damien took a deep breath and hit the buzzer for her

apartment. His foot tapped impatiently on the sidewalk. The June evening air was humid but breezy, and it felt like rain might fall before the morning.

No one answered the buzzer. He hit it again, holding it longer than was courteous. But damn it, he knew she was in there, and he needed to talk to her. After his tattoo was completed, he'd finished up his business with George and caught the first plane back.

He needed to look her in the eye and tell her to stop feeling whatever she thought she felt for him.

Before he admitted that he loved her as well, however flawed that love was. Before she tried to convince him that it would be enough. Before he believed her and then later hurt her.

"Who the hell are you and why are you ringing my doorbell at two in the goddamn morning?"

That most definitely wasn't Mandy's voice. Damien had forgotten about her roommates. He'd also forgotten that most of the world was asleep at two in the morning.

"Uh, sorry. This is Damien Sharpton. I'm looking for Mandy. Is she there?"

"Of course she's here, but she's sleeping. Like a normal person who has to go to work the next day is."

"Can you wake her up for me?" He was her boss, after all. He wasn't going to dock her pay if she slept in tomorrow.

There was total silence for a good sixty seconds.

Damien hit the buzzer again. It got a reaction.

"Stop it, jerk! There are three other people still sleeping in this apartment."

"They'll all be awake if you don't go get Mandy for me." So he was being the jerk she'd labeled him, but there was no way he could go and wait until the morning. He just couldn't. "Please? I really need to talk to her."

The voice sighed into the intercom. She groaned. "You really won't leave, will you?"

"No."

With a slur on the character of his mother, she hit the buzzer to open the door. Damien grabbed it and ran up the three flights of stairs at top speed so she wouldn't change her mind. He knocked on the door.

It yanked open, and a woman with long brown hair and even longer legs glared at him. "You're a lunatic, you know that?"

"No, I'm just assertive."

She rolled her eyes. There was only one muted lamp on behind her in the apartment and a dim hall light, but Damien could read the antagonism on her face. "Assertive . . . asshole. Same difference."

"I'm sorry I woke you up. But I just got back from Chicago and I really, really needed to see Mandy, and I sort of forgot she has roommates."

Damien suddenly became aware that she was basically in her underwear, and he started to question the wisdom of this impromptu visit. Not that she looked worried about the fact that she was in bikini panties and a tank top, but he felt something like embarrassment.

"Allison, did I hear the doorbell?" A blonde with white spots of cream all over her face stumbled down the hallway in blue satin pajamas with fat pink pigs on them.

"Yes, you heard the doorbell. Damien wants to see Mandy."

The blonde's head snapped up, and her eyes widened. "Mr. Sharpton? Oh, my God!"

Yep, this had been a bad idea. "Hi, Caroline. I, uh, didn't recognize you there at first."

Her hand flew to her head and the hair that normally was so well contained and was now puffy and flyaway.

He realized what a stupid thing that was to say.

Her hand moved to her face and touched one of the white spots.

Feeling extremely uncomfortable, he cleared his throat.

"Sorry to wake all of you up. I just wanted to see Mandy for a minute."

Caroline dropped her hand. Her eyes narrowed. "She was worried about you. I'm sure she'll be glad to see you."

It was a reprimand, plain and simple, for leaving without telling Mandy where he was going. He didn't know what to say since she was most likely right, so he set his suitcase down and pushed down the expandable handle.

"Are you moving in?" Allison asked, sounding amused.

"I came straight from LaGuardia."

Allison yawned. "First door on the right. Go for it. I'm going back to bed."

She went down the hall, tugging her tank top down. But he'd already seen way more than he'd meant to, including her left butt cheek. With a grimace, he glanced at Caroline, who did not look pleased with him.

"You share a room with Mandy, don't you?"

"Yes. Just let me grab my pillow and a blanket and I'll sleep on the couch."

"I'm not going to be that long," he protested.

She snorted. The pink pigs on her shirt wiggled as she stomped into her bedroom and reemerged with a huge comforter and double-wide pillow. Passing him, she clipped him with her shoulder and stumbled a little. Damien reached out and tried to steady her, but she shook him off.

Feeling like a gigantic jackass, he went into the bedroom and stood still for a minute, adjusting to the dark. He could hear Mandy breathing in her sleep to his right. Some light filtered in through the white wood blinds and cast stripes on her legs, covered by a sheet.

They had their air-conditioning running, yet Mandy still looked warm, her hair matted to her forehead, her legs scissoring like she was trying to kick the covers off in her sleep. He thought she was amazingly beautiful.

"Mandy." She didn't stir, so he took a step toward her and spoke louder. "Mandy."

She rolled over. Damien cursed, rubbing his temples. He dropped to his knees next to her bed and shook her shoulder a little. Her flesh was hot, with a sheen of perspiration, which he knew was normal for this stage of pregnancy. Night sweats, the book called them.

"Mandy." Feeling desperate and ridiculous, he shook her again and kissed her lightly.

With a jerk, she came awake, her eyes wide and unfocused. "Wha . . ."

"It's me, Damien."

"Damien? What's the matter?" Mandy tried to sit up, but he held her shoulders gently.

"Shh. It's okay, nothing's the matter. I just needed to see you."

He had needed to see her, to touch her, to remind himself what could never be. To stare her straight in the eye and tell her that love was pain and he didn't want any more of that ever.

Yet it was so hard to remember any of that when she blinked up at him and all he wanted to do was kiss her, hold her, love her.

Chapter 21

Mandy fell back against her pillow, thinking she was having a really vivid dream, that annoying pregnancy side effect that had been plaguing her nearly from conception. But Damien looked real enough, even if she couldn't see his face clearly in the shadows. And if she were dreaming he would be naked. "I thought you were in Chicago. And what time is it?"

She was struggling to figure out why he was in her bedroom in the middle of the night. Not that she was complaining, mind you. But it struck her as a little odd, to say the least. She was hoping it was odd in a good way, as though he'd had an epiphany that he reciprocated her feelings.

"I was in Chicago, but I just got back. It's two in the morning. After you called this afternoon when I was getting the tattoo, I finished up my business and took the first flight back." He brushed her hair back off her forehead.

Sitting up, Mandy grimaced. Her hair was sweaty. Nice and sexy. Not that Damien seemed interested in sexy when she studied him in the dim lighting. He looked as if his dog had died. Which meant anything he might say was probably not going to involve his own vow of love and wish to remain by her side through better or worse, richer or poorer, having another man's child, whatever.

"We need to talk."

Swallowing, she felt sadness rush over her. Those words were the kiss of death for relationships. *We need to talk* meant one of two things. *You're clinging to me and I'm not ready, so I need some space*—aka *We're breaking up*. Or *This just isn't working anymore*—aka *We're breaking up*.

"Okay," she said, because she didn't know what else to say. While she loved Damien, if he didn't want a relationship, she wasn't going to pursue him. She was too old and too pregnant for that kind of futile and desperate effort. "Why were you in Chicago, Damien?"

"I needed to take care of a few things."

He paused and she waited. The one thing she wasn't going to do was settle for cryptic, not now, when he'd woken her up in the middle of a REM cycle. He did at least owe her some answers, about why he was there and how he felt about her.

"I needed to talk to a Realtor about selling the house I had with Jess. I saw my parents. I gave Jess's parents some of her things." He put his hand over his forearm. "And I got my tattoo . . . redone."

It wasn't smart to feel hope, but she did, a bright burst of hope that took her breath away and made her heart pound. Maybe, just maybe, he wasn't there at two A.M. to deliver the break-up speech. She reached out and touched his cheek, ran her finger across his lip. "Why, Damien? Why do all those things now?"

"It's time . . . I'm trying." He drew a shuddering breath. "I need to try and let it go, move forward somehow. I want . . . people back in my life."

Mandy watched him for a moment, wishing the light was on so she could see into his blue eyes, read in them what he was really trying to say. She stroked across his skin, felt him lean toward her into the touch, his thigh pressing against her hip as he sat on her bed.

There was so much he had shown her, given her, yet so much she still didn't know. "Tell me how she died," she whispered. That was really what it was all about. There was something about Jessica that still held him captive, his emotions strained and contained, his heart unreachable.

Damien shuddered. He dropped his head so that her hand fell away. "She was murdered." His voice was raw and hoarse, nothing more than a whisper, but loud in the quiet room.

Mandy froze with her fingers on the sheet she was bunching about her waist. That was not what she'd expected to hear, and his words arrested her. "Oh, Damien! That's awful. God, how did it happen?"

His head lifted and went slowly back and forth. "You don't want to know."

Tears sprung to her eyes. "I do. I want to know what you've been through."

There was hesitation, but only for a second or two. Then Damien started to speak.

"Jessica and I had an argument about her spending habits." He could still hear her voice. *Fuck you and your fifty bucks*, she'd said, when he had complained that she'd bought another pair of shoes, pushing their credit card over its limit. "Sometimes when we fought, she'd leave and go out with her friends. Spending lots of money, getting drunk, and flirting with guys was her way of getting back at me, her way to get me jealous and piss me off. It always worked."

Damien dug his fingernails into his legs. He never said these words out loud. It hurt to do it now, it ripped and clawed and shredded at him, but if he wanted to make Mandy understand why he wasn't lovable, he had to tell her the truth about him. "It wasn't a healthy way to deal with her anger, I guess, but then neither were the bribes and begging that I alternately used to try and get her to see my side of things. I think we both wanted the other to be something we just weren't. But anyway, she took off that night, and while I was mad, I wasn't surprised. Later her friends said when they left the club they'd gone to, Jessica had refused to go with them. They went on to the next party place and left her there."

Mandy's hand closed over his, forcing his grip on his pants to relax.

"It wasn't the first time she'd stayed out all night, but in the morning I asked around and no one knew where she was. I called the cops right around the same time a restaurant owner was throwing his trash out in the alley and found her body. She'd been raped and strangled."

The words meant nothing, could never convey anything as horrible as the sight of his dead wife that had greeted him in the morgue. The crime scene photos had cemented the knowledge that Jessica had suffered tremendously and had sent him retreating in his head to the safety of logic. Cold, hard survival. Never emotion. He had shut all that down like a pool at the end of a summer season to protect himself.

"Oh, dear God."

Tears rolled down Mandy's face, and her fingers jerked on his. Even in the dark, he could see the shock in her eyes, the horror. The pity.

"Damien, I'm so sorry. I can't imagine what you've suffered."

"I don't want you to know!" he said, voice shaking. Biting the inside of his cheek and hardening his hand into a fist, he tried to regain control of himself. "I don't want you to see the dark places I've been, I don't want to expose you to that. I don't want to hurt you or your daughter. I want you safe. I want you happy."

"I want those same things for you. You deserve to be safe and happy, too." She took his face in her hands, shook him a little. "It wasn't your fault."

He almost laughed. He'd heard those words so many

fucking times, if he strung them together they'd stretch from Chicago to New York three times. He was trying to hold on to his anger, to his conviction that he couldn't have Mandy, but it was so damn hard when she was looking at him like that.

Like she loved him.

"I love you, Damien. Please don't dismiss that."

"You don't even know me." He took her arms, moved them to her lap to distance her, to distract him from his pounding heart and stupid foolish hope.

"Yes, I do. I know everything that matters about you. I know you're a wonderful man of integrity. I know that you're complex, driven, and that you're compassionate. I know you." She ignored the wet stains on each of her cheeks and met his gaze straight on. "And I know that you didn't come to my apartment at two in the morning to tell me to kiss off."

He had thought he had. He had thought he was here to warn her away from him. But he wasn't sure he could convince her when he was desperately wavering himself.

"What do you really want, Damien? If there was no past and no guilt and no fear? What do you really want?"

That was brutally easy to answer. But he wasn't sure he could say it out loud. Wasn't sure it would be smart to put into words feelings that couldn't, shouldn't, matter in the long run. Eyes closed tight, he drew in a painful breath.

Mandy kissed his forehead, her dewy lips gliding back and forth, her whispered words muffled against his skin. "It's okay . . . just tell me what you feel. Tell me what you want."

He couldn't stop himself. He couldn't keep his fingers from drawing up her back, pulling her into him. He couldn't help the words that tumbled out of his mouth.

"I want you . . . I want you to love me."

Her mouth shifted on his forehead, kissing over to his temple, with a tenderness that made his throat constrict.

"That's easy enough. I do love you."

It sounded so true, so right, so pure when she whispered that to him. "What else do you want?"

"I want you to be mine." His voice got stronger, the lump in his throat easing up. He rubbed his lips along her cheek. "I want to love you."

Her lips met his, briefly, tantalizing. "Then love me, Damien. Love me."

He did. With all of the shards and damaged pieces of his heart, he did truly love Mandy. In a way he'd never thought possible, with a desperate sort of ache and a quiet joy.

"I do. I will." And he covered her mouth, kissed her softly again and again, wanting the moment to stretch and last and allow them both to hover in that place of promise.

He touched her—arms, waist, shoulders, neck—questing, intimate touches, the need to feel Mandy's flesh everywhere, to caress and worship every inch. Their tongues met as they kissed, a slow, leisurely mating that sent of kick of hot desire through his body.

"I want to feel you closer," she said, pulling back to yank her tank top off. In the shadows, he could see the full roundness of her breasts.

It had been over three weeks since he'd seen her without her shirt, and then he'd only known her body for two days, but he knew she looked different. The change to her breasts was subtle, the dark pinkness around her nipples larger, her belly a little rounder. She looked incredibly sexy to him. But she also looked beautiful, wonderful, vulnerable in her love for him.

He was in absolute awe that she could look at him and think there was anything for her inside of him. "Mandy."

She started to tumble back onto the bed, reaching for him.

"Don't lie that way, remember," he said, mentally referencing the *Everything Guide* as he took off his own shirt. "Lie on your side and just let me hold you. I just want to hold you."

She did as he asked, her head falling onto the sleep-squashed pillow, a soft smile on her face as she settled onto her side. Damien stood up, took his shoes and pants off. He left his boxers on as he slid in alongside her. This wasn't about sex. It was about feeling her, being near her and cherishing the idea that they could be together.

That love could be enough.

Mandy sighed when he reached for her and shifted closer until they were touching from shoulder to toes, her soft curves nestled against his hard flesh, her belly resting above his pelvis.

They shared her pillow, faces hovering inches apart.

"This could work, Damien," she whispered. "It's honestly all up to you whether we should try or not."

He knew she wasn't talking about sleeping arrangements or sexual positions, but about them. The future. Rubbing his lips across her forehead, he asked, "Why is it up to me? You're the one having a baby. That's the most important thing we need to think about."

"Exactly. I know that you'll be wonderful with my baby. I don't doubt that for a minute. But I need to know if this is temporary or long-term. If we need to take it slow . . . or we need to leave it at this tonight."

The words tickled his ear as she spoke. He could smell the floral scent of her lotion, feel the dampness of her hair as he drove his fingers through her curls.

"I don't want to pressure you or rush you or be insensitive to what you've been through, but I do have to think about my baby, and I just need to know what it is you want."

What he wanted and what he should do seemed to be two different things. It wasn't fair to ask Mandy to wait for him to heal the wounds he had. It wasn't fair to ask her to take him on as he was, more liability than asset. It wouldn't be fair to ask her to allow him into her daughter's life.

He closed his eyes. He didn't give a shit about fairness. If he couldn't have Mandy, tonight, here, now, love her and feel her love for him, if he couldn't have a life that included her in it, then he wasn't sure he could face that empty future.

Selfish or not, he needed her.

"I want you. I want your daughter. I want *us.*"

"I was really hoping you'd say that," she whispered.

It wasn't clear to him who moved, but their lips were together, coaxing, pressing, begging, tasting each other, and he gripped the side of her cheek, desperate in his desire, his feelings.

He loved her. She loved him. And Mandy said it could be that simple. Here, in the dark, with her in his arms, her taste on his tongue, he believed it.

Mandy kissed Damien for all she was worth, trying to push into his mouth all the feelings, the love, the tenderness she felt for him. She knew it wasn't easy for him to open up to her. He had been living in emotional solitary confinement for three years.

But this was right, so very, very right, and she wanted to show him that.

When she started pushing down her knickers, he broke their kiss. "Need help with those?" His voice wasn't urgent, but slow, sensual, achingly intimate.

"Yes, please. I want to be closer to you. I want to be inside your skin." She slipped into his boxers and held his bum, wedging him closer against her, even as he skimmed her panties down.

"You feel so good," he said, brushing his mouth over her shoulder, her arm, as he pushed the panties to her knees.

Mandy kicked her legs and got them off the rest of the way. They were hot flesh to hot flesh, the moonlight reflecting off his glossy black hair, the hair on his legs tickling over her skin.

She drew in a deep breath. "You smell so good. Like a man."

He laughed softly. "I don't think that's a good thing."

Hearing his laughter always pleased her on a fundamental level because she didn't think he'd had much to laugh about before she'd met him. It seemed such a small thing, but every time she heard it, she had to smile.

"Oh, but it is." She licked his chest, enjoying the startled little jerk he gave. Shifting her hands, she maneuvered his boxers down to his hips. Desire was building between her thighs, and when his erection pressed against her, she groaned softly.

Damien disposed of his boxers using the same kick-and-flick method she had, until they were both on their sides, locked together like a couple of Legos. His kisses rained down her neck, shoulder, and breast while she rocked against him slowly, the tip of his penis sliding along her slick folds.

They teased and touched and kissed until their breathing was loud and ragged and their rocking movements desperate. Mandy ached to feel him inside, ached to show him what he meant to her.

"Lift your leg over my hip," he said, hands cupping her backside.

She did, and he slid inside her at the same time his tongue entered her mouth. A shudder tore through her, the groan she gave captured by his kiss. She had never been this close to a man, in this way, this total, complete joining of heart, body, and soul.

"Damien." She tore her mouth from his, unable to take so much at once. She buried her face in his neck, grasped his shoulders with trembling fingers as he moved inside her over and over, his thrusts coming stronger and faster.

Hands holding her in place on the bed, Damien moved inside her as he whispered along her cheek. "I love you, Mandy."

"I love you, too." Her swollen flesh wrapped around him, received him, and she came with a cry, jerking backward with the violence of her orgasm. "Oh, damn!"

He held her to him, wouldn't let her leave him, escape

him, as he sank into her again and again, stretching out her pleasure until she thought she couldn't take another stroke. She ran her fingers into his hair, gasping for breath, certain she was going to die, when he paused. Then he exploded in her with a fierce growl wrenched out through clenched teeth.

Mandy watched him, reveled in the pleasure on his face as he pulsed deep in her body. Satisfaction, elation, power, love all coursed through her, and it wasn't until she tasted her tears that she realized she was crying.

He noticed, too, as soon as his shudders slowed and his eyes refocused. "You're crying. Oh, baby, why are you crying?"

She sniffled as she squeezed the small of his back, keeping him in her when he would have left. "Damn, I'm sorry. They're good tears, honestly. I just can't believe how happy I am."

Damien relaxed again, his chest sinking toward hers. "I believe it. And I know how to appreciate it now."

He pulled out of her, but now he arched a finger back and forth over her clitoris, which tingled with aftershocks. "I'd like to appreciate you all over again in a minute," he said.

She smiled at him. "Can you appreciate it in the morning instead of now? I can't keep my eyes open. The orgasms you give me seem to act like warm milk."

With a laugh, he moved his hand to her belly and rested it there. "That's not really a flattering analogy, Mandy. My lover is like a glass of warm milk—knocks me out cold every time."

"What did you say?" she teased, letting her eyes drift shut. "I've fallen asleep."

Damien laughed again, pulling the hot rumpled sheet over them. "Nothing. Go to sleep." His wandering hand traveled north to her breast, stroking over her nipple. "Dream of me between your legs, licking you, sucking your clitoris, and stroking my tongue along your hot wetness."

Oh, my, there was an image.

"Cunnilingus, you mean?"

He gave a wicked laugh, low and near her ear as they lay on their sides facing each other. "Oh, yeah. In your dreams just imagine me cunnilingusing the hell out of you."

Mandy fell asleep with an anticipatory smile on her lips.

Chapter 22

Damien was in the kitchen trying to rustle up some coffee when someone knocked on the door. He glanced toward it, debating whether to open it or not. Mandy was still sleeping. Caroline was gone from the couch and the second bedroom door was still firmly shut.

He didn't want to disturb Mandy or be presumptuous in her place, but the knock came again, so he went to the door.

There was a thin guy standing in the hallway looking politely startled. "Oh, good morning. I'm looking for Mandy."

Mandy? Damien felt a green tidal wave roll over him. This was Ben, the Brit. Ben, the father of Mandy's baby. Ben the bastard.

"She's sleeping," he said in the voice that had made many an assistant cry.

"Really? Well, that's a bit surprising." Ben glanced at his watch. "It's a quarter of nine, and she starts at her office in fifteen minutes. I think you must be mistaken. Perhaps you can get Allison to check?" He held out his hand. "I'm Ben Hurst, by the way. You must be Allison's new boyfriend."

He was a friendly enough chap. Too bad Damien hated his guts already. But he gave him a quick handshake, putting excessive force into the pump.

"No, I'm not mistaken. I just left Mandy sleeping in the bedroom five minutes ago."

Ben's smile faltered. "You're not Allison's boyfriend?"

"No." Damien stepped back to let him in, thinking this was a golden opportunity to square things away between them. Let Ben know he was sticking around. He hitched up the wrinkled pants he'd pulled back on, in deference to Mandy's roommates. He hadn't bothered with a shirt, though, and he could feel the scratchy beginnings of a beard. He knew he looked like a man who had just dragged himself out of a woman's bed. Good. "I'm Damien Sharpton. I'm here with Mandy."

Ben raised an eyebrow. "Are you saying you and Mandy are . . . involved?"

"Yes." Damien fought the need to cross his arms over his chest and spread out his legs like a bouncer denying admittance to a popular nightclub. Instead, he leaned against the arm of the couch and tried not to glare.

"But she's pregnant." Ben glanced down the hallway toward the bedroom, apparently shocked.

Damien thought that was stating the obvious. And he had just about used up his ability to be nice before his first cup of coffee. "Pregnant women like sex, too."

Ben's mouth fell open. "You're saying . . . ?"

"Yep." He just knew he looked smug, and he wasn't the least bit ashamed of himself. Mandy was his. He loved her and her baby.

After a second, Ben laughed—not a raucous laugh, but a chuckle of amusement. "My ex-wife never did. She was forbidden territory for nine months."

Damien crossed his feet. "Not Mandy."

Then he shut himself up before he started bragging like a teenager in the locker room. Ben needed to know how serious they were about each other, but anything beyond that was private. "But look, I know you're the baby's father, and Mandy has every intention of letting you get as involved in her life as you want to be. But you should know that Mandy and I are very serious about each other, and I'm going to be around. Permanently."

Ben sat down and crossed his leg. He didn't look perturbed by Damien's announcement. "Damien Sharpton . . . that name is familiar. You're Mandy's boss, aren't you?"

Damien nodded, wary. Ben should look angry and he didn't. At least Damien thought he should. If it were him, and his ex was pregnant, he wouldn't want her involved with another man.

"And you're permanent, you say?"

He gave another jerk of his head.

Ben flashed him a smile. "I can't tell you how relieved I am to hear that."

Damien stared at Ben. There was something wrong with this man. "Why is that?"

"Look, can I be straight with you?" Ben uncrossed his leg and tapped his knee. "I don't want to bring up another baby. I wasn't so keen on it the first two times, but my ex-wife insisted. And this bit with Mandy, it was a total accident as I'm sure you know."

Words didn't quite come to Damien, so he just nodded again.

"I'm trying very hard to be supportive because I know Mandy's all alone here in New York and she hasn't got much in the way of money without her parents' help. But I really don't want to be involved with this child. And if I know that she's got someone to look after her, I think maybe I should just bow out of the whole mess."

Damien took a deep breath and tried to suck back his anger. This mother-fucker had just called his daughter a *mess*. He didn't deserve to be a father. He didn't deserve a woman like Mandy. He didn't deserve anything but a boot up his ass.

He managed to control himself, speaking in a cool voice. "Feel free to bow out. I've got the situation covered."

"I can still offer financial support, of course, but the little chap's probably better off if I don't pop in and out of his life."

"Her," Damien forced out through clenched teeth. He couldn't stop his hand from curling into a fist.

"Hmm?"

"Her. The baby is a girl."

"Oh, right. Of course. Anyhow, perhaps I should see if Mandy's up and we can discuss this."

Damien pushed off the couch. "She's exhausted. Don't wake her up. I'll let her know you stopped by, and we'll see if between the three of us we can resolve the situation to mutual satisfaction."

"Perfect." Ben stood up and held out his hand. "I'm so glad we understand each other, Damien."

Oh, Damien understood a lot of things.

He understood that Ben was giving him his daughter. He really could have everything.

A wife. A family.

The thought nearly cut him off at the knees.

"I don't think it's any of our business." Jamie looked to Allison for support, but she was frowning just as fiercely as Caroline. "I'm serious, guys, this is Mandy's life."

Caroline set her carrot stick down on a plate on the kitchen counter. "Mandy is flooded with endorphins or pheromones or whatever they're called. She's pregnant and clearly not behaving rationally."

Jamie stared across the breakfast bar at her. "Why is falling in love with her boss irrational?" Personally, she thought it was really romantic, sort of a *Maid in Manhattan* kind of thing, only Mandy wasn't poor. Or Latina. She forced the image of Jennifer Lopez in shlubby gym shoes out of her head.

"Because men don't fall in love with pregnant women. Because Damien Sharpton is the most unemotional man I've ever encountered, and suddenly he's head over heels? It doesn't add up."

Caroline blotted her mouth with a napkin, though Jamie

couldn't see what a carrot stick could leave behind on her lips.

"But Beckwith predicted Mandy would be happy—"

Allison cut her off. "Oh, God, here we go." She rolled her eyes and tossed her hair back over her shoulders as she headed for the refrigerator. "I need some ice cream if we're going to discuss fortune-telling crap."

When she pulled out a pint of mint chocolate chip, Jamie's mouth watered. It so wasn't fair that Allison was five-ten and weighed like two pounds, and never had to watch what she ate. Jamie fought the battle of the bulge on a daily basis.

Caroline whimpered. "Put that thing away! I'm getting married in six weeks! I can't even *look* at ice cream until I get back from my honeymoon."

"You can have one spoonful. You can't deny yourself indefinitely or you'll leap on a Ben & Jerry's like a lion on a gazelle carcass. Better to just have one spoonful and get the craving out of your mouth."

Jamie thought that sounded reasonable. She leaned over the top of the breakfast bar and tried to reach the drawer. Her breasts stopped her. "Damn, I can't reach. You'd think after like fourteen years lugging these things around I'd be used to them."

"I should have your problems." Allison tapped her metal spoon left and right on her chest. She was braless in her tank top. "Nothing. I'm a plastic surgeon's dream."

"Can we talk about your breasts after we've decided what to do about Mandy?" Caroline dipped a spoon into the ice cream and stared at it with obvious longing.

"I don't think we should do anything, y'all. I think it's wonderful she's found happiness after what's-his-name dumped her." Jamie grabbed the spoon Allison was holding out for her and figured it didn't matter if she gained five pounds. No one was seeing her naked lately anyway.

"She's y'alling us." Allison turned to Caroline. "There's a down-on-the-farm story coming, I just know it."

Jamie laughed. "Shut up. I wasn't going to say anything about Kentucky, but now that you mention it, I have an aunt whose no-good drunk husband left her with nothing but a double-wide, three kids, and a baby in her belly. And when she went on down to that bank to argue for mercy when they were on the verge of foreclosing, the loan officer took one look at her and fell in love."

Caroline swallowed, her lip curled. "What the *hell* does that have to do with Mandy?"

"It means that love can come when you least expect it and you shouldn't close the door on it." Jamie shoved a big mouthful of mint chocolate chip in her mouth and sighed, taste buds bursting into an alleluia chorus.

"So your aunt didn't close the door of the double-wide on love?" Allison grinned.

"Nope. And she's been happy ever since. Why can't the same be true for Mandy?"

"Because something is weird about Damien." Caroline set her spoon down, ice cream uneaten.

The willpower was admirable. Jamie bent back for another scoopful. She wasn't the one who needed to wear a wedding gown in six weeks. Though she did have to put on a bridesmaid dress and walk down the aisle in front of a hundred people. She set her own spoon down with a sigh.

Caroline looked at both of them. "I think we should run an Internet search on him."

"Google him?" Allison asked thoughtfully. "I like it. That's a good idea."

Jamie was horrified. "You can't do that! It's unethical." She glanced toward the front door, even though she knew Mandy was out at dinner with Damien and probably wouldn't be home for another hour. Prying into Mandy's business didn't sit right with her. "And there's nothing wrong with Damien, he's just a little reserved. I've met lots of weirdos doing social work, believe me, I know the signs."

She could also spot a cockroach at twenty paces, but that was another story.

"You want weirdos? Try working retail." Allison shuddered. "God, I hate my job."

Caroline was heading into the living room, still dressed in a pale gray suit from work. She picked up her computer case and whipped the machine out.

Jamie abandoned her spoon and rushed to Caroline's side, tripping over her ankle-length skirt in the process. "I don't think this is such a good idea. Mandy won't like it."

"Mandy will never know we did a search unless something is wrong; then she'll thank us for warning her before the baby is born."

"I think you're smart to do it." Allison perched on the corner of the couch, ice cream carton in hand. "He could be a deadbeat dad for all you know."

Caroline was biting her lip, clicking away. Jamie tried to follow on the screen, but computers weren't her thing, and Caroline was opening windows too fast for her to catch but a glimpse.

Suddenly a big newspaper article popped up and Caroline paused.

"Holy shit," Allison said, her words mumbled behind a mouthful of ice cream.

"What?" More than a little nervous, Jamie read the headline. "Husband arrested in Southloop slaying . . . What is this all about?" But somehow she knew what it meant, and her heart started to pound. It couldn't be, it just couldn't.

Caroline sucked in a sharp breath. "The cops arrested Damien for killing his wife! Oh. My. God." The computer went unbalanced on her legs and toppled to the floor with a horrible crash. "I never thought, I mean I never, oh shit, oh shit, what are we going to do?"

"He must not have done it." Jamie swallowed hard, shock sending a shiver through her. "Otherwise, he'd be in jail, right?" She gripped a throw pillow. "Right?"

Allison reached for the laptop. "That's a damn good question. One we should answer. Then we need to see if Mandy knows Damien's fascinating marital history."

Somehow Jamie didn't think that would lead to the enrichment that Beckwith had assured Mandy was right around the corner.

Chapter 23

"There's something I meant to tell you about this morning," Damien said, straightening the silverware on his napkin. "But you were in such a hurry to get to the office I barely got a word in before you shoved me out the door."

He grinned at Mandy sitting across the table from him, thinking how ironic it was that she had been the one eager to rush off to work and he'd been thinking that just once in a while it would be nice to spend the day lounging in bed.

"Well, really, no one was expecting you to be there today, since you cancelled all your appointments, but if I didn't show up, it would look really bad. Like I don't go to work when my boss is out of town."

Mandy had a tight black top on with a black-and-white floral skirt, though he couldn't see the knee-length skirt under the table. But he had a great view of the top and her healthy cleavage spilling from the open neck. She had put on a necklace, a little oval encrusted with diamonds, and it dipped enticingly toward her breasts. When she sat back, her belly rounded under the stretchy shirt, and he thought she was the hottest, sexiest woman in existence.

"For all they know, you could have taken a personal day." He knew she was right, but it had been difficult to walk away from her to head home and change his clothes.

Then when he'd gotten to the office, she had hidden from him. It had been a long, torturous day where he had walked around with the knowledge that he loved Mandy and she loved him. It had seemed like something so momentous should call for at least one day off, and he'd paced around the eighteenth floor restlessly, until Rob had told him he was scaring the employees and could he just stay in his office if he was going to pace and scowl?

He was starting to think that Mandy had set up a cubicle in the woman's rest room, because he hadn't seen her all day. And now he was starved for her.

"Damien, executives can do what they want. Secretaries can't. Everyone talks and watches and gossips and they already think it was odd that I went to Punta Cana with you. And they are all catching on to the fact that I'm bursting out my clothes."

"And quite beautifully." He couldn't help but glance at her chest again.

"Oh, stop it, you lecher," she said, laughing. "You know, I'm going to have to quit this job. If we're going to be involved, that is."

"We are." He was firm on that point. Beyond firm. He was concrete-solid, steel determination.

"There are too many conflicts of interest. I don't want everyone in the office talking about me."

"So we'll just switch you with someone else's assistant. You don't have to quit." He didn't want to be the cause of that. He didn't want to give her any stress or cause to worry about her health benefits. "Though it brings me to tears to give you up, I can see the wisdom of us not working directly together."

She laughed. "What a gesture. You mean, you'll be willing to go on the Great Assistant Hunt all over again? Just for me. How sweet."

"Sweet is not normally a word used to describe me. But

yes, I'll suffer through another Lanie for you." He was starting to think he'd do just about anything for Mandy. "Anyway, I'm trying to tell you something."

"What's that?" Mandy took a sip of her Diet Coke and licked her lips.

Damien frowned. He'd been so busy staring at her breasts he hadn't really noticed what she'd ordered. "Should you be drinking that? They're really not sure about the safety of aspartame."

She was still smiling, but her eyes got a little sharp. "I'm just going to pretend you didn't say that."

"What? You read the book—didn't it say that?" He hadn't dreamt that. He hadn't even slept the night before.

"I'm not giving up Diet Coke." Her fingers tightened around the glass. "I've given up coffee, deli meat, sushi, sleeping on my back, taking an aspirin when I have a headache. I've given up all pretensions of modesty, I've given up my shop, and I've given up wine and all other forms of alcohol. I am not giving up my Diet Coke when there's no proof whatsoever that it's harmful."

Me-ow. Geez, here was the irritable thing, apparently. Damien reached for a compromise. "So, just drink regular Coke, then. It doesn't have aspartame."

"It only has about five thousand calories that I do not need since my bum is spreading even as we speak."

"Your butt is not spreading." The very thought made him smirk. The look on her face caused him to straighten up and slap a sober expression in place of the grin.

She didn't appear placated.

"Instead of talking about my backside, what is it you wanted to say?" Mandy looked around the restaurant, which was a sterile and cool Pan-Asian place. "And when is the food going to get here? I'm absolutely starving."

She was being snarky, she knew it. But she was hungry and tired. Staying up all night having sex had sapped her energy. It was one more thing to stress over. She was having a little trouble picturing herself waking every two hours to feed an infant.

Plus she was worried about Damien. He loved her. She believed that he did, sincerely. But he wasn't discussing the future with her, and while she couldn't blame him, since they were just getting started on their relationship, she felt a sense of urgency. This wasn't the same for her as it was for him.

He probably needed to take things slowly, cautiously. After all, his wife had been killed, violently. Mandy was the first woman he had made love to in all that time, the first woman he had expressed feelings for.

But while he needed to adjust, she felt the need to know her future now. She had enough concerns and fears and life changes, she just didn't think she could wait around and see how all this was going to turn out.

She wanted a commitment or she didn't want anything at all. Her heart, her willpower, wasn't strong enough to continue on dating him indefinitely, waiting for him to figure out what he might want. Regardless of how she felt, her child was her number one concern.

Her daughter.

The very thought of her baby made her flush with happiness.

"We can order an appetizer. I'll flag the waitress down and see how long it's going to be."

He was trying, she'd give him that. She was being peevish, and he was just concerned about her.

"I can wait a few more minutes."

"Ben stopped by the apartment this morning while you were sleeping," he said, before she'd even completely finished her sentence.

"What?" That startled her stomach off thoughts of food. "What did he want?"

"He never did say what he came by for originally once he realized that you and I . . . that we . . ." Damien cleared his throat.

"Oh, God! You let him know we're sleeping together?" She could only imagine what Ben must have thought. That she was a slut was the first thought that came to mind.

"Well, it was kind of obvious."

She had no problem picturing it. Damien in his underwear, looking sexy and rumpled and giving Ben that cool, *I'm in charge* stare that he had perfected. "And instead of waking me, you told him to stop back later?"

"Well . . ." Damien's fingers drummed on the table. He had trouble sitting still, the way he always did. A part of his body was always moving. He didn't look as though he'd been up all night expending energy instead of conserving it in sleep. "Maybe you should talk to Ben about what he said."

Oh, that sounded promising. And distracting. And infuriating. Given that she'd come to realize she didn't know Ben at all or what he might say, she couldn't even begin to imagine what he had said to Damien. And she wanted to know. "You can just tell me. I promise I won't kill the messenger."

"He said he was relieved that you were seeing someone."

No, she couldn't have predicted that. "Oh, really? And why is that, I wonder?"

Damien's blue eyes were unreadable. "Because he said he's not really all that interested in being a father the third time over, but he was reluctant to leave you on your own. He felt if I was serious about you—which I am—that he could bow out of the situation and leave you in, ah, good hands."

Mandy felt as if she'd been dealt a good swift kick to the shins. "Oh, did he now?" Her voice wavered and she blinked hard to dispense tears that had risen without warning. Damn, why should it matter? But it hurt. It bloody well hurt to hear Ben talk so callously about her. As if she was a baton to pass off from one runner to another. *Here you go, thanks, chum, your turn now*.

Damien reached for her hands. "I'm sorry. I didn't mean to tell you all this here. I just wanted to tell you he'd stopped by so you could call him."

"You're not the one who needs to apologize." Damn, was she really such a poor judge of character that she'd never seen that kind of weakness in Ben? And what did that say about her feelings for Damien? What was she misinterpreting or choosing not to see there?

Knowing she was about to cry for real and embarrass the hell out of herself, she stood up. Damien got to his feet, too, startled.

"I'm just going to the rest room. I need a second. I'll be right back." She bent over and grabbed her purse. "And if my miso chicken isn't here when I get back, I'm storming that kitchen for it myself."

Then she bolted before he could stop her.

Damien stared after Mandy, her skirt twitching around her legs as she walked quickly toward the rest rooms.

He had messed that up. He hadn't meant it to sound so cold, but then, Ben's words had been cold. Maybe there was no way around that. He was certain that she didn't have feelings for Ben the Bastard any longer, but that didn't mean it wouldn't still hurt.

He rearranged his silverware for the third time, took a sip of his Coke. Stared at her Diet. Then switched them. She didn't need to worry about ass spreading.

But he wasn't sure what his role was in relation to her ass spreading or anything else for that matter. Did he have the right to be involved in her pregnancy?

Did he have the right to be the baby's father?

Father. The word alone had him choking on his ice cube.

He'd never thought much about having kids. Jess had

never wanted children, and since he'd never spent a lot of time around them himself, it hadn't seemed like such a big deal. Besides, they had been young, just in their twenties, and he'd thought maybe later Jess would change her mind and they would talk about it. He would have been happy either way, he'd figured, but had always kind of secretly hoped Jess would go for kids eventually.

There were good memories from his childhood, a lot of good memories, and he had wanted to repeat that.

But then Jessica had been murdered, and there had been no thought to anything but getting through one long, painful day at a time. Kids became unfathomable. An impossibility. An alien concept in his frozen, hard, minimalist existence.

But for a man who had spent three years clamping down on every emotion, his seemed to have all burst out in one great greedy rush, a tidal wave of want and desire crashing over him.

He wanted Mandy. He wanted her baby. He wanted to get over his past and be given the chance to live again, a real life, with love and laughter and someone to share his home.

Was he ready? No, he was sure he *wasn't* ready. He was sure that he was going to make mistakes, sure that he was going to smother Mandy with his needs and wants and neuroticisms. Sure that the thought of calling another woman his wife again would send him into a cold sweat. Sure that it was too easy to expect everything to be handed to him all neat and tidy and wrapped with a bow.

Mandy came back, pale but composed. Their food was still MIA.

"Why don't I just get the food to go?" This wasn't really the place to say what either of them needed to say.

"That's a good idea. How close are we to your place?"

Damien gestured to the waitress. "Just a block." That had been the reason he'd chosen this restaurant. He'd been hoping to entice her home with him, where he had a nice large bed, air-conditioning, and thick walls that muffled any screaming in pleasure she might be inclined to do.

"Perfect."

He handed his credit card to the waitress, who promised to expedite their departure when he explained Mandy wasn't feeling good.

Mandy touched her stomach. "Oh, that was weird. She knew I was pregnant, didn't she? People look at me and see a pregnant woman." Her cheeks pinkened.

Damien wasn't sure what the correct response was to that, so he just nodded. Mandy took a sip of her soft drink and made a face. Then she stared down into her glass, eyes narrowed, and took another pull on her straw. Her voice was outraged. "Did you switch our drinks?"

Oh, shit. Her hand reached for his glass, but he pulled it out of reach, which was stupid, because he was already busted. "Maybe you just picked the wrong one up."

Mandy rolled her eyes, but she was laughing, thank God. "Nice try. You are very lucky that I love you, or you'd be wearing that Diet Coke in your lap right now."

But her threat didn't bother him in the least. He stared at her, amazed at how those words could change his every perspective, every thought, every day. "I am lucky that you love me. I don't deserve this much luck."

Her mouth opened into a surprised O. Then she wet her lips and gripped her purse. A sensual sigh drifted over to him. "Take me home, Damien, so I can show you what you deserve."

Chapter 24

Mandy strolled down the pavement, leaning on Damien's arm. It was a fabulous night, the air warm and balmy on her bare arms. Traffic was light in this neighborhood, trees tucked into little squares of dirt curbside, and flowers spilled out of window boxes. For having spent most of her girlhood in the English countryside, she really did love the city, and this was a quiet, well-established area.

In the restaurant rest room, she had splashed water on her face and got a handle on her emotions. Now, strolling along on a beautiful summer night, she realized she was feeling at peace with the world. With herself. So Ben didn't want a baby. That was not new information, and if he took himself off now before the baby was born, all the less complicated everything would be.

None of that mattered. It would all work out. She was certain of it.

"Don't faint from hunger. My building is right here." Damien pulled her toward the front doors and led her inside. Since he actually looked worried, she gave a smile to reassure him.

"When I was sick in my first trimester, my doctor told me not to ever worry about the baby. That if need be, my body will give to the baby first, consume my fat stores, then attack my own muscles to provide the baby with nourishment."

"That's kind of gruesome. But biological maternal instinct, huh?" Damien stopped in front of the elevators after hitting the button. He opened the bag of food he was holding and pulled out a spring roll. "Eat it. We don't want your muscles being cannibalized."

They got on the elevator, and Mandy laughed. "Don't worry, I have a few fat stores left before they get to the muscles." But she bit the roll anyway. She was starving.

"Elevator, upset stomach . . . if I had any coffee, this would remind me of the day we met."

"Should I bend over? Then it would really be romantic."

"Yes, it would." His eyebrows went up suggestively and his eyes darkened. "Though hot is probably a better word than romantic."

Mandy clamped her mouth shut so carrot and water chestnuts bits wouldn't fall out. "I was joking! I meant it wouldn't be romantic, like the day we . . . oh, never mind. I know exactly what you were thinking, you bloody pervert."

He just laughed.

After eating, Damien showed Mandy around his apartment. It had been built in the sixties, so it was sparse on details, with chopped-up rooms and low ceilings. He had been working on fixing that, adding molding around the windows and working on plans with a contractor to knock out the walls that created narrow hallways. The end result would be an open, airy flow from three principle rooms, instead of the five tiny rooms he had now.

Except he was thinking some modifications to the plans might be needed.

"It's a great apartment, and so amazingly quiet."

"That's why I moved here." He paused in the doorway of

his bedroom. "I was planning to knock this wall out into the other bedroom and make this room bigger and the other into a walk-in closet, but I'm rethinking that."

"Why?" Mandy went into the room and turned around, taking in the space as her fingers trailed over his bed, lingering on the soft downy white pillows. "And why am I not the least bit surprised that this room is so clean and neat you could probably eat off the floor?"

Because he had become slightly neurotic. He knew he couldn't control a lot of things in the world, in his life, but he could control his personal environment. He could wrestle order and tranquility into this apartment.

"I'm a neat freak. I'm man enough to admit that. And it's something that you need to think about—whether or not you can live with that." He meant that literally. He wanted her to live with him. "And I'm rethinking my plans because I'm hoping that I'm going to have to accommodate a nursery."

Her head turned sharply back to him.

Damn, that wasn't right. He had meant to start with her, tell her how he loved her, propose to her. Then discuss living together, the baby, eloping over the weekend.

But he was feeling a little sick, and it wasn't the chicken. He wanted these changes. He wanted Mandy. But he was terrified she'd say no. Terrified she'd say yes.

God knew he didn't want to hurt her, and he didn't want to make the same mistakes he'd made the first time with Jessica.

Mandy stared at Damien, searching his face for something, anything that would reveal to her what he was really saying. He had a way of putting out words that masked what was really going on underneath.

He wanted to build a nursery in his apartment. Did that mean marriage? Living together? A guest room for her baby when she came over to visit Uncle Damien?

Heart pounding, she was about to ask when her cell phone rang in her purse. She had been hauling her purse around to freshen up her makeup when Damien showed her the bathroom. She absently glanced down toward the sound.

"Let it ring." His voice was urgent, harsh almost.

"It might be my mother. Or Ben. Just let me check." Mandy pawed through her purse and pulled the phone out. It was the number to the apartment flashing. She answered it, not sure what her roommates could possibly want since they knew she was out with Damien.

"Hello?"

"Mandy, this is us." It was Caroline's voice, so Mandy wasn't sure what the *us* entailed. All of her roommates, she had to assume.

"Hi, Caroline. Listen, I'm a bit busy. Can I ring you later?"

Damien was giving her a most frightful scowl.

"No! Just listen to me. I have to tell you something about Damien . . . Honey, this will come as a shock I know, but you need to know this."

Mandy was only half listening, waiting for that moment when she could interrupt Caroline to tell her it would have to wait.

"Damien's wife was killed. Murdered."

Mandy turned toward the window, startled. "I know that, Caroline. But how do you know that?"

"I read it on the Internet in the *Chicago Tribune*'s articles. Damien was charged with killing her. The cops were certain he did it, but the grand jury didn't indict him."

Mandy almost dropped the phone. Damien had been arrested? Good God. She felt a hot flush start up her neck. "Why are you telling me this?"

"So you can get yourself away from him. Just go to the rest room and sneak out the front door of the restaurant. You don't want to be involved with a man like this." Caroline's voice was urgent.

Mandy swallowed hard, her heart aching. "I'm with Damien at his apartment right now. I'll talk to you later."

She hung up the phone.

Jamie shook her head at Caroline, who looked as flustered as she'd ever seen her. "That was not a good thing to do for a lot of reasons."

Allison tucked her hair behind her ear impatiently. "What did she say? Was she horrified? What restaurant is she at? We'll go pick her up."

Caroline bit her lip, another gesture that indicated extreme agitation. Caroline didn't have bad habits. She froze bad habits with the force of her will.

"She's not at a restaurant. She's at Damien's apartment."

Jamie clapped her hand over her mouth. "Caroline! She's at his apartment and you told her that he's a murderer?"

"Well, I didn't know when I told her!" Caroline's cheeks flushed an angry red.

"Okay, this could be bad." Allison's long legs ate up the living room as she paced back and forth. "What did Mandy say?"

"Nothing. She just hung up on me."

"Well, she must not think he did it. And she knows him better than we do. She's probably right." Jamie looked at both of them. "Right?" She didn't want to think that the man who'd shown such interest, such concern for Mandy could be a cold-blooded murderer. "They didn't indict him, after all."

"Because they didn't have any evidence, not because he didn't do it!" Caroline dropped the phone on the couch. "Damn, I've made a mess out of this. What if she confronts him and he . . . does something to her?"

Jamie didn't think that was likely, really, she was sure he wouldn't. But what if he did?

"Oh, shoot. We have to call her back!"

* * *

Mandy's phone rang again as she sat heavily down on Damien's bed. A glance at it showed it was Caroline again. She turned it to vibrate and ignored it.

Damien was staring at her. "What's the matter? You look all flushed. Is talking about a nursery here too soon? Am I rushing you?"

"Why didn't you tell me?" she whispered, though she supposed she knew the answer. It was something of a miracle that Damien had shared with her what he had. But she wished she had known the full truth about Jessica right from the start, because it explained so much.

"Tell you what?" A cautiousness slid over his face.

"That you were arrested for killing Jessica."

Shock sprang into his eyes. "Who the hell told you that?"

"Caroline. Just now. Apparently she saw a newspaper article."

He turned away from her, paced the room, voice bitter. "And do you think I did it?"

That startled her. "No. Of course not. Absolutely not! But why didn't you tell me when you talked about Jessica last night? It must have been so painful for you . . . so horrible to be accused like that."

She could only scratch the surface of imaginings of what he had been through. He had loved his wife. She had been killed, after they'd argued. And then in that intense, soul-shattering grief, he had been arrested for doing such a heinous act.

His thumb twitched, but he stopped walking. "Horrible? Oh, yeah, it was horrible. That's why I didn't tell you, Mandy. How do I find the words to tell you that the cops thought I followed my wife, angry that she'd spent too much money, angry that she flirted with other men, and I raped her, and closed my fingers around her neck and squeezed the life out of her?"

His voice cracked.

"Damien . . ." Even she could hear the pity in her own voice.

"Don't." He raised his hand. "Please don't feel sorry for me. I saw that so many times at first, the deep pity people felt for me. They meant well, but it was smothering to look at so many faces and never feel normal, never have them understand that my life was over just as sure as Jessica's. Then the looks turned, and they started to suspect, started to question, started to remember all the times that Jessica and I had fought, how she'd complained about my stinginess, how she ran around with other men, and really who could blame a husband for being angry about that? But murder . . . it was there in all their eyes, in the cold, hard stare of the detectives, in the prosecutor. They all thought I did it."

Damien clamped his mouth shut to stem the words. He hadn't meant to tell her this, any of this, ever. But he couldn't stop it all from spewing out of his mouth. "I didn't tell you because there's nothing to tell. It's ugly, it's bitter and hateful, and it's thankfully over. But if you want, I'll tell you all the evidence they supposedly had against me, and I'll tell you why they didn't indict if that would make you feel better. Tell you all about forensic evidence and how my semen was found in her, and my skin under her fingernails, because before our argument we had sex—I mean, how crazy is that? A man sleeping with his own wife?"

It still rankled that they had used that against him, his desire and love for Jessica. That the only thing that had saved him had been a lack of conclusive evidence, a few stray fibers on her body that didn't match anything he owned, and a damn good defense attorney.

"I don't *need* to hear any of that," she said in a quiet voice. "I only need to hear what you're willing to tell, what you want to share with me. But if we're going to spend the rest of our lives together, which I'm sincerely hoping we will, then you need to trust me with the ugliness as well as the good things."

Her dignity, her calm, controlled tone, jerked him out of his ranting. His shoulders fell and he leaned back against the wall, then sank to the floor, too tired to stand anymore. It was just as exhausting now as it had been three years ago. He wasn't over a damn thing. "Christ, Mandy, I didn't want to ever bring you into any of this. You deserve better than this."

"Better than what? A man who loves me? A man who loves my child?" She stood up and came toward him, dropping onto the floor in front of him. "It's not your fault, damn it. You didn't do anything. You didn't kill Jessica and it doesn't matter what those cops thought. You know the truth here." She jabbed her finger in his chest, right over his heart. "And *I* know the truth."

"Then why can't I let it go?" He touched her cheek with longing. "All I want is to be with you. All I want is just a sliver of happiness. Why can't I have that?"

"There's no reason you can't." Her mouth turned into his palm, her lips brushing across his flesh. "You can have whatever you want."

He closed his eyes, everything in him aching. "There are people who will always think I did it. The publicity wasn't as bad as it could have been since it was in the aftermath of 9/11 and there were more important news stories. But there will always be a question in some people's minds. Do you want that for you and your daughter?"

"I don't give a damn what anyone else thinks."

Somehow, he believed her. He could see her resolve, feel it, and her strength, conviction, belief in him, made him feel weak all over again. He kept wrestling his demons, and they kept winning, and he didn't know how to fix that. "I'm sorry I didn't tell you. I wasn't trying to keep secrets from you, but it's so hard to talk about it . . ."

Her finger pressed against his lips. "Someday, when

you're ready, you can tell me. You can tell me about Jessica then, too. But for now, I just need to hear that you love me."

There was no doubt about that. None at all. If he knew anything, if anything made sense, it was that he loved Mandy. He kissed her fingertip. "I do love you. So much. In a way I never thought I could again. In a way that's more mature and stronger than what I felt for Jessica."

He needed to say that, to acknowledge that. It wasn't his fault, and it wasn't Jessica's fault that their marriage had been riddled with problems. There had been mutual blame and circumstances and two selfish people who hadn't wanted, or hadn't been willing, to change.

"Jess and I had our share of problems, but she didn't deserve to die like that."

"Of course not." Mandy stroked her fingers across his forehead, his cheeks, and he was comforted, strangely and completely comforted. His knees were up in the air, but she had inserted herself between them, using his left leg as support. Yet he had the feeling she was the one holding him up.

He couldn't stop himself from stroking a soft curl that fell across her shoulder. Couldn't stop himself from asking. "What do you see, Mandy, when you look into the future? What do you really see?"

She gave him a soft smile. "I see me marrying you quickly, before I look like a white inflatable pool toy floating down the aisle. I see a nursery, right on the other side of this wall in that second bedroom. I see pink gingham and white eyelet curtains, and a baby named Rebecca Sharpton who grows into a little girl who loves her daddy just as much as I love him."

Pain and want and love rose up in him so sharp that he felt his vision blur. "Do you really want that? After everything you know about me? I have scars, Mandy, that will never completely go away."

Mandy hadn't felt confidence a lot of times in her life.

She couldn't say the right thing at social events, she couldn't keep her clothes neat, and she couldn't seem to figure out how to balance her checkbook.

But this she was sure of. She and Damien were meant to be together. They complemented each other, they brought out the best in each other. They had both been given a second chance and she was going to take it if she had to wrap her arms around it and wrestle it to the ground.

"You seem to think that I'm getting the bad end of the bargain in this. You're forgetting that I have quite a few flaws of my own. I'm forgetful, a borderline slob, hopeless with money, and lousy in bed."

He gave a startled laugh. "Are you joking?"

"No, just fishing for a compliment." She snuggled into his arms, rather liking sitting on the floor between his legs. She felt surrounded, safe, loved. "But to answer your question, yes, I most certainly do want this. And I want this because I know everything about you that's important. You're a damn good man. Scars fade with time. And the ones that never go away, well, they build character, maturity, caution."

"And you're an amazing woman." He kissed the side of her mouth. "Who happens to be fantastic in bed."

The way he stroked her back, her temples, as he kissed her, with such tenderness and awe, had her longing for physical intimacy to match the emotional closeness she was feeling. She needed to have Damien in her, to see him give up control and succumb to their love. To trust her and her feelings.

"Let's test how good I am in bed, just to make sure." Mandy could hear his breathing change then, move from anxious to relaxed to aroused, as she flicked her tongue across his bottom lip. "But first you need to ask me to marry you."

Damien breathed in her scent, soft and floral. He had never thought he would say the words again, but when he did, they were easy. They were strong. They were hopeful. "Mandy Keeling, will you marry me? I love you with all of my heart, such as it is."

Her brown liquid eyes were tender, round. "It's a good heart, even if it's been kicked around a bit. It's always been a good heart, that's why it was so easily bruised. A lesser man wouldn't have cared as much. So yes, I will marry you. And this baby . . ."

She took his hand and placed it on her stomach, under hers. "This baby is already *our* daughter."

He kissed her then because he had no words. He needed to pour all his passion and emotion and love into her. There was so much feeling, so much emotion, more than he could have ever believed possible. She had given him a life back. She had given him everything that mattered.

Mandy shifted as they mingled hot, wet, tongues, so that she was facing him. "Put your legs down."

"Why?" Even though he knew why, even as he obeyed her. Their hands were tearing over each other, pulling at clothes, shoving fabric and buttons and zippers out of the way.

"Because I can't wait for the bed. Just love me, Damien."

"I do. I will." Damien skimmed her panties off as she went on her knees and shoved her dress up to her waist. She had already unzipped his pants, and he pulled her forward with a desperate groan.

Now, everything had to be now. Mandy was his, going to be his forever, his wife. They were going to share her child, and he had to climb inside her, blend all of him with all of her in frantic mating.

He eased her down onto him, her slick, hot body wrapping around him as they both panted in out-of-control pleasure. Mandy gripped his shoulders and they moved, together, with no words, in perfect unison and perfect understanding and perfect love.

* * *

Vaguely, somewhere in the back of her sex-soaked brain, Mandy heard her cell phone going off.

"Maybe you'd better answer that. Your phone has vibrated about twelve times in the last hour."

Mandy peeled her head off the bed with a groan. "It's got to be my roommates. They're worried about me." Which was sweet, but incredibly annoying.

"I'll get it." Damien reached over to the nightstand. "I tossed it over here when we ripped the covers off the bed."

Mandy let her head drop back down, sighing with satisfaction. She reached out and ran her finger across his tattoo. He had turned Jess's name into a rather erotic looking dragon, his tongue licking at the flames he threw. It was amazingly sexy, just like Damien. The man she was going to marry.

Damn, that sounded fantastic.

"Hello?" Damien said, his voice low and scratchy from their lovemaking.

A woman's shattering shriek pierced Mandy's ear. And she was three feet away from the phone. Damien's eardrum was probably damaged from that volume.

"What the hell?" Damien jerked his head back and dropped the phone.

Mandy grabbed it. "Jamie? What's the matter?"

"Mandy?"

"Yes?" Maybe she should have answered the phone earlier. Maybe something was wrong and they were trying to reach her.

Jamie sighed. "When he answered your cell, I was so sure he'd killed you. He scared ten years off my life."

It took Mandy a second to figure out what Jamie meant. Then she rolled her eyes. "I'm fine. Wonderful, in fact. Damien's proposed to me and I accepted."

"Really?" Jamie's tone completely shifted. "That's awesome, Mandy! I told these guys he was a nice man, just right for you."

Mandy grinned. "Thanks, Jams. Now we're in bed, so I'm going to hang up."

"Oh! Absolutely. Bye, sweetie."

Mandy dropped the phone and met Damien's gaze. "They were a bit concerned, since they found that article and I wasn't answering my phone." No sense in beating about the bush.

There was a long awful moment where her words hung between them.

Then he gave a brief smile, rubbing his hand over his chin. "I guess they really care about you."

Mandy nodded. "They're good friends."

"I can't wait to get to know them and give them a more accurate impression than those articles must have given."

Mandy was concerned that Damien might retreat from her, but he just put his hand squarely on her bum and hauled her over to him.

"But I won't be meeting your roommates tonight. Or tomorrow. Or even Sunday."

"Why not?" She tried to sound nonchalant, but her ragged breathing and tightening nipples gave her away as he stroked, stroked, stroked.

"Because we'll be busy getting married, that's why. In Punta Cana."

"Oh, Damien, that's just bloody brilliant."

Chapter 25

"How do I look?" Mandy smoothed her dress and wished she'd worn something without a pattern. God only knew what these yellow flowers looked like on her backside, which was spreading, no matter what Damien said.

Damien kissed the side of her head, messing up the hair she'd just tried to tame in the taxi. "You look fantastic. And why are you so nervous? It's just my family."

"Spoken just like a man." Mandy went up the front walk with him, taking in the trim lawn, the tidy flower beds, and the stone duck sitting by the front door. This big Victorian house was where Damien had grown up, and she could just picture him running through the shady backyard in his baseball uniform, not a speck on it anywhere.

"I'm meeting my mother-in-law for the first time, and the initial sixty seconds are crucial. I already have strikes against me."

"What strikes?"

"We eloped in the Caribbean and you told your parents two days after the fact. You were in Chicago two weeks ago and never once mentioned that I even existed. And they have no idea that I'm pregnant." She wasn't calming herself down. Mandy felt worked up into a regular lather.

At least her parents had greeted their news with aplomb.

Her father had said, "Marvelous," and her mother had given up a prayer of thanks after Mandy had reassured her that Damien owned real estate and was in the top tax bracket.

"The baby's a surprise. It'll be fun."

Their idea of fun apparently didn't match. Fun was a circus clown, not a five-months-pregnant daughter-in-law. She glanced at her watch. "Damn, we're late, and we didn't even bring any food."

"It's just a Fourth of July barbeque. They do this every year with family and friends and it's casual. We said we'd be here around five."

"And it's five-oh-seven now." Mandy bit her lip, feeling hot and flustered and swollen, and not in a good way. "This is all your fault for forgetting your wallet in the hotel room, then suddenly getting it in your head to have sex."

"I didn't hear any complaints from you at the time." And the man had the nerve to squeeze her bottom.

She whacked at his hand. "Oh, my God, stop that! You're insatiable. We're on your parents' front porch." Then she glanced at him and saw that while he was grinning, his eyes were vulnerable, raw. This had to be hard for him, too, and here she was snapping at him. "That's not to say I didn't enjoy making love to you, because I did. And having me kneel while holding the headboard seemed to work quite well."

His nostrils flared. He was really so damn sexy. Mandy felt herself growing warmer in the summer heat, and forgetting to worry about first impressions.

Damien stared at his wife—his *wife*. It felt so goddamn good to say that. Mandy was gorgeous, loving, and hopeless with money.

And she was all his.

"My mother will love you, just like I do."

"I hope so." She took his hand. "I do love you, Damien."

He gave her a searing kiss, running his thumb over the

platinum wedding band he had placed on her finger standing on the beach in Punta Cana.

And then he opened the front door and led her inside a cool, hushed living room. The house was quiet, empty. He had expected to feel that pang of sorrow, that longing that had characterized his thoughts about his family, his childhood home, over the last few years. He had always been conscious that he could never go back, could never be that child again with all his innocence, who knew his place in the world and was loved.

But now, it didn't feel that way. It felt good, exciting, like coming home with all the hope for the future, all the happiness of the now pushing him forward. He wanted to see his family, he wanted to smile and laugh and be a part of it again, instead of always standing outside looking in.

Damien headed down the hall, squeezing Mandy's hand, ready to show her off, to let everyone know that he had managed to snare an amazing woman, and they were having a baby. "They're all in the backyard, I'm sure."

Even better. Mandy had to descend off a back porch while thirty people gawked at her. And the yellow flowers on her breasts.

But first they passed through the cozy feminine kitchen—and it wasn't empty. A woman was bent over in the refrigerator.

"Mom."

The woman straightened up so quickly she almost dropped a glass bowl. "Damien!"

His mother turned toward them, and all of Mandy's fears evaporated. His mother was taller than she was, with short, black hair peppered with gray. Her eyes weren't blue like Damien's but a deep rich brown, almost black. Those eyes were raw, naked with worry, hope shimmering out of them.

"Hi, Mom." Damien leaned forward and kissed her cheek, taking the bowl from her hand and setting it on the counter. "Mom, this is my wife, Mandy."

But his mother was already moving toward her, enveloping her in a welcoming hug that stiffened immediately. She pulled back, looked down at Mandy's stomach, looked over at Damien in astonishment, met Mandy's gaze.

Mandy smiled, though her heart was somewhere up around her nostrils. "Damien thought it should be a surprise."

"Oh, it is." His mother blinked, tears rapidly forming in her eyes. A shaky hand fluttered over Mandy's stomach, touched briefly, then pulled back. "It's a wonderful, wonderful surprise. When are you due?"

"October twenty-first," Damien said, looking puffed up and proud. Which she knew he was.

She was, too. Proud that she was his wife. Proud that her daughter would have this man for a father.

His mother swiped at her eyes and sniffed, rapidly losing control of her emotions, which made Mandy's heart warm. She had a bond with this woman. They both loved Damien and wanted to see him happy.

She hugged his mother again, overwhelmed with emotion. "I'm so pleased to meet you, Mrs. Sharpton."

"Oh, please, honey, call me Rebecca."

Mandy started and glanced over his mother's shoulder at Damien. He winked at her.

Oh, damn, the man was enough to make her melt.

Just as predicted.

Here's a sneak peek at
GET A CLUE
by Jill Shalvis,
available now from Brava . . .

Cooper's deep blue eyes sparked, *flamed*, and the oddest thing happened to her. In spite of everything, a little ball of heat swirled low in her belly.

She had to be delirious. From the cold. From exhaustion. From her life sucking big-time. Awkwardly she hopped again, trying to pull her jeans back up, but they weren't going anywhere. Then she made one too many hops and caught her boot heel on the hem of the jeans. Waving her arms wildly, she struggled for balance.

Cooper merely stepped forward and caught her.

Fine. He could help her and she could die of mortification later.

But he didn't help. He put a hand to the middle of her chest and gave her a little push, making her fall gracelessly to the couch. Once again, the pink vibrator hit the floor and rolled to a stop at his feet.

They both stared at it for one beat before Breanne tried to bounce back up.

"*Stay*," he commanded.

Oh, no. *Hell, no*. She scissored her legs, meaning to kick him, either in the chin or the nads, she didn't care; she was going to take him down. *Now*.

But he just laughed low in his throat, and then again when she struggled to karate-chop him with her legs caught together by her own jeans. *Laughed*, as he crouched besides her, a big hand on either of her thighs and said, "Give in, Princess."

"I never give in."

Holding her down with ease, he reached for the fallen vibrator, lifting it up. The obnoxious thing still glowed neon-pink. "Never say never." Then he grinned at her in the firelight, looking just like the devil must look in the dead of winter with no one to torture. "This thing keeps showing up. Maybe you should claim it."

"It's *not* mine!"

"I don't know . . . earlier you were gripping it like it was your long-lost best friend." With a flick of his wrist, he turned it on.

The low hum filled the air, and with it came a buzzing in Breanne's ear—the sound of her brain coming to boiling point.

"Ready for use," Cooper said, suggestively waggling it in her face.

"Good." She struggled to get free, trying not to think about the picture she was presenting him with. "You can shove it up your—"

"Oh, no," he said. "Ladies first." He dropped the thing to the couch next to her, where it rumbled against the soft, buttery leather while he slid his hands down her legs to the jeans pooled between her knees.

"Don't even *think* about it," she choked out.

But he wasn't only thinking about it, he was doing it, fisting his fingers into the wet denim and yanking them past her knees to her ankles, where they caught on her boots.

His gaze met hers, intense and raw, and along with it a heart-stopping heat.

Did he have to pack such a sexual energy? She felt her entire body clench with a punch of shocking yearning.

"High-heeled boots," he murmured. "Ever so practical out here."

She stared down at the top of his head as he worked on stripping her. Her little triangle of white satin had not only slipped sideways, it was now riding up into parts unknown. She'd had a bikini wax two days ago—again for the rat bastard Dean—and judging from the very soft, very rough sound that escaped Cooper at her movements, he'd caught an eyeful up close and personal. "If I wasn't so tired," she murmured, sagging back, suddenly exhausted, "I'd kick your ass."

"Next time," he said, trying to untie her boots. The laces were iced. "I guess you were all prettied up for the honeymoon."

No. She'd prettied up for herself, to feel sexy, but she was not going to argue with a man when her pants were around her ankles; when she had a vibrator bouncing on the couch next to her, taunting her; when she had bigger worries, such as her panties, and what they still weren't covering. Shoving the sweatshirt down as far as she could, which was to the tops of her thighs, she leaned forward to hurry the process along.

And don't miss
FANGS FOR THE MEMORIES
by Kathy Love,
available now from Brava . . .

Why would a gorgeous hunk like Rhys be fascinated with her? Sebastian had to be mistaken. But she had been in bed with Rhys. And he'd . . .

Her cheeks flamed, making her complexion a colorful pink, looking mottled against the purple under her eyes.

She closed her eyes, releasing a hitched breath. She couldn't remember last night, but she could certainly remember the feeling of Rhys's hands on her when she woke up.

Heat drained from her flushed cheeks to pool in her belly, then lower. She'd never felt anything as wonderful as Rhys's fingers against her.

As if by their own will, her fingers moved to the buttons of her blouse. Not opening her eyes, she pretended it was Rhys's fingers loosening the buttons, parting the white cotton. The wisps of steam from the hot water filling the tub moistened her skin, and she pretended it was Rhys's kisses warming her flesh.

What was she doing? She'd never been the type to fantasize about men. And especially fantasies like this. But she'd also never had a man touch her like Rhys had. It had been so . . . thrilling.

She let her blouse fall to the floor, and she moved her fingers to the front clasp of her bra. The filmy material separated, and her nipples peeked against the humid air.

Embarrassed, but unable to stop herself, she brushed her fingers over them, trying to remember exactly how Rhys's lips had felt suckling her.

Her eyes snapped open at the sound of a quiet cough, and she spun toward the open doorway.

Rhys stood there, watching her.

She crossed her arms over her chest, trying to hide herself and to somehow hide what she'd been doing. But she could tell from the smoldering glow of his eyes, he'd seen it.

The burn of embarrassment mingled with the fire those intense eyes created inside her. She so wanted this man.

His gaze left her covered chest, and he held her eyes with his.

She shifted slightly under the hunger she saw there.

"Sorry," he said, his voice was huskier than usual. "I thought I heard you calling me."

She stared at him. Well, her body had been calling him, but she didn't think her voice had. "I . . . No."

He nodded sharply. "Then I will leave you to your bath."

They stared at each other for a moment longer, then Rhys bowed slightly and left, pulling the door shut behind him.

Jane sagged against the sink, still clutching her breasts. This was impossible. It had taken every bit of her rational mind not to invite him to join her in the tub. What was wrong with her? She'd always been so practical, so reserved. Now she was acting like a wanton.

Rhys shut both Jane's bathroom and bedroom door, and he still seemed to sense her desire pulling at him, begging him to come back to her. He stopped in the hallway, his own desire telling him to go back. She was his betrothed after all. They weren't married yet, but they would be soon, as soon as he could arrange it, and then that delectable body of hers would be his.

He nearly groaned, thinking about what she'd been doing

when he arrived at her bathroom door. Her hands caressing her creamy skin, shaping themselves to the rounded curves of her breasts, her fingers teasing her swollen pink nipples.

He still remembered the taste of them. The heat of her body. His cock pulsed painfully in his trousers.

She was already his but—soon, he'd have her beside him every night.

Forcing himself to ignore his overly enthusiastic body, he searched for Sebastian. His brother had left him after their celebratory drink to talk with Jane again. Rhys was curious to see what Jane had told his brother.

Sebastian was in his room. He finished buttoning his shirt, then shrugged on a jacket.

"Where are you off to?"

"To the club." Sebastian combed his fingers through his blond hair. The locks fell into their usual, unruly tangle.

Rhys nodded. "I would join you, but I'm certain Jane already believes me a complete reprobate. I believe I should stay with her this evening and try to convince her otherwise."

Sebastian smiled, a puzzlingly amused twist of his lips. "Yes, I think you should."

Rhys frowned slightly, then went over to pick up a tie lying on Sebastian's bureau. How on earth would anyone get a proper cravat out of that skinny thing? He tossed it back onto the bureau.

"Where is Wilson?" Rhys had not seen their valet all evening. Not that any of the brothers utilized the man much. They all agreed that if a man couldn't dress himself . . . well, he was truly inept.

Sebastian frowned, then his eyes widened. "Oh, Wilson. We gave him a holiday—for Christmas."

Christmas? That was right. Today was Christmas. Good Lord, Jane must think she was the one about to wed a savage. He hadn't even wished her a happy Christmas. And what of a proper Christmas meal? Surely the staff hadn't forgone the meal because Elizabeth and Christian were away. And they had left on Christmas, too?

Rhys frowned. How very curious.

"I won't be at the club long," Sebastian said. "But I thought it would be nice for you and Jane to have a little time alone."

Rhys glanced at his brother, no longer bothered by his siblings being away. In fact, he quite liked the idea of having Jane to himself, too. He just wished he had thought to arrange a proper Christmas celebration, even if it was only for the two of them. He had so much to make amends for, he hoped she was an understanding woman.

"Have fun," Sebastian said. Again that knowing little grin was on his lips.

Rhys supposed his brother found him actually being taken with his betrothed quite humorous—especially after all the objections he'd had. Rhys had to admit it was mildly amusing. If he'd known what he was missing, he would have arranged for her to join him sooner.

The bath didn't have the desired effect Jane had hoped it would. She was too unnerved by all the events of the past two days to relax. Not that she wasn't tempted to hide in her room the rest of the night, but she was supposed to be watching Rhys.

She finished drying her hair, then brushed on a little mascara, hoping it would make her look a little less tired. Examining her reflection, she decided it didn't help much, but at least she was suitably clad, her turtleneck and jeans very modest.

She took a fortifying breath, then exited her room to find the "beautiful brothers."

She walked down the hall toward the living area. She pushed open one of the dining room doors, but no one was in there. She paused, her hand still on the door and listened.

The whole apartment was silent as if not another living soul was there. Worry filled her. What if Rhys wasn't here? What if he left the apartment?

She softly closed the door and hurried farther down the hall. The hall opened out into a large living room. It was as lavish as the rest of the apartment, with more dark antique furniture covered in rich upholstery. But other than a cursory scan of the room, she didn't stop to study the decor too closely.

She rushed straight to another door at the far end of the living room. The door was ajar. She pushed the wood panel open and stepped inside.

Rhys stood in front of a huge stone fireplace, his profile to her, a drink held loosely in his hand.

She didn't say anything for a moment, too captivated by how gorgeous he was. The firelight glinted off his hair. The simplicity of the black sweater and black pants he wore seemed to enhance the width of his shoulders and the narrowness of his hips.

After a few moments, he glanced over at her. "Do come in. I promise I won't bite."